A Wreath for the Bride

A WREATH FOR THE BRIDE

by

Lillian O'Donnell

G. P. PUTNAM'S SONS
New York

G. P. Putnam's Sons
Publishers Since 1838
200 Madison Avenue
New York, NY 10016

Library of Congress Cataloging-in-Publication Data

O'Donnell, Lillian.
A wreath for the bride / Lillian O'Donnell.
p.   cm.
I. Title.
PS3565.D59W74   1990   89-10245 CIP
813'.54—dc20
ISBN 0-399-13478-6

Printed in the United States of America
1   2   3   4   5   6   7   8   9   10

A Wreath for the Bride

Chapter ONE

The ceremony took place four days after Christmas, a Wednesday, in the bride's home.

An awkward date, Anne Soffey, mother of the bride, thought as she watched Mary, her only child, swaddled in the satin and tulle of the hastily fitted, off-the-rack gown, perched like a nervous bird at the top of the imposing cantilevered staircase. Graham Dussart, member of the board of Soffey Cosmetics, great and good family friend, stood beside her. The Christmas season was no time for a wedding, Anne Soffey thought. There were too many parties, too many social events and family obligations. There was absolutely no gap in the calendar into which to fit a wedding. Even a couple of weeks into January would have made things easier. But Mary had been adamant. Her usually tractable daughter had held firm. Exactly one week ago, on December twenty-second, in the midst of the routinely hectic preparations for Christmas, her Mary and Clark Langner, son of a neighbor, had presented themselves to Anne. They'd stood before her hand in hand like children and announced they were getting married. Tomorrow.

Mary's chin had quivered slightly, but only for a moment. They would be married at City Hall, she'd stated. They'd taken their blood tests and they had the license.

"You're welcome to come, if you want," she told her mother.

Anne Soffey struggled with a variety of emotions. First, surprise—no, shock. Mary was twenty-four, attractive, with all the advantages of health, money, and a good education. But she was not outstanding. Her mother admitted it. Her glossy brown hair was expertly cut to best frame her small, angular face. Through the resources of Soffey Cosmetics Mary had learned the art of makeup and knew how to emphasize her gray eyes so that attention was drawn to them and away from a weak mouth and recessed chin. She dressed in the current style, whatever it happened to be, but wore the clothes without conviction. Through high school and college she dated as much as any of her friends, but she'd never had a steady boyfriend or a "relationship," though she wouldn't admit that. After graduation from Radcliffe—which she regarded as a release rather than an accomplishment—she took a job in the New York office of her mother's company but performed by rote. She seemed content to remain in the shadow of her glamorous, successful, and assertive mother.

There appeared to be no prospect of success in a career for Mary. As for marriage, her mother had no idea where the girl had set her sights or what dreams she might cherish. She supposed that eventually Mary would find a young man of equal mediocrity with whom to share her life. That wouldn't necessarily be a bad thing, Anne Soffey thought; not everybody was destined to set the world on fire. She had to accept that her daughter was a nonachiever. But where did she get the complacency? Not from her and not from her father either. Then suddenly there was Mary with Clark Langner the local heartthrob and the last man in the world she would have been expected to attract.

Langner was thirty, a clean-cut, all-American, Olympic athlete type. The image was misleading. Clark had no interest in sports. In school he had participated only because it was expected and because it enhanced his undergraduate record and would look good later on his resumé. Clark Langner was prudent regarding certain aspects of his future, but also careless and irresponsible in the present. He had studied just hard enough to get a good job as a management trainee in one of the big Wall Street investment firms and he performed, if not with dedication, certainly with diligence. He was known to be wild, though not more so than the other restless sons and daughters of the privileged with whom he played but with whom he didn't really belong. He could have any girl he wanted—and usually did. So Anne Soffey's shock was followed by anxiety. How had Mary snared him? And why were they in such a rush? She decided she didn't want to know. That meant being careful not to show curiosity which might be construed as disapproval. She was distressed that Mary had not confided in her, but at least she wasn't being completely shut out.

"Of course, I want to be there!" Anne Soffey exclaimed and hugged her child and held her close. Then relinquishing Mary, she opened her arms to Langner marveling, even as he returned the embrace, that her introverted girl had got him.

"Have you told your parents, Clark?"

"Not yet."

Anne Soffey licked her lips; she was picking her way through an emotional minefield. "You are going to?"

Clark looked to Mary and shrugged. "When it's done," he said. "Mom would want to make a big deal out of it, invite half the club and Dad would use it to pay off as many obligations as he could. Who needs it?"

"It's our day," Mary mumbled with a pout she seldom used, but which her mother recognized as a sign of this new independence. She couldn't know whether her child had had sex with this man, but she was blossoming with the knowledge of being desired.

"Yes, it is," Anne Soffey agreed. "Yours alone. And you

should fill it with memories you can cherish through the years. Don't cheat yourselves to spite someone else."

She herself had no memories of what was considered to be the happiest day in a woman's life. She had fallen in love and nothing else had mattered. *The Feminine Mystique* had just been published and Anne had been swept up in the wave of Women's Rights. She had enthusiastically spurned the atavistic trappings of marriage, even the legality of a marriage certificate. She knew now that the ritual was important. So she wanted Mary to have it all—the engraved announcements, the parties, the showers, luncheons with the bridesmaids, the selection of the gown, the registering for gifts at Tiffany's and Steuben's; the fun of being, if only for a few weeks, the center of attention. The girlish giggling and the solemnity of the minister's instructions. Then, whatever happened, however the marriage turned out . . .

At this moment, as the hundred and twenty-five assembled guests waited for the familiar chords of the wedding march and for the bride on Graham Dussart's arm to begin the slow measured descent, Anne Soffey felt the smarting of tears. She saw a lot of herself in Mary. At her age she had been almost as colorless. She'd had to learn to market her abilities. Appearance was her billboard. She'd set about making herself over. She tinted her hair to a rich auburn, put on enough weight to be elegant, taught herself to walk, head high, as though she owned everything in sight, which after a while she did. Successful as she was, skilled in getting what she wanted, it took all of her considerable power of persuasion to talk the young couple into waiting one week.

So the red Christmas bows came off the wreaths and garlands and were replaced with nuptial white and silver. Invitations were rendered by telephone, or, in extreme cases when the parties could not be contacted, by telegram.

Let the guests think what they wanted. As long as they came.

The modern, split-level house of cedar and glass was set on a knoll overlooking the Lawrence Yacht Club and Bannister Creek. The glass wall of the front was directly opposite the glass sliding door at the rear so that the panorama of inlets and marshes and the Atlantic Beach peninsula were dramatically presented as one came up the walk. Though the boats were gone into southern waters, nevertheless, the club house and docks gave the scene a nautical atmosphere. The sea was unusually calm, Anne Soffey thought, the breeze gentle, and the sun's refractions off the rippling water dazzling. It boded well. She would have preferred a summer wedding, of course; the back lawns sloping gently down to the pool and tennis court, banded by beds of roses, Anne's particular pride, would have been the perfect setting. Yet even as she regretted the season, the mother of the bride took pride in the arrangements. The twenty-five-by-thirty-five living room had been cleared of furniture and the oriental rugs taken up. The cherry floors, taken from an old house in Maine which Anne had bought only to dismantle, glowed with the authentic patina of a hundred years of loving hand buffing. She had made sure the rented gilt chairs were rubber-tipped so as not to scratch them. Light streamed in from the south flooding the room, bathing the altar banked with white poinsettias. After the ceremony a simple luncheon would be served in the conservatory, library, and family rooms. By the time the meal was over, the chairs were to have been cleared from the main room and the five-piece orchestra that played for the ceremony would play for dancing.

And now the moment had come. The chords were struck. All heads turned toward the bride. The staircase on which she stood was designed to appear to float without support. And her Mary, usually so awkward and self-conscious, seemed to float too. An aura of eagerness enveloped her. She was transformed by the moment's happiness as she and Graham Dussart started down.

In the front row on the other side of the aisle, Edith and Owen Langner, parents of the groom, sat erect. They were both large, not merely in height, but in the heaviness of their frames. Edith Langner wore a two-piece cream lace gown from Bergdorf's which she'd been lucky to find at the last minute, and the ruby and pearl brooch which she had received from Owen's mother on their wedding day and which she intended to pass on to Clark's bride. She hadn't done it yet; something had held her back. Just as well, Edith Langner thought; the brooch would have been lost on Mary in the incredibly frumpy dress she was wearing. Anyway, there was no rush. Meanwhile, it sparkled on her own bosom. She held her head high, short silver hair coiffed into a halo, blue eyes shining but thin lips tight. She was experiencing mixed feelings—partly relief and partly disappointment.

Clark, their only son, in whom she and Owen had always taken great pride, had recently become a cause for concern. He had a good job, a job that could lead him as far as he wanted to go. He'd seemed happy in it and was performing well. Then his attitude changed. Nothing tangible. He didn't miss a day's work, didn't call in sick or report late, didn't take long lunch hours or leave early—as far as she'd heard and she would have heard. No, the trouble, whatever it was, hadn't shown up in the job yet. Though Clark no longer lived at home, Edith Langner knew that he stayed out late and knew what condition he went home in. Her friends made sure she knew. He was drinking too much, and Edith Langner was even afraid he might be using drugs. She didn't voice her anxiety to her husband; to do so would have been to give it substance.

Clark played around. She knew it and that didn't bother her. She and Owen were of the generation that accepted the double standard. A young man had the right to sow a few wild oats. As for the girls, nowadays they knew what they were doing. She had no concern for them.

Then suddenly, Clark was out of a job and apparently not making much effort to get another. He didn't come around to ask for money and that made Edith Langner all the more uneasy. When he had the good job he'd left home for a fancy apartment in Tribeca. He was out of that now and living in a squalid walkup on the upper East Side, but even that didn't come rent free. Where was he getting the money? Edith Langner tensed for the inevitable disaster. Instead, Clark announced he was getting married.

It was the last thing in the world she'd expected and Mary Soffey was the last person she thought her son would choose. Edith Langner frowned as she watched her handsome son take his place beside his plain bride at the altar. Maybe marriage was the best thing for him. It might curb his other cravings. As for the bride, Edith Langner was not displeased by her lack of looks and poise. On that level, at least, they wouldn't have to compete. It lessened the natural rivalry between wife and mother-in-law. Clark and Mary had grown up right here in the Five Towns. They had gone to the same schools. Clark had gone on to Dartmouth and graduated with honors. Mary had somehow got into Radcliffe where she'd performed without distinction. Edith Langner didn't care. She wasn't interested in a brainy daughter-in-law either. She would have wished for better social credentials.

Anne Soffey was a neighbor. She and the Langners had homes here and apartments in town and in Palm Beach. They moved in the same circles; the difference was that the Langners, husband and wife, had been born to it, while Ms. Soffey had worked her way in. That was all right. Nowadays few people differentiated between old money and new. Some even professed to admire those who had made it on their own like Anne. Edith Langner had reservations. Anne Soffey had never married. The story was that she had been engaged to a Navy pilot. He was killed in a training accident three days before the wedding. Touching. Sad. Some believed it and admired Anne for remaining faithful to the one love of her life. Others pointed out she had never mentioned the man's name and so the affair was more likely to have been sordid than romantic. Most didn't care.

Owen Langner watched with considerable satisfaction as his son took his place at the altar. They were alike, father and son, both big men with bold features and deep-set brown eyes. The father had worn well. At fifty-eight he looked ten years younger. The son, at his present pace, would not be so fortunate. Owen Langner had always been fond of Mary Soffey. It didn't matter to him that her background was misty. She had gone to the right schools—not that he cared about that either, not when it related to girls. What mattered was that she would be content to stay home and look after Clark. Give him babies. Lots of babies. Also, she had money or would have. In the weeks since his son had announced his intention to marry, Langner had looked up the latest financial statement put out by Soffey Cosmetics and found it entirely satisfactory. Being a banker, he hoped now that they were family, Anne Soffey would throw some business his way.

Owen Langner was encouraged. The boy had done well. His decision to marry showed a strong determination to dissociate himself from the singles drink and drug scene into which he'd been sinking. His choice of Mary Soffey underscored that. Langner, Sr., hoped there was more to it. He stole a glance at his wife, her haughty profile etched in the winter light. Their marriage had been based on shared interests and a common background. Love had come later. Maybe what they had wasn't even love, he thought, but companionship, friendship, the buildup of years of shared experiences, of making a home and raising a child. Whatever it was, he valued it and he hoped Edith did too. Nevertheless, he wanted more for his son. The urgency of the marriage suggested there had already been passion. Owen Langner, set and dignified, a man of scruples, hoped it was so.

Reaching the altar, Graham Dussart handed the bride over to the waiting groom, made a formal bow, and stepped back.

Alongside the Langners, father, mother, son, almost everyone was diminished, but not Dussart. His abundant silver hair was a beacon. He was at ease in any group. He carried himself with the assurance of an unquestionable background and hid the financial instability. At the moment he basked in the glow of his role. He and Anne Soffey were lovers, had been for years, were accepted by their friends as a couple and invited everywhere together. But they maintained separate residences. For Mary's sake, Anne had always said. That was understandable when Mary was a child, but even after she grew up and went to college and could be assumed to know very well the nature of their relationship, Anne refused to let him move in. Of course, he'd offered marriage. Time after time. She turned him down. Now maybe with Mary in a home of her own, Anne might change her answer. That she had asked him to give the bride away seemed to Dussart a public confirmation of his position. As for Mary, he was not too optimistic about her future with Clark.

These four, though they were the closest to the young couple, were not the only ones to speculate about their future or to ruminate about their past. As the minister

looked out over the assembled guests and intoned the hal-
lowed words:

"Dearly beloved, we are gathered together here in the
sight of God, and in the face of this company, to join
together this Man and this Woman in holy Matrimony. . . ."
no one really listened until he reached:

"Into this holy estate these two persons present come
now to be joined. If any man can show just cause, why they
may not lawfully be joined together, let him now speak,
or else hereafter for ever hold his peace."

At that there was the usual, instinctive hush, the almost
breathless waiting. And knowing the groom's reputation,
there were perhaps a few guests with specific knowledge
who tensed in expectation that indeed someone would cry
out. Sensing the mood, the minister's eyes swept the as-
semblage sternly. But no one spoke and the moment
passed. He picked up where he had left off and continued
briskly to the end: "Forasmuch as Mary and Clark have
consented together in holy wedlock, and have witnessed
the same before God and this company . . . I pronounce
that they are Man and Wife. In the Name of the Father,
and of the Son, and of the Holy Ghost. Amen."

Mary Soffey, now Mary Langner, turned to her husband
and tilted her thin, pale face up for the nuptial kiss. As he
bent to her, the moment's anxiety was forgotten. Her face
was suffused with a joy that enveloped the two of them
and spread out to include everyone present as he gently
and possessively folded his lips over hers.

The triumphant recessional burst forth along with ap-
plause as the newlyweds walked back up the aisle to stand
at the foot of the stairs and receive the congratulations of
their friends.

Toasts had been drunk, luncheon was over, and the dancing begun. The bride and groom had gone upstairs to

change. Stella Blanchard, bridesmaid and cousin of the bride, put on a coat and stepped outside, took a deep breath of the cold air and felt better. Stella hadn't wanted to be a member of the wedding, but she hadn't been able to find a reasonable excuse to get out of it. Now, to cap the irony, she had been asked to make sure that all the luggage was in the bridal car. Well, why not? She had nothing against Mary. It wouldn't be much fun for Mary to discover on her wedding night that part of her trousseau had been left behind. That could be the least of her disappointments, Stella Blanchard thought. She looked around squinting in the bright sunshine. Cars were parked everywhere—by special permission of the police department—but the bridal car, of course, was at the front door. For all the champagne she'd drunk, Stella could hardly mistake it—it was the one with the ribbons and tin cans and old shoes.

But she couldn't get the trunk open. The key stuck. Damn. Soon Mary would be tossing the wedding bouquet. Stella had no desire to be present. Her lovely, sultry face, flushed with wine, darkened, her hazel eyes smoldered. No, she'd just as soon miss that. And she certainly didn't want to be standing here to face the happy couple when they came out. She tugged at the trunk handle.

Usually Clark kept an extra key taped to the back of the sun visor. She walked around to the front and saw right away that there was a key in the ignition.

One knee on the seat, the bridesmaid reached for the ignition key. It wouldn't come out. Maybe the car wasn't firmly in Park, she thought. She jiggled the gear lever. Nothing. What *was* the matter with it? Damn, damn.

She got out, slammed the door shut, and started for the house. She was walking around the hood when the car exploded.

Stella Blanchard was torn apart. Arms, legs, torso tossed into the air, blood and bones splattered everywhere.

The gasoline ignited.

The explosion shook homes within a six-block area. Inside the Soffey house, pictures fell, glasses shattered in the hands of the wedding guests. The music stopped. So did the dancing. The sound reverberated and when finally it stopped was replaced by crackling flames.

The guests, most of whom were gathered at the foot of the stairs waiting to say goodbye to the newlyweds, turned their backs to stare in horror through the cracked glass of the window wall at the flaming pyre.

On the landing above, Mary and Clark Langner froze in horror.

Somebody screamed.

Fire sirens shrieked in the distance.

Chapter

TWO

It was December thirtieth and the long holiday weekend loomed ahead. Most companies were closing early. Gwenn Ramadge decided to give herself the rest of the day off. She had caught up with her paper work; she was ready to close the books. Why not take the extra time? The only reason Gwenn hesitated was that she didn't know what to do with it.

Gwenn Ramadge had just turned twenty-seven but she didn't look it, probably wouldn't ten years from now. She was a bouncy, cheery five foot one. She had a mop of blonde curls that bleached to silver streaks in the sun. Her fair skin refused to tan. It burned and peeled and burned again so that for most of the summer she was a bright red, yet she loved the beach and all kinds of outdoor activities. She was astute, resourceful, persevering. She was carefree but not careless, lighthearted but not irresponsible. Born on the West Side of Manhattan, bred on the East Side where she attended the Cummings School for Girls, a prestigious private school on Madison near Seventy-second, she was an authentic New Yorker. She grew up in a seven-room apartment on Fifth Avenue. Her friends were the live-in maid, Helene, and the various doormen of the building. Central Park was her backyard. Spring and Fall she roller-skated on the Mall. In winter, when the pond froze, there was ice-skating—the Wollman Rink was not even a gleam in Donald Trump's eye. Summers, she went to camp so that her parents were free to travel, mostly through Europe. Gwenn Ramadge had a happy childhood. She thought visits to museums and art galleries were fun and considered the city the finest place in the world in which to grow up. True, she was a privileged child and the city had changed since, but she continued to love Manhattan. She had never lived anywhere else and didn't want to.

Bad investments, however, caused her parents, Oscar and Paula Ramadge, to give up the apartment on Fifth Avenue and join the expatriate colony in Cuernavaca where the dollar still purchased luxury. Gwenn stayed behind and faced earning a living. She found to her dismay that it wasn't easy. She'd expected to get a job after graduating Barnard, to work at something—not out of need, not because she had any particular ambition or even enthusiasm—but because that was what everybody did. She'd had vague notions of working as an assistant to the curator in one of the big museums; that way she could continue the life-style she was accustomed to. Unfortunately, she didn't have the requisite qualifications. Her knowledge was superficial. Next, she fixed on interior design. There were interviews arranged through contacts, mostly through the law firm of which Oscar Ramadge had been a senior partner. She was courteously received and courteously turned down. The problem was the same—she had no training for a real job, no marketable skills.

Gwenn knew she wasn't beautiful. Because of her height, she had no hope of impressing with elegance or dignity. She didn't try. In a society that puts so much value on appearance she was at a disadvantage. She refused to fade into an anonymous job behind a desk or counter.

She met a photographer. You couldn't hope to be a model unless you were tall: Gwenn knew that. But Ray

Eagan liked her. Tall was for fashion models, he said. So were sunken cheeks. He liked her verve. He could use her for ads. Height didn't show in close-ups, but vitality, energy, enthusiasm did. The money was good. The work was not as exciting as she had at first expected, but far from boring. She was doing all right. She actually made the cover of *Mademoiselle*. She and Ray Eagan became intimate. Then the bubble burst. She got pregnant. Eagan was not interested in marriage. Since he was the source of most of her assignments, the bookings fell off. The money stopped coming in.

She couldn't go to her parents. They'd stand by her, she was sure of that. Though they couldn't approve, they would accept that new times brought new standards. At this point, Gwenn wasn't so sure she did. She'd had a sound religious upbringing and the morality which had been ingrained in her childhood now brought a sense of guilt. She acknowledged she hadn't really loved Eagan. She had fallen into the affair casually, as a line of least resistance. If she admitted that to her mother and father—and she couldn't lie to them—they would be even more upset.

There were, of course, organizations that took in unwed mothers. My God! Gwenn Ramadge with her private school background and her degree from Barnard thought, is that what I am? Is that the label I have to wear? My scarlet letter? If she applied to a church-sponsored service, it might not be so bad. They'd see her through the pregnancy and birth. And then what?

She thought about abortion. Each year a million teenage girls in the U.S. became pregnant and half of those pregnancies ended in abortion. But she was no teenager; she was old enough to take responsibility for her actions.

When she was little, seven or eight, she remembered a woman in the building who had a cat. The cat somehow got out of the apartment and disappeared. It came back a couple of weeks later—thin, dirty, bedraggled. The woman welcomed it, overjoyed, till it was apparent it was pregnant. She offered the kittens to her neighbors and those for which she couldn't find takers, she ordered the handyman to drown. Gwenn's parents had not allowed her to adopt a kitten and when she heard what happened, Gwenn cried for days. Nobody blamed the woman for getting rid of the kittens. Nobody would point a finger at Gwenn for having an abortion but she couldn't regard a human fetus as the same as a cat's or a dog's. She didn't want the baby, but she couldn't kill it.

Having made the decision, Gwenn had to find some way to sustain it financially. In other words, she was back at the starting gate. She needed work. Forget about the glamorous, prestigious jobs; she needed a real job that would bring in a regular paycheck, would cover the rent, and put food for two on the table: a job in a department store, a restaurant, doing whatever unskilled work was available, and there was work available to those not too fussy or proud to take it. Forget the influential contacts, visit the employment agencies, answer the ads in the newspapers. Unfortunately, Gwenn was beginning to show her condition and the answer she got everywhere was: come back—afterwards.

She didn't know for sure what Hart Security and Investigations did. The three-line ad said it needed a "gal Friday." Gwenn understood that to mean a jack-of-all-trades, a gofer, skilled at nothing and willing to tackle anything. Exactly her job description, she thought.

The office was consistent with that assessment. It was located on lower Broadway near City Hall and around the corner from the New York State office building. It was small, appearing to consist of a tiny vestibule and a single inner office. The vestibule had bright blue wall-to-wall carpet, the standard metal desk and filing cabinet, and a row of molded plastic chairs. Strictly functional. Nobody sat at the desk; presumably she would if she got the job, Gwenn thought. The door to the private office was ajar. Before she could approach to knock, a cheery voice called.

"Make sure you close the hall door and come on in."

The woman who sat behind the desk was fat. There was no kinder way to put it. However, her face was fresh and smooth. Her chestnut hair was cut bluntly at the chin line; it was thick and shining. She was pretty and probably younger than Gwenn had at first thought. No more than thirty-five.

She smiled. "I'm Cordelia Hart. What can I do for you?"

"I came in answer to your ad."

"Ah . . . I thought so. Take a seat."

The inner office was as unpretentious as the outer and not much bigger. In contrast, Cordelia Hart was almost exotic. She wore a loose tent of a dress, a swirl of lavender shades. Chains of gold were draped around her neck and gold hoops hung from her ears. She carried it well. The flamboyance suited her.

"As you can see, this is a one-woman operation." Bracelets jangled as she gestured. The hair flipped from side to side. "I've been in business for myself close to three years. Hart Security and Investigations designs security systems for small businesses, offices, and factories. I run personnel checks and investigate business crimes."

Gwenn nodded. Probably all she'd be doing would be answering the telephone and running errands.

"The recent rash of mergers and takeovers has encouraged corporations to hire pros to scan their offices and meeting rooms for phone taps and transmitters planted by their competitors. That's expanded the field and I've decided I can now afford some help." Cordelia Hart sat back, folded her arms, and smiled encouragingly. "Tell me about yourself."

Gwenn sat tall, as tall as she could. Why not be straight and up front? she thought. This woman was smart; she wouldn't be fooled. Gwenn didn't want to fool her; she liked her. Instinctively and without knowing why, she felt a *rapport*.

"What you need is someone who can do a little bit of everything," Gwenn began. "A little typing, dictation, a little filing, bookkeeping, answer the telephone . . ."

"Right."

"I can't do any of those things," Gwenn told her. "Except answer the telephone; I can do that. I can take messages. I can keep your appointment schedule. I guess I can type, but I'm slow. Probably take me half the morning to get out a letter, that is if you want it without errors. I guess I can file."

"And you need a job," Cordelia Hart said.

"I do. But I'm not qualified. I can't take dictation any better than I can type."

"Most young women, especially the attractive ones, want to work in a big office with lots of eligible young men. You'd be cooped up in here from nine to five with nobody but me. A lot of the time I'm out visiting clients."

"I'm pregnant," Gwenn told her. Her eyes filled as she awaited the inevitable response.

"And alone?"

"Yes."

"How long do you think you could go on working?"

"Six, seven months."

"And then?"

"It would be up to you."

"I don't offer medical, dental, or retirement plans."

"I'm healthy. I've got good teeth, and I don't plan to retire for a while."

"We could give it a try."

"Yes, ma'am."

Cordelia Hart held out her hand.

Gwenn grasped it and held on to it.

* * *

That was not quite five years ago, Gwenn thought, as she prepared to lock up. From the start Cordelia Hart was more than an employer. She encouraged Gwenn to go beyond the routine of office work. Though installation of electronic equipment when required was subcontracted, she urged Gwenn to take a course so that she understood the principles and could check out the work. She personally trained Gwenn in investigative procedure.

She stood by her during the miscarriage.

"I'm relieved," Gwenn confessed from her hospital bed. "And I'm ashamed because I'm relieved. I didn't want the baby." She would not have admitted that to anyone but Cordelia.

"But you were willing to have it and take on all the responsibilities that entailed."

"I didn't want it," Gwenn insisted. "And I think subconsciously I was hoping something would go wrong. I had no business swimming that day. It was too rough. I knew it. The lifeguard warned me about the undertow. He didn't need to. I know the area. I've been swimming off that beach since I was a child." She paused. "When the wave slapped me down and the undertow sucked at me, I didn't think of the baby, only of myself. 'I'm going to die,' I thought. I didn't fight. I didn't care. Then another wave dumped me on the beach and that was when I thought of the baby. 'I've lost it,' I thought. And deep in my heart, it was what I wanted."

"You're not the only woman caught in an unwanted pregnancy who's had such feelings."

Losing the baby was the first tragedy in Gwenn Ramadge's life. With her new friend's help she would get over it, but she would never be completely rid of the guilt. Nor would she ever be rid of the uneasy sense that somehow she'd willed it to happen. She could never again be totally carefree. Her natural ebullience lessened but she still had the ability to raise the spirits of others.

The two women became like sisters. Cordelia Hart had learned the business from her father at a time when listening devices and computers didn't exist. The tools of the detective were intelligence, patience, and instinct. Had electronic equipment been invented, Roderick Hart might have used it as adjunct, never as substitute. It was her father's knowledge and his ethic that Cordelia passed on. When Gwenn had served her apprenticeship of three years, Cordelia Hart sponsored her application for a private investigator's license.

The work entailed none of the glamour and excitement portrayed in movies and on television. There were no heart-stopping moments of danger on sinister streets. The surveillance Gwenn undertook didn't lead to exciting night spots. But she wasn't disappointed. She was now an accredited member of a profession and she was determined to be more than competent. As her skill increased, so her instincts became more reliable and Cordelia Hart began to rely on her. Gwenn was glad to take on more responsibility. She particularly enjoyed personnel investigation. In doing a routine background check she discovered that an applicant for a sensitive post in a defense-related firm had a criminal record. She had performed a real service there, she thought.

Then there was the assignment from the toy company on the verge of bankruptcy because its newest and most innovative designs were finding their way to a rival. In the middle of the investigation, Cordelia turned the whole thing over to Gwenn. Gwenn started by comparing the life-styles of the employees to salaries. One employee was living too high for what he brought home in the pay envelope. Presenting herself as an agent for a European toy company, Gwenn approached the suspect. She set up the meet, alerted the White Collar Crime Squad, and then

"made the buy." The police moved in and "made the bust."
It was exciting, but afterwards it was back to the periodic
checking of equipment, keeping the books, writing the
reports. And answering the telephone. Hart S and I was
prospering, but not enough to hire a third person.

Gwenn had noticed for some time that Cordelia wasn't
looking well. She was coming in late. Her color was high.
She was always tired.

"Change of life." Cordelia dismissed it.

She was putting on more weight. She was short of breath.
She was sending Gwenn out more and more to renew
contracts with old clients and make the pitch for new ones,
a job she had heretofore reserved for herself. However,
on a bright September day when she was looking better
than she had in a long time, strong and energetic, Cordelia
elected to go uptown for some research at the main branch
of the public library at Forty-second Street. She was tracing
the real owner of a commercial waterfront company by
checking the actual history of the area. Two hours after
she'd left the office, Gwenn got a call from St. Luke's-
Roosevelt Hospital. It was Cordelia.

"It's nothing. Now don't worry. I've had a slight heart
attack, but I'm okay."

Gwenn's heart jumped.

"I'm all right," Cordelia repeated. "They say I can go
home."

"I'll come and get you. You wait till I get there. Cordelia,
promise?"

She did wait. She sat in a chair in one of the cubicles of
the emergency room with her coat on and her purse in
her lap till Gwenn located her. Cordelia sighed. Her eyes
fixed on her friend. And closed.

Cordelia Hart left everything to Gwenn, everything she
owned in the world—a few pieces of antique jewelry, the
gold chains and bracelets which Gwenn had never seen

her without, some E Bonds and shares in the Ford Motor Company, a co-op on East Seventy-second Street, and the business. The business consisted of the rental lease, the office furniture, and the client list. And the goodwill. It was almost as though by sending Gwenn out to the clients in those last months, Cordelia Hart had been preparing for this eventuality. In the will she had added almost diffidently the request that Gwenn keep the business going. It wasn't necessary. Gwenn never for a moment had any intention of doing otherwise. She informed the clients individually, personally, that Cordelia was gone and she intended to continue. She offered the option of staying with Hart S and I or going with another firm. Not one left.

Gwenn was still not settled in the comfortable two-bedroom apartment she'd inherited. The building was pre–World War II, which meant soundly constructed. You didn't hear your neighbor's stereo or his late parties. Not that there were many late and/or loud parties in that building. Most of the tenants were of the same vintage as the building. The furnishings had belonged to Cordelia's parents, and Gwenn was still in the process of replacing them. A modern sectional covered in beige linen dominated the room with a Sarouk rug in soft hues of red and blue in front of it. Brass lamps with fringed silk shades were set on butcher-block tables. There were pictures from Gwenn's home on Fifth still stacked along the walls and waiting to be hung. Books, which Gwenn cared enough about to have kept in storage while she moved from one shared apartment to another, also waited to be arranged in newly installed walnut shelves. This was the weekend to do it, Gwenn thought. She was looking forward to it.

It wasn't till the next afternoon on her way out to do the marketing when Harry, the doorman, wished her a Happy New Year, that Gwenn remembered it was New Year's Eve. For a moment she was deflated. She had no plans. Nothing to do and nobody to do it with. Since the loss of the baby, Cordelia and learning the business had filled her time. Taking over the business and moving in here had occupied her since Cordelia's death. Well, she could call Mom and Dad in Cuernavaca at midnight, their time. She would tell them she had friends over; television in the background would support that. Not that she wanted to deceive them, but they would worry if they knew she was alone. Gwenn enjoyed solitude but she was also gregarious. Why be alone? she thought. Why not ask some of the neighbors in? She didn't know any of the other tenants except to nod pleasantly in the elevator or lobby. But it was a big building, and she was sure she wouldn't be the only one sitting alone behind a closed door tonight. Why not knock and invite them over?

Everyone she asked came and more. *Open House*, Gwenn said, and the word spread. Without her suggesting it, everyone brought something—a bottle, a cake, cheese, crackers, pretzels. It was all spread out on the dining room table for people to help themselves. Their very own loaves and fishes, Gwenn thought. By New Year's Eve standards the party broke up early, but everybody had had a great time.

Gwenn woke after eleven on New Year's morning with a feeling of satisfaction. It was one of the best New Year's she could remember. She got up, went to the kitchen to fix herself toast and coffee, and brought a tray back with her. All she had was yesterday's paper, but she hadn't read it so she brought that back too. Leafing through it, the single-column story on page four caught her eye.

BRIDAL CAR EXPLODES
BRIDESMAID KILLED
GUESTS WATCH IN HORROR

Lawrence, N.Y.   Guests dancing in celebration of the marriage of Mary Soffey and Clark Langner were startled by the sound of an explosion on the street outside the Soffey home where both the ceremony and reception had been held. They had a clear view through the picture window and saw the car in which the newlyweds had intended to drive away enveloped in flames. Some said they saw the bridesmaid thrown into the air. The victim was dismembered by the force of the blast. She was identified as Stella Blanchard. Miss Blanchard, 26, and a cousin of the bride, had helped decorate the car and had gone back to make sure all the luggage was stowed.

The cause of the explosion was not known, police said. Mr. Langner, the groom, stated he'd been having trouble lately with the ignition.

First the locality, Lawrence, then the names of the bride and groom caused Gwenn to read the brief piece. As a child she'd spent weekends at the homes of school friends in the area. More to the point, she knew Clark Langner, had even dated him a couple of times. That was long ago, long before Ray Eagan, the baby, Cordelia. A couple of dates with Clark had been enough, Gwenn recalled. But he had gone on calling even though she kept turning him down. Finally she'd had to tell him straight out to leave her alone. Then he'd turned nasty. Gwenn didn't know the bride, but she wished her well.

What a way to start a honeymoon.

Chapter

THREE

Mr. and Mrs. Clark Langner checked in late at the Plaza Hotel, but Anne Soffey had called ahead to make sure their suite would be held for them.

There had been some uncertainty about whether they should keep to their schedule. Death had brushed close. Clark saw nothing to be gained by giving up their trip. Both sets of parents agreed and Mary was persuaded. Arrangements were made for another car. Their clothes were in cinders, so Anne Soffey made a hurried selection from the bride's wardrobe and they stopped at the groom's bachelor pad so he could pack a bag.

It was no wonder that the wedding night was less than wildly successful. It was not the first time they'd been together. The groom was less disappointed; it was Clark Langner's experience that the pleasure was in inverse ratio to the frequency—with the same partner. The bride—thinking the marriage legalized or sanctified, according to viewpoint, the relationship—freed of the guilt and fear attendant on the clandestine meetings, had expected to reach ecstasy as never before. She was therefore deeply dismayed. However, under the circumstances, she shouldn't be surprised, Mary rationalized. The explosion had brought her running out of her room. By the time she'd reached the head of the stairs, the car was a fireball. There was nothing left of Stella.

After the fire department put out the flames, Mary heard a woman sobbing because her car parked on the other side of the street was splattered with Stella Blanchard's blood.

How could either of them forget that?

The police had been gentle with Mary. Sergeant Todd Pennock of the Nassau Detective Division asked her if she or her husband had any enemies. It wasn't till then that it occurred to Mary that she and Clark had been the targets, that they were the ones who should have been killed. She didn't discuss it with Clark. She was too upset. He was upset too; she could see it. Undoubtedly, Sergeant Pennock had asked Clark the same question. Later, Mary thought, they'd talk about it. Once on the ship, once in the warmth of southern waters, they would relax. Everything would be better.

That morning, neither admitted to anything other than ecstasy. They breakfasted in the living room of the suite at noon, presenting an image of connubial bliss to the waiter who served them. They dressed and in the early afternoon took a cab to the pier on the Hudson River and boarded the SS *Serena*—Italian registry, cruise capacity 974 passengers, 500 crew, gross tonnage 31,500. The *Serena*, a part of The Island Star Line fleet, usually sailed out of Fort Lauderdale to Caribbean waters with the passengers flying down from northern points. She entered New York harbor only on the first and last cruises of the winter season in order to undergo refurbishing and repairs. Recently, those cruises had become so popular that it was decided to make New York the point of departure and return for the Christmas and New Year's cruises as well.

The *Serena* was scheduled to lift anchor at 5:45 P.M.. There was plenty of time to unpack, stroll around the ship. There was no formal dress required for dinner on the first night out as there would not be on the last, so Mary didn't bother to change. They had a couple of drinks before departure, during and after dinner. They went out on the deck to admire the moon on the water, but it was very cold. They went back down to the cabin.

Clark undressed her impatiently, roughly. "Why do you wear all these contraptions? You don't need them. You've got great boobs and a sexy bottom. Did you know that?"

Mary flushed, but she was pleased.

"Damn," he muttered, struggling with a hook of the bra. "Help me, will you?"

She reached back. She had barely loosed the bra when his hands grabbed her breasts, cupped them, and he bent to them sucking, biting. He pushed her down on the bed.

"How about the pants? Are you going to take them off or what?" He straddled her ready to plunge into her.

He had never been like this. Mary flushed again, the heat coursing through her whole body.

"Come on, babe, I can't wait much longer."

Suddenly, Mary pulled up her knees, rolled over to the side of the bed, and out from under him. "No. I don't want to."

"What?"

"I'm tired."

He started to laugh. "It's a little early in the game for that, isn't it? This is our honeymoon. Come on, sweetheart." He reached to pull her back down.

She edged away.

"Don't play games with me, Mary. You're not the shy bride and we both know it. You were willing enough before, so what's the matter now?"

Standing naked before him, Mary was suddenly embarrassed. "I don't know. I keep thinking about Stella. I can't get what happened out of my mind."

"It was an accident. There was a problem with the ignition. I told you that. You've got to forget about it. Put it out of your mind."

"It could have been us."

"But it wasn't."

She shivered. "It was meant to be."

"Who says so?"

"The police. Oh, that sergeant didn't come right out with it, but . . ."

"Listen, he wants to make a big case out of this. Get his name in the paper. Get a commendation. I don't have any enemies. I've got a couple of old girl friends who are disappointed that I'm out of circulation, but they don't care enough to try to kill me. How about you? Is anybody that mad at you?"

Mary shook her head. Tears brimmed in her limpid eyes. "It's a bad omen."

"Shit. I'll tell you what's a bad omen—the way you're acting. Hell, you were the one set on getting married. You couldn't wait. So now you've paid for it, enjoy it."

Harsh words, but he was smart enough to say them softly, to make them almost caressing.

"I can't."

"Want to bet?"

He reached. She backed away. The cabin was small and there was nowhere to go. He grabbed her by the arm and drew her slowly, inexorably down on the bed. "Come on, sweetheart, relax and enjoy."

And after a while, she did.

They awoke the next morning at sea. This time there was no pretense. Clark was glum, openly dissatisfied; Mary, ashamed and a little frightened. Neither wanted to tarry in the cabin so they dressed quickly and had breakfast in the main dining room. The rest of the day was spent in normal shipboard fashion—strolling, playing shuffleboard, miniature golf. The tension between them eased. Clark was again ostentatiously attentive, and the word quickly spread that they were newlyweds. Nods and smiles were directed their way. Clark acknowledged with a grin or by putting an arm around Mary and giving her a quick hug. She responded with a return of optimism. The explosion had surely been an accident, she told herself, and Clark's behavior last night was due in part to delayed reaction and to heavy drinking. Tonight would be different. At lunch they decided not to go down to the salon but to try the buffet in the Mermaid Lounge.

Clark knocked back two scotch old-fashioneds before even looking at the food.

"Honey?"

"What?" There was an edge in his tone that had not been there all morning.

"Please don't drink any more."

"Why?"

"Because . . . it's not good for you."

"I'll be the judge of that. Waiter." His arm shot up. "Waiter, another one of these for me, and my wife will have . . . What do you want, sweetheart?"

"Nothing."

"She'll have the same," he told the waiter. "It'll help settle your stomach, darling." He waved the waiter off.

"There's nothing wrong with my stomach."

"Something's wrong. You're not much fun to be with. Maybe a drink will cheer you up."

"I'm sorry."

"What good is that? Are you going to mope for the rest of the trip?"

"No, of course not."

"Then smile, for God's sake. People are going to think I'm beating you."

The first day and night were spent at sea, but there were plenty of shipboard activities available—planned and unplanned. For those who could brave the cold there was jogging, shuffleboard, skeet shooting, deck tennis. An indoor pool and gym were popular. The more sedentary spent time reading or at the movies shown in the two-hundred-seat theater, or in the bar. That night featured the captain's Cocktail Party, Gala Welcome Dinner, Gala Review, Midnight Buffet. At 8 A.M. the next morning, Sunday, the *Serena* put in at her first port of call, Fort Lauderdale. The day was spent ashore sightseeing, shopping, on the beach. Then back on board for dinner while the ship sailed on. The cruise itinerary was planned so that the ship would dock at a different island each morning. The nights were spent at sea. *Warm equatorial nights resplendent with stars, nights of dining and dancing, nights for romance*: the brochure had promised.

Mary came to dread the nights.

The nights were filled with humiliation. From the first, Clark had been demanding; now he merely used her. He was drinking more and more, but Mary no longer tried to stop him. On the contrary, she welcomed his drinking. The more he drank, the sooner he passed out. Then she would slip quietly out of the cabin and go up on deck. She slept in a steamer chair under the velvet, star-spangled skies till dawn. At first light, before the crew could discover her, she crept back inside. She slid to the edge of the double bed as far from her drink-stupefied groom as she could.

Inevitably the tension between them was noticed. A ship is a small, self-contained world in which the action of every inhabitant is under scrutiny. It didn't take long for the gossip to start. Mary felt the pitying glances cast at her. A couple of women seemed on the verge of approaching her, but she indicated she would consider it an intrusion. It was none of their business, she thought. She only hoped nobody would go to Clark and confront him with the fact that she was sleeping on deck. He continued to play the loving husband in public. It surprised Mary that he bothered.

Nassau was their last port of call, and then the SS *Serena*

headed north and home. On the last night she and Clark
had dinner, the routine brief nightcap, and then went
down to the cabin as usual. Traditionally, the night before
had been the culmination of festivities with a masquerade
and dancing till dawn, while this night was left open for
packing and getting ready for the early morning debarkation. However, it wasn't turning out an early night. The
cruise had been very successful and the passengers were
reluctant to see it end. The various bars were in full swing.
On this night, instead of ordering drinks in the cabin, Clark
told Mary he was going back up. He didn't suggest she
should go with him.

She didn't know what to do. She sat alone in the cabin
for about half an hour. When would he be back? What
condition would he be in? She decided she wasn't going
to sit around to find out. She got her heavy winter coat
and a couple of steamer rugs and left.

The night was unexpectedly mild with only a light
breeze. Several couples were out taking a last turn around
the deck. Mary had to climb all the way up to the sports
deck before she could find a place in a corner near the
jogging track where she could be unnoticed and undis-
turbed. Nobody was likely to be jogging at this time of
night.

But she couldn't rest. She kept thinking about Clark.
The marriage had been a bad mistake. She might as well
admit it and call it off. The decision should have eased
her, but it didn't. She didn't like not knowing what Clark
was up to. When he got back to the cabin would he be
sober enough to notice she wasn't there? And drunk
enough to come looking for her? He'd never find her up
here, of course. Mary threw off the blanket, got up, and
walked over to the rail. He'd never think of looking for
her up here.

Leaning out, she looked at the frothy wake on the dark

water. Tomorrow the ship would dock and it would be all over. She heard a step behind her. A shadow fell between her and the moon.

"Clark?"

Clark Langner was awakened by the hubbub. People were talking in loud voices and walking back and forth in the companionway outside the cabin. Of course, they were getting ready to debark. He looked at his watch which lay on the night table: seven-thirty. God! His head ached; his mouth was dry; the taste was indescribable. He swung his legs over the side of the bed. After a couple of tries he managed to get himself on his feet, and lurching, made it to the bathroom in time to vomit into the basin. He rinsed out his mouth and looked at himself in the mirror. He hadn't had that good a time, not that he could remember. He stumbled back to the cabin. He was in his shorts; the clothes he'd been wearing were on the floor. The rest of the clothes still in the wardrobe. Along with Mary's. Looking out the porthole, he could see the ship was already docked, but, what the hell, there was plenty of time before he had to get off. He rang for the cabin steward.

"I want some coffee."

"For one, Mr. Langner?"

"Yeah, I guess. My wife's probably having breakfast in the dining room."

The steward nodded and eyed the unpacked bags. "Passengers are requested to report to immigration by nine. In the main lounge, sir."

"I know that. I know that. We'll be there."

He shaved but didn't bother to shower. He dressed in dark slacks and gray cashmere jacket. He threw his clothes into the shabby suitcases he'd picked up at home after the explosion destroyed the new ones he'd bought particularly for the trip. Should he pack Mary's bags? The hell with it, he thought, and went up to the dining salon.

"Have you seen my wife?" he asked the maitre d'.

"No, sir, Mr. Langner. She didn't come in this morning."

Breakfast wasn't being served anywhere else that morning. The bar wouldn't be serving liquor since they were in port, but they might be serving coffee. Clark looked in.

"Have you seen my wife?"

"No, sir, Mr. Langner."

He went up to the promenade deck and presented himself to the purser.

"I can't find my wife," he said.

The purser took him to the captain.

"I can't find my wife."

Captain Francesco di Steffano was a graduate of the Livorno Naval Academy and came from a long line of seamen. He was aware that as master of a luxury cruise ship his duty was not merely the safety of his ship and its passengers and crew, but also the comfort and pleasure of the passengers. Passengers on holiday, out to have a good time, were not always good-humored. They could be arrogant, overbearing. Often, very often, they drank too much. Yet he had to be considerate, to handle them gently.

"I don't understand," Captain di Steffano replied warily.

"She wasn't in the cabin when I got up and I can't find her anywhere."

"Where have you looked?"

"All over."

Captain di Steffano knew what was going on on his ship. He knew about Clark Langner and Mary Langner so he was very careful.

"When did you last see Mrs. Langner?"

"Last night when we went to bed. When I woke this morning, she was gone."

"She's not gone, Mr. Langner; nobody has debarked as yet." The captain ventured a smile which earned a scowl from Langner. "Have you checked the sauna? Sometimes passengers use that the morning after. Or even spend the night there."

"My wife doesn't drink," Langner stated coldly. "I want you to institute a search."

Di Steffano suppressed a sigh. "Very well. The ship will be thoroughly searched." He cast a look at his purser. "See to it."

"I've already done that," Langner protested. "She's not on the ship. I want you to turn around and search for her at sea."

"That is impossible, Mr. Langner." Francesco di Steffano no longer pretended geniality. His dark eyes gleamed with a hard lustre. "First, I must convince myself that she's not on board. If we can't find her, then I will notify the coast guard." The harshness of authority in his tone.

It didn't cow Langner. "You'll be wasting valuable time."

"I think it is you who have wasted time, Mr. Langner."

Chapter ———— FOUR

BRIDE OVERBOARD?
Husband Reports Wife Missing
Tragedy on Honeymoon Cruise

On the morning of Saturday, January 9, shortly after the SS *Serena,* returning from a New Year's cruise to the Caribbean, had docked, Clark Langner, a passenger, reported his bride, Mary Soffey Langner, missing from their cabin. Debarkation was delayed while a search was made.

Langner, 30, of New York City, stated that his wife had not been feeling well the night before and had gone up on deck for a breath of air. He fell asleep and when he woke the next morning, she had not returned to their cabin. According to Langner, Mrs. Langner, 24, daughter of Anne Soffey, head of Soffey Cosmetics, was not a good sailor and had been spending part of every night up on deck. He suggested she might have lost her balance and been blown overboard by the high wind. The coast guard has been notified and boats are being sent to

examine the area where it is thought she might
have gone over the side.

Benjamin Cryder gasped. His heart pounded, reverberating in his ears. The newsprint blurred and the bright day turned gray.

The story, a last minute filler in the Sunday editions, was given more space on Monday. Cryder saw it by chance as he idly perused the paper and enjoyed the warmth of the newly completed conservatory while he waited for the car to be brought around. He'd purchased the twenty-two bedroom, Gothic-style mansion in Harrison, New York, on the occasion of his marriage two years before. It was built in the twenties at a cost of one million dollars. Benjamin Cryder had paid twelve million for it and could probably sell it at twice that. It was furnished with eclectic lavishness, reflecting the taste and profligacy of a series of previous owners, self-made billionaires, all of whom gauged value by the price tag, and who had married women with the same standards. Not Cryder.

Cryder had married late and chosen carefully. Patricia Garvé, twenty-six at the time, was beautiful, graduated from Vassar, and of impeccable social background. Her only lack was "serious money." He provided that. Their wedding was performed at St. Thomas's on Fifth Avenue and the reception held in the Great Hall of the Metropolitan Museum of Art on Fifth Avenue and attended by five hundred guests, including high society and the "smart money" crowd.

Benjamin Cryder noticed the story because it was on the same page as the announcement of an auction of American art to be held at Christie's East in which he was interested. It was the name, Soffey, that caught his eye. Not a common name and the reference to Soffey Cosmetics left no doubt as to identity.

He let his gaze roam past the glass wall out over the spread of terraces, the sloping lawn and English-style hedges, the Italianate urns and statuary that was part of the thirty-acre estate. Though brown and sere on this January day, it was an impressive vista. He dwelled particularly on the artificial lake which, like the conservatory, was his own addition. Its blue waters threw off scintillas of light even at this distance. He derived satisfaction from the sight and from what it represented. Sustained, he went back and read the story once more.

Sad, he thought. A tragic accident. No one could help but grieve for the abrupt ending of a young girl's life as she stood at the threshold of marriage. But he couldn't weep for a stranger. Regret was unproductive. He had never allowed the past to be a burden. If ever before he had reason to think of the future, he had it now.

Cryder had been a very sick man. In mid-September his doctors, and there was a battery of them, had diagnosed cancer of the prostate. They had assured him that of all malignancies this had one of the highest cure rates, when caught early. They operated immediately. Then they told him this one had not been caught early enough. They recommended chemotherapy. Then radiation. Platinum injections. His thick, tough hair fell out. From two hundred and five pounds he shrank to a hundred and forty. He was bent and walked with a cane. His brilliant eyes were sunk deep into his head. His skin was brittle. But he didn't give up. Then, suddenly, a change began to take place. Apparently, the platinum injections were working. A series of nauseating, debilitating ordeals, they offered the first glimmer of hope. The growth of the tumor had been arrested, the doctors told him. They were cautiously optimistic. Benjamin Cryder was ecstatic.

He had come a long way. His father was a butcher with a small shop in Bayside, Queens. He married a school teacher and they lived over the shop. Elena Cryder felt herself intellectually superior, and was. When Benjamin was born, she had to give up teaching to stay home and raise her only son. She could and did help out in the store, but she felt demeaned. So it was from his mother that Ben Cryder got his ambition and determination to become "somebody." From his father he got bodily strength and stamina. His mother wanted him to go to college. His father wanted him to work in the butcher shop, but if he preferred other work, Joseph Cryder didn't care as long as the boy brought money home at the end of the week.

Ben Cryder went to work as a busboy in the dining room of the Staffordshire Hotel. To some it might seem on a par with what he'd left behind, but to the eager young man it was entering another world. Then, as now, the Staffordshire was one of the finest independently owned hotels in New York. From the first day the hotel fascinated Cryder. He was eager and learned quickly. Soon he was promoted to waiter, then captain. His next move was to get out of the dining room and into the management office. Actually it meant less money, counting the loss of tips, but he had a goal. He knew what he wanted—to be manager of the Staffordshire and to make it not merely the best in the city, but internationally recognized.

Just as it seemed he was about to achieve his aim, the manager under whom he'd served and who was about to retire called him in to inform him that the Staffordshire would close. Cryder knew, of course, that they'd been losing money. But he hadn't realized how much. The board of directors intended to file for bankruptcy. Dismayed, Benjamin Cryder sought a way out. He believed he could turn the operation around and make it profitable. He had to convince the board. He asked to appear before them. He came with facts, figures, plans for remodeling, refurbishing, rescaling of rates, and a new advertising campaign. The board saw more money going out. They were not inclined to trust a young man and inexperienced manager. The answer was no.

Frances Oppenheim, grande dame of society and administratrix of one of the largest family philanthropies in the nation, was the only one who gave his plan serious consideration.

"I'd be willing to invest a million," she announced. But no one around the long, polished table offered to join her.

After the meeting broke up, she came to Cryder in his tiny assistant manager's office on the mezzanine. "I'm sure we can round up seven or eight outside investors. You shouldn't have any trouble getting a loan for the rest. I'll put in a word for you at Chase."

Chase held the hotel's current account. "Morgan Guaranty might be better."

She understood his desire to start afresh with a bank where he would not be regarded as the subordinate he had been. She nodded. "I can do something for you there."

He'd known that before putting up the name.

"This is a fine old building," Mrs. Oppenheim said. "I'd be sorry to see it go under the wrecker's ball. We should put in motion the process for having it declared a landmark."

Their eyes met; the deal was made.

Only one other member of the board, not present at the time of the final meeting, was impressed enough with Cryder and his plan to risk real money. Cryder had no other contacts. Mrs. Oppenheim, however, did. She introduced him into the elegance and ruthlessness of fund-raising, to society and the world of high finance. She guided him through the acquisition of the Staffordshire and once he'd turned it into a success, she said:

"That's our first. Have you picked out the next?"

They were good friends. Frances Oppenheim, slim, with fine features, and a royal deportment, was sixty-nine years old. There were no young Mrs. Oppenheims around, so Ben became known as a perennial bachelor.

With Frances Oppenheim as silent partner, he acquired a chain of luxury hotels across the country. The Cryder name and signature, his initials intertwined with a laurel wreath, were the stamp of service and the ultimate in luxury. He went international, at last expanding to Europe, even behind the iron curtain. There were Cryder hotels in Budapest, Bucharest, Prague.

Then Frances Oppenheim died. With her passing and his forty-eighth birthday looming, the man who was assumed to have everything discovered that not much of it counted. For one thing, the challenge was gone. He had no interest in further expansion. He had postponed a personal life, given up more than he cared to admit. Wasn't it time finally to enjoy the fruits of his work? He decided to get married. He set about it methodically as he had done in selecting and then acquiring each of his properties. And he chose well. Patricia Garvé was perfect. They had two years if not of passion, certainly of loving contentment, and then he was stricken.

After the initial shock, Cryder rallied his forces. This was only another kind of fight and he had never lost a fight. Never. He would not lose this one. After the disappointment of the operation and the various treatments, it was now beginning to look as though once more he would win.

Each day he was stronger. He was beginning to regain some of the weight lost. The hair was coming back in darker and thicker than before. His personal therapist, who lived at the mansion and worked with Cryder twice a day, said his muscle tone was improving. Soon he'd be out on the golf course again. He was fifty and aiming for eighty-five at the very least. He had married a young wife and intended to continue enjoying her. Might they have children? Suddenly, the thought of having children, of keeping his name alive, was very appealing.

A light knock at the door interrupted his thoughts.

"Good morning, darling."

Patricia Garvé Cryder, now twenty-eight, a sparkling, blue-eyed brunette, entered the conservatory and went straight to him. She put her arms around his neck and bent down to place a soft, but lingering kiss upon his lips. "How are you?"

He looked her over, appreciating her anew. She was wearing an artfully draped wine jersey dress from the couture collection of the new fashion sensation, Christian Lacroix, set off by a single brooch of rubies and gold. Her complexion was like fine porcelain. For all the care she took not to crack it and cause lines, Tricia Cryder managed to show a great deal of expression.

"You're all dressed up," he remarked.

"I thought I'd ride in with you. Okay?"

"You have an appointment in the city? Shopping?"

"No. I thought it would be nice to ride in with you and go to the doctor's with you."

"Not necessary. Everything's fine."

"I know that. I can see it."

"Never felt better in my life. I'm going to get a good report."

"Of course you are. And then I'm taking you out to lunch to celebrate. To your old Staffordshire. What do you think of that?" Her blue eyes danced. The sun brought out the red highlights in the mass of chestnut curls.

He smiled up at her. "It's a date."

Nevertheless, there was anxiety in Tricia Cryder's eyes while she waited outside the consulting room. As soon as Cryder came out she got up and went to him, the question unspoken.

"I hope you ordered champagne," he said.

"Oh, sweetheart!" She reached and took his hands into hers. Eyes brimming, she kissed him.

"No more treatments, injections, radiation. I don't have to come in for another six months."

They entered the Staffordshire and were greeted by the current manager, escorted by him and followed by a retinue of lesser management personnel, some of whom knew Benjamin Cryder from the early days. Everyone commented on how well Mr. Cryder looked. They formed a triumphal procession into the dining room.

At the end of the simple but exquisitely prepared and served meal, Tricia took her husband's hands once again into hers. "So where shall we go? Las Haciendas? Or would you rather go skiing—Aspen or Saint Moritz? Maybe a cruise? You decide."

"Whatever you want, but I have some business first."

"Oh, Ben . . ."

"I've let so much slide."

"Let it slide awhile longer. Let's get away. Come on, darling, we both need it. I say we go someplace warm. It will do us both good."

He considered. "You're right. Okay. We'll open the house in Palm Beach. How about that?"

"It's not really getting away, but . . . I guess it's the next best thing."

"We will get away. There's something I want to take care of first. After that, it's around the world, if that's your pleasure. I promise."

He raised his glass to her. She leaned across, took the glass out of his hand and kissed him full on the lips, hard, without restraint for doing it in public. Then she returned the glass to him and raised her own.

"To us."

Chapter
FIVE

The search of the SS *Serena* failed to turn up any trace of Mary Langner or to suggest what might have happened to her. Her husband continued to insist she had fallen overboard. Captain Francesco di Steffano had no choice but to notify the coast guard that one of his passengers was missing and that he had reason to believe she might have gone over the side some time during the previous night. He couldn't say when.

The call was taken by the OD (Officer of the Day), who in turn notified the local authorities. That was precisely what the captain had tried to avoid, knowing it would delay debarkation and cause confusion and indignation among the passengers. However, the tedious hours and dogged questioning by the detectives who came on board did elicit some information. Mary Langner had been seen wandering around the decks at about 3 A.M. One couple saw her heading up to the sports deck. They were sure it was she because the Langners were assigned the table next to theirs in the dining room. The *Serena*, like most cruise ships, had been making her approach to New York harbor in the early morning. Therefore, it was calculated that the missing woman might have gone into the water two or three miles southeast of Ambrose Tower. All shipping was notified to keep a lookout for a "person in the water." The coast guard would continue to refer to her in this manner until recovery because, technically, no matter how obvious the indications might be when she was sighted, they were not qualified to determine life or death.

Not that there was much hope of recovery, not now in midwinter. Bodies had a tendency to go down and stay down because of the cold. In spring, the water warms, the gasses in the body cavities swell, and the body comes up. Bodies long forgotten come up in the spring. Mary Langner's could have been one of these. Or she could have sunk to the bottom and stayed there for years or forever. Or been carried away to who knows where by capricious tides.

However, the next moring, in response to the coast guard request, the captain of an oil tanker reported a sighting about a quarter of a mile outside the channel on the right side and heading up. This position put it in Station Rockaways area. The tanker captain, John Petrus, using his binoculars, determined that it was floating face down. Therefore, with less concern for semantics, he referred to it as the "body."

The coast guard requested he remain nearby till they got there in order to be sure the position didn't change. Captain Petrus was disposed to be agreeable. The seas were calm enough so that the coast guard was able to send a forty-one-foot motor life boat to make the recovery.

By late morning on Sunday, thirty hours more or less after she'd gone into the water, Mary Soffey Langner had been passed from boat 41382 to coast guard Station Rockaways to a slab in the Queens medical examiner's office. There her husband went to make identification.

The condition of the body, even after such a relatively short immersion, was quite dreadful. Already crabs were on her face. Already portions of the body had been consumed.

Clark Langner threw up, but he verified it was his missing bride. He left as soon as he could.

Advised that her daughter had been recovered, Anne Soffey insisted on going to see her. She would not be dissuaded. Graham Dussart, who had been with her almost constantly since the news that Mary was missing, tried, but failing, finally agreed to drive her over on condition that he stay at her side. One look was all Dussart could bear. The mother, however, after a gasp of horror, could not take her eyes away. She stood and stared immobilized at what had been her child. Anne Soffey had no sense of time. Finally, Dussart recovered himself enough to forcibly turn her away and walk her out.

He told her Mary hadn't suffered. After the moment of shock when she hit the icy water, it was over for Mary. None of the rest affected her in any way. Mary had felt nothing, Dussart insisted, repeating it like a litany. He had no idea whether it was true, but he convinced himself so he could convince Anne.

"Where's Clark? What are they going to do about Clark?" Anne Soffey demanded.

Dussart grimaced. "He'll be questioned again, of course."

"He killed her. He pushed her overboard. I know that. He has to pay."

"He will." Dussart strove to calm her. "He will."

Somehow, Anne Soffey got through the funeral, sustained by the fact that Langner was in fact being closely questioned, as were his friends and the people he'd worked with both on Wall Street and his part-time job at the upper East Side bar. A clear picture of Clark's character and lifestyle emerged. In addition there were the accounts gathered at the original interrogation of passengers testifying to the bad situation between the newlyweds. The DA believed he had enough probable cause to charge Langner with murder. Five days later Clark came up before the grand jury. He asked to appear and give evidence in his own behalf, thus giving up immunity. The gamble paid off. He charmed them. The grand jury refused to indict.

When Anne Soffey heard, she broke down. The thought that her daughter's killer was back home living his normal life was more than she could bear and she eagerly reached for the sedation she had heretofore refused. For days that turned into weeks, she gulped down the Valium. Then one morning as she put her hand out for the oblivion contained in the bottle of pills beside her bed, Anne Soffey found she could hardly unscrew the cap because her hand was shaking so badly. She looked at the calendar. It was one day short of three weeks since Mary had been reported missing. Three weeks less one day since her child had been murdered. And the grand jury had let her killer go, citing *insufficient evidence*. That phrase was clear in her scrambled mind. Mary's killer was free. Living his life without remorse. Thinking he'd gotten away with it. Well, he had a surprise coming. Anne Soffey's hand still shook, but instead of the bottle she picked up the hand bell on the night stand and rang.

"I want some coffee, black, Agatha," she told the housekeeper. "And toast. And eggs." Just the thought of eating brought a wave of nausea, but clenching her teeth she fought it back. She needed to be strong physically so she could be strong emotionally. Everything she had tried to forget about the tragedy she must now force herself to remember. She had sought oblivion in drugs; she must now shake off the effects and get to work.

She went right to the top, to Queens District Attorney Nathaniel Hirsh, not an assistant, certainly not the assistant who had presented the case against Langner, but all Anne Soffey got for her efforts was regret and sympathy.

"It's very difficult to make this kind of case," the district attorney explained. "It's difficult to prove it was murder and not an accident—regardless of the emotional environment. In fact, forgive me, the emotional environment suggests it might have been suicide."

Anne Soffey's ravaged face turned to stone. She got up. "Thank you, Mr. Hirsh. I won't take up any more of your valuable time."

Hirsh got up too and saw her to the door. Neither said any more; there was nothing more to say.

But Anne Soffey wasn't ready to give up. Far from it. She'd go to the police next. Who did she know connected with the police? There was a deputy commissioner of Public Relations . . . what was his name? He had once worked for an advertising agency that handled the Soffey Cosmetics account. Ah, yes, Kreizler, Jan Kreizler. He was glad to take her call and seemed eager to assist. He arranged an appointment with the chief of detectives.

Chief Eugene O'Malley immediately called in Captain Pablo Salazar. In her presence he instructed the captain that Ms. Soffey was to be kept fully informed of the progress of the case.

"Who's carrying?" the Chief wanted to know.

"Lieutenant Wellesley, sir, at the 101."

"Oh, yes. Good man. Very good man, Ms. Soffey. I'm sure he's doing a thorough job, covering every possible angle."

"I'd like to speak to him, please."

"Of course. Certainly. Set it up," he told Salazar, "at Ms. Soffey's convenience." He got up, came around the desk, and walked her to the door. From there Captain Salazar took over and escorted her as far as the elevators.

"Captain, could we do it now? I mean, set up the appointment with Lieutenant Wellesley?"

"As you wish."

So he walked her to his office, sat her in a chair, and they both had coffee while the sergeant at the desk outside the door put the call in to the precinct. Informed the commander was on the line, Salazar picked up, spoke, listened, put his hand over the mouthpiece, and addressed Anne Soffey:

"Lieutenant Wellesley is on vacation. He won't be back for another ten days."

"What happens to the investigation meanwhile?"

Salazar scowled. "Who's covering for Wellesley?" He looked at his visitor. "Detective Daniels worked with Wellesley on the case. If you wish . . ."

She didn't know whether to laugh or to cry or to scream. She merely got up. "Don't bother, I'll wait for the lieutenant to get back."

Relieved, Salazar got up and started around the desk.

"No, no, don't trouble. I can find my own way."

And that, Anne Soffey thought as she walked alone down the long corridor, was just what she would have to do.

She'd started up too high. The people she'd appealed to were administrators, formulators of policy, symbols. The actual work was done by the little guys at the bottom. What she had to do was find the man who had done the legwork, had chased down the evidence, conducted the interrogations, who was familiar with the day-to-day routine details of the case. Once she found him, would he be willing to tell her what he knew? The big shots had offered sympathy. That didn't compromise them. But sympathy and compassion for her loss might prove too expensive for a Detective Daniels: might cost him a promotion, even his job. What she needed was a private detective.

As always, it was a matter of choice. She could afford the best. The best would provide a large organization and would certainly be dedicated to her interests. But she would be one of many clients. So she should heed the lesson she'd just been taught and choose someone at the bottom. She would look for a small agency and a detective not distracted by other clients. Someone for whom Anne Soffey and her needs would be paramount. Anne had a good memory; she especially did not forget those who had served her well. She turned her Rolodex to Hart Security and Investigations.

She was dismayed to discover that Cordelia Hart was dead. The Hart Agency in the person of Cordelia Hart had handled an industrial espionage problem for Soffey Cosmetics four or five years back. Their research discoveries, a breakthrough in the field of collagen application, were being leaked to rival companies. The loss amounted to millions. Cordelia Hart had not only discovered the culprit, not all that difficult since Anne Soffey had suspected him from the start, but had got the evidence to convict. In recalling Cordelia Hart and her quiet competence, Anne Soffey had felt a surge of optimism. She believed she'd solved her problem. Now, not knowing where else to turn, she made an appointment with the woman who had inherited the business from Ms. Hart. Gwenn Ramadge. She could have had Ms. Ramadge call on her, but Soffey decided she could better gauge her in her own surroundings.

By then Ms. Soffey had herself well in hand. She was her usual composed, authoritative self. Under a dark sable coat she wore a conservative, exquisitely tailored light gray suit. Her auburn hair, simply brushed back from her forehead, gleamed with salon highlights. At last she was able to recount the story of Mary's death with equanimity, though not without bitterness toward Langner and those involved in the investigation. Probably she would never be rid of the resentment. At this moment, seated opposite Gwenn in the office that had been Cordelia Hart's, she let it all pour out. She wanted this young woman to know exactly what she felt and what she expected to get for her money.

"I believe that Clark Langner killed my daughter and that the grand jury made a mistake when they let him go."

"Precisely why do you think that?"

Anne Soffey frowned. On entering the small office across from City Hall park, she had been reassured to find things much as she remembered. It suggested the new head of the agency walked in her predecessor's footsteps. Then Gwenn Ramadge appeared. Her youth and looks were unexpected and disappointing. In the business of personal appearance, the older woman acknowledged that Ramadge was appropriately dressed and her manner entirely professional. Certainly, the question was in order. As long as she was here, she might as well go through with the interview. As she started to recount the events that led to her daughter's death, Anne Soffey found herself not merely retelling but re-exploring her own deep feelings. In turn, this led to recounting facts she had not been consciously aware of knowing.

Gwenn Ramadge, green eyes intent, remained silent and let Anne Soffey unburden herself.

"They were quarreling, Mary and Clark—had been since the start of the cruise. There were witnesses," the mother hurried on to explain before being asked. "Passengers gave statements to that effect. Clark was drinking heavily. Mary spent the nights in a steamer chair on the deck." Her throat tightened; she paused to fight back the anguish. "Can you imagine spending the nights of your honeymoon alone on deck? What does that suggest to you, Ms. Ramadge?" She didn't wait for an answer. "I'll tell you what it suggests to me—it suggests she was afraid to spend the night alone with him."

Gwenn didn't comment.

"According to Clark, Mary wasn't feeling well. She was seasick. She found the cabin too close and that's why she went outside. But that's a lie. Mary was a good sailor. She knew all about boats. She grew up near and on the water. She was used to rough seas. He claims she used to go up on the jogging track, and that on the last night she'd been drinking. According to him, she must have lost her balance and the wind blew her off."

Anne Soffey paused for a moment to indulge her indignation. "Mary didn't drink, not more than a couple of glasses of wine. She was no athlete and would not have had any reason to be up on the track. And finally, the captain says the wind wasn't strong enough to blow anybody overboard." Now she looked to Gwenn and waited.

"There is another possibility, Ms. Soffey," Gwenn responded. "You acknowledge the fact that your daughter and her husband were not getting along. It's possible they were up on deck together. They had an argument. It became violent. There was a struggle and in the course of it Mary fell overboard. Were there any marks on her body to indicate she might have been slapped or punched or injured in any way?"

"If you had seen the condition of . . . the state Mary was in . . ." Anne Soffey couldn't finish. She turned her head away.

"I'm sorry." Gwenn was upset at herself. She hadn't needed to ask that; the information was available elsewhere. "Can I get you a glass of water?"

Ms. Soffey shook her head. She took a few more moments to compose herself. Then she got up, drawing the mantle of sables around her. "Thank you for your time, Ms. Ramadge. If you'll send me a bill."

"We would need to prove intent, Ms. Soffey. Without intent, even if Langner did push Mary overboard, say during an argument, it's only manslaughter in the second. It can be plea-bargained down to a few years in jail."

"I see. I was hoping you'd feel empathy with Mary."

"I do. More than you realize. Some years ago I dated Clark Langner. He's all the things you say, but that's not evidence."

"We can get the evidence."

Anne Soffey meant to be positive, to show assurance, but the façade was cracked once again. The woman has been under tremendous strain, Gwenn thought. She sensed that proving her daughter's death was not an accident but premeditated murder—and that Clark Langner did it—was necessary to Ms. Soffey's recovery, if there was to be a recovery.

"Maybe," Gwenn replied. "But this is out of my field. I haven't had the training nor the experience . . ."

"You know Clark and you know his friends. You understand their life-style. They'll talk to you."

"I dropped out of that scene a long time ago, Ms. Soffey. Since . . ." She was about to say *since I lost the baby.* "Since Cordelia took me in and taught me the business. Anyway, the most I could get from Clark and his friends and Mary's friends would be background, affirmation of what we already know. They can't tell us what happened between them aboard ship.

"It's not a matter of ringing doorbells or canvassing a neighborhood," Gwenn continued. "The incident took place at sea . . . The shipboard passengers were interviewed before debarking. Those interrogations were necessarily brief. Now these people have returned to their homes. They've scattered in every direction. Tracing them isn't a problem, but it will certainly take a lot of time and money. Probably, they'll have little if anything to add to what they've already stated."

"You never know. There may be some who kept silent, who purposely held something back—for whatever reason."

"It's always possible."

"I want you to go through the entire passenger list, the crew, the officers. Hire as many men as you need. I'll pay."

"Police detectives went on board the morning the *Serena* docked," Gwenn reminded her. "They interviewed Langner and they talked to the passengers. After Mary was

found, they brought Langner in and intensified the interrogation. They thought they could make a case, but the
grand jury disagreed. I doubt very much any team I could
put together would do any better."

"I want you to try."

"As for physical evidence, the ship has turned around
and made—I don't know—three or four crossings since."
Even as she detailed the obstacles, Gwenn found herself
getting interested. "May I ask you something, Ms. Soffey?"

"Anything."

"You told me that Mary and Clark hadn't been going
together for any length of time before the marriage. Not
insofar as anybody knew. So the marriage was sudden,
unexpected to both families and friends of the couple."

"Yes."

"Did there seem to be any reluctance on Clark's part?"

"No. They were both eager. Determined. Couldn't wait."

She had to ask. "Was Mary pregnant?"

Anne Soffey flushed. "No. I thought myself she might
have been, that it might have been the reason for their
marrying, but no—they tell me she wasn't."

"Does Clark stand to inherit a lot of money?"

"Not at this time. Under her grandmother's will, Mary
would have inherited when she reached her twenty-sixth
birthday. She had two years to go."

"He must have known that," Gwenn pointed out quietly.

"I'm sure he did," Anne Soffey sighed with bitterness.

"Is it possible then that he loved her?"

"Anything's possible. What we know for certain is that
he mistreated Mary. He was a known womanizer. He might
have flirted in front of Mary even though it was their
honeymoon. Mary wouldn't have kept silent. So they argued. But not on deck. Mary wouldn't make a scene in
public. It happened below deck, in the cabin. The argument became physical. Clark is a bully. He hit her. Maybe
he hit her harder than he intended; anyway, he killed her.

He was scared. He didn't know what to do. He decided finally that he had to get rid of her. He carried her up on deck and threw her over the side." She paused, hoping for encouragement, but got none. "He waited as long as he could before reporting she was missing. He never imagined, of course, that she would be found."

"Lucky for him that she was," Gwenn said.

"Why?"

It couldn't be easy for Mary's mother to discuss these details, to summon up the images of Mary's last moment, Gwenn thought, but if she wanted an investigation they couldn't be avoided.

"According to the news reports, there was seawater in Mary's lungs. That means she was alive when she went over the side."

Anne Soffey went dead white. "But not conscious? It's not likely she was conscious?" she begged.

"It happened very fast, Ms. Soffey." It was the only consolation Gwenn Ramadge could offer.

"Clark killed her," Anne Soffey repeated doggedly. "Whether she died in the cabin or in the water, he's responsible and he's not going to get away with it." She clenched her fists and placed them on the edge of the desk in front of her, hammering as she spoke. "I came to you because Cordelia Hart did a big job for me once. I assumed since she had enough confidence in you to turn over her company to you no other recommendation was necessary. But if you won't help me, I'll find somebody else."

"You'll find someone to take your money; I'm sure of that."

"What I do with my money is none of your business."

"I'm sorry, I shouldn't have said that," Gwenn apologized. According to Roderick Hart, Cordelia's father and the firm's founder, the investigative method was the same regardless of the type of crime. Petty theft, industrial espionage, embezzlement, murder, all were subject to the same technique—interrogation. The good detective talked to people, asked questions, and listened to the answers. Mary Langner's death, just when she stood at the threshold of a new life, at a time of what should have been her greatest joy, touched Gwenn. She felt a strong emotional pull to find out what had happened. She wanted to take the case.

"The agency isn't equipped to handle this big an investigation," she told Anne Soffey. "You can see for yourself . . ." She indicated the cramped quarters. "I don't have anybody working for me. But if you would be satisfied for me to make some inquiries, handle the job on a very personal level, I'll do my best."

Anne Soffey hovered between a smile and tears. The smile won out. "Nobody else has offered me that much."

"About the explosion of the bridal car and the death of one of the bridesmaids . . ."

"Stella Blanchard, Mary's cousin."

Gwenn made a note. "Have the police discovered who was responsible?"

Anne Soffey shook her head. She wasn't interested.

Gwenn was. She thought it was the logical place to start.

Chapter_____
_____ SIX

First thing the next morning Gwenn rented a car and drove out to Lawrence, Long Island. As a child she'd spent many weekends with school friends out here, but that was long ago and the area was much changed. She took half an hour or so reacquainting herself with that section of wealth and privilege tucked between the Atlantic Beach peninsula and the tract development of the western midsection of Long Island. Once, before the railroad extended from the city, it had all been farmland. Trains brought people, and because of the magnificent stretch of beach, the equal of any in the world, Gwenn thought, it turned into a resort area. As transportation improved, the Five Towns developed into a bedroom community. A light snowfall the night before eased the midwinter bleakness, and the nearer she came to the vast ocean glistening as far as the horizon, the less Gwenn was affected by the barren landscape. Following the route she'd mapped out, she turned left at the Causeway and headed to the Soffey house.

It was set on a knoll overlooking the empty yacht basin. There was no one around. Gwenn stopped at the foot of the circular drive, then got out, and walked to the front door. The bridal car had been parked right here, she thought. Cars had been lined up, bumper to bumper on either side and well back along the grass verge of a two-way blacktop. It was a miracle that the shower of sparks and flaming metal hadn't ignited other fuel tanks to start a series of explosions.

All physical traces of the explosion were gone. No sense of the violence that had occurred there lingered, no trace of the emotions that had erupted. All was tranquil. Gwenn got back into her rented Toyota and drove to the Nassau Fourth Precinct police station.

She'd called ahead to find out who was carrying the case and then again to make sure Sergeant Todd Pennock would be on duty, but she hadn't spoken to Pennock nor even left her name. On those rare occasions when Hart Security had to deal with the police, Cordelia had always made an appointment with the officer in charge. She'd been respectful and got good cooperation in return, but, of course, she'd been dealing with white collar crime, not homicide, and she hadn't been invading their turf. Anne Soffey had already warned Gwenn about her own experience with the police. It was because of their resistance that she'd hired Gwenn. So Gwenn had decided to drop in on Pennock, to catch him off guard.

At the threshold of the squad room she paused for a moment. She'd been told his was the desk nearest the window. A sandy-haired man sat bowed at the typewriter with his back to her. Though she held herself very straight and walked firmly, Gwenn was nervous. She hadn't expected to be.

"Sergeant Pennock?"

He looked around. He had pale gray-blue eyes and freckles. He was wearing slacks and a plaid flannel shirt. He was about thirty-five and looked easygoing.

Attractive, Pennock thought, and classy. He was used to dealing with the upper classes, knew when to placate, and when to stand firm—but politely. He wasn't exactly sure how to handle this one. Civilians who walked into police stations brought their troubles with them and this one was no exception, but she seemed in control of herself.

"Yes ma'am. What can I do for you?"

Gwenn had counted on instinct to guide her, only no approach suggested itself. She opened her handbag and fished out a business card.

Security and Investigations. Pennock formed the words silently. He looked Gwenn Ramadge over a second time. "You're Ms. Hart?"

"No, that's me." She pointed down in the corner where her name was printed. "Cordelia Hart was the head of the agency. She died. I've taken over."

He waved her to a chair. "How may I help you?"

"I'm investigating the Langner case."

"It's not in our jurisdiction."

"I know that. Actually, I'm interested in the explosion that took place in front of the Soffey house on the day of the wedding. All I know about it is what I read in the paper. I wondered . . . the car was bombed, wasn't it? I mean, it wasn't any sort of freak malfunction or anything?"

"Oh, it was bombed all right. It was a very ordinary device linked to the ignition."

"I see. Do you have any suspects?"

"No."

"I suppose you've traced the components of the bomb?"

"Stuff you can buy in any hardware store, Ms. Ramadge. Except for the dynamite. We don't know where that came from yet. Probably stolen from a construction site. We'll find out."

She nodded. "You know that the bride, Mary Soffey Langner, was drowned at sea?"

"I do. Yes."

"I thought there might be a connection between the explosion and Mary's death." She put it tentatively and waited.

But instead of giving information his hitherto friendly eyes narrowed. "You have a reason to think that?"

She hadn't expected to be challenged. "It seems logical." Then she added anxiously, "Doesn't it?"

"In other words, you have a hunch."

She was just about to say yes, then realized that if she did, the interview would be over. If she admitted that's all it was, she'd be giving up. Also, she was tired of being humble. She met Pennock's look straight on. "No, Sergeant. It's a lot more."

"Oh? What then?"

"Common sense, that's what. Look, Sergeant, this is my first homicide case. I admit that. I admit I'm feeling my way, but that doesn't mean I should ignore the obvious. Whoever planted that bomb meant to get the newlyweds and got the bridesmaid instead."

He nodded. "Stella Blanchard."

"Mary's cousin," Gwenn added. "That was in the papers."

"And Clark Langner's longtime girl friend. That was not in the papers."

Gwenn gasped. "Are you sure?"

"I'm sure. I talked to friends of both parties. The bride may or may not have been aware of the relationship, but everybody else was. Langner and Blanchard had been going together on and off for a couple of years. It was a volatile affair. They'd break up, find other partners, then come back together again. The last rift occurred right after Thanksgiving. Langner told her they were finished and that he was marrying Soffey for her money. Made no bones about it. Blanchard told him he wouldn't live to enjoy it."

Gwenn frowned. "But there was no money. Oh, Mary had an allowance, but the real money wouldn't come till later. He must have known . . . he should have known. But maybe he didn't. Maybe he found out after they were married, when it was too late . . ."

"Not so fast, Ms. Ramadge," Pennock warned. "Stella Blanchard told her roommate she was going to break up the wedding. The roommate pleaded with her to let Langner go. Said all the things you might expect—that he was no good, a womanizer, an alcoholic, that she was well rid of him. But Blanchard wouldn't listen."

"You think she could have rigged the bomb and somehow inadvertently set it off and killed herself?"

"It's possible."

"But then who went aboard the ship and killed the bride?" Gwenn asked. "And why only the bride? Why not both of them if that was the original intent?"

Gwenn returned to Manhattan, turned in the rental car at Avis on East Sixty-fourth, and walked the short distance uptown to Clark Langner's bachelor pad. It was a brownstone tenement surrounded by high-rise, luxury condominiums. As she entered the dark hallway, she was immediately assaulted by the rancid mix of unventilated rooms and the heavy application of roach spray. The paint was peeling from the walls, the linoleum cracking underfoot. She could well understand that Clark would have done just about anything to get out of there. She wasn't sure whether he would be at work, but whether or not, the places he was likely to get a job and the set he ran with didn't get started till ordinary people, like his parents, were already in bed. She felt reasonably certain of finding him.

She rang and after a short wait he answered the door, opening it a crack. He didn't recognize her. She recognized him though, different as he was—the flab flopping over his belt, the heavy jowls, the hooded eyes and sluggish skin. His good looks were fast becoming a memory, Gwenn thought.

"Yes?" His manner was surly. He scowled at her and then a light came into his eyes, turned into a smile and with that smile he was once again the charming all-American she had once dated. "Gwenn? Gwenn Ramadge?"

"Hello, Clark."

"Gwenn! What a surprise. What are you doing here?"

"Aren't you going to invite me in?"

"Oh. Well, sure." He actually showed a trace of embarrassment. "This isn't my place. I . . . actually . . . a friend is letting me use it till I can find something. The rental market in New York is something else. You wouldn't believe how hard it is to get anything halfway decent. Here." He cleared a gray sweat suit from a Naugahyde-covered armchair beside a lumpy studio couch. Gwenn noted there was a bedroom, very small, off to the right. The kitchen, part of the living room, was equipped with a roller blind if the tenant should care enough to bother to use it. Apparently, Clark did not.

"So." He stood off and looked her over. "Well. Good to see you, Gwenn. Can I get you a drink?"

"No, thank you."

"I think I'll have a beer." It was only a couple of steps to the refrigerator. He took out a can, broke the seal, and swallowed greedily. "You're looking great, girl. Blooming. Got yourself a lover?"

She shook her head.

"Not still a virgin, I hope? I always told you—don't hoard it." He took another swallow. "So? I don't suppose you just dropped in?"

"I'm a private investigator."

He gaped. "You're kidding."

She handed him a card.

"I can't believe it. Who're you working for?"

She'd already decided it would be okay to tell him. "Ms. Soffey."

"Figures," he grunted. "She never liked me. None of the mothers like me. Not funny. Sorry." He had some more of the beer, the gulps not quite so desperate. "Well, she's wasting her money. If you know your job you know that and you shouldn't be taking it."

Gwenn ignored that. "I've just come from talking with Sergeant Pennock of the Nassau police. He's in charge of the investigation into Stella Blanchard's death."

"Poor Stel." He sighed. "I don't know anything about that. I had nothing to do with it."

"Not directly."

"In no way. No way. Stella knew the score. From day one. It was never meant to be forever with us and if she couldn't handle that . . ." He shrugged. "If you want to know what I think, I think she tried to kill us and ended up blowing herself away. Poetic justice."

It was a possibility she and Pennock had already considered, but she didn't tell Clark that. "What happened the last night of the cruise?"

"It's all on the record. Go read it."

"I'd like to hear it from you."

"So you can punch holes? Forget it. I've already been exonerated by the grand jury. I'm clear. No matter what you think, what you find, you can't touch me. That would be double jeopardy."

"Wrong. It's only double jeopardy if you've been brought to trial and found innocent. A grand jury hearing isn't a trial. The district attorney has the option of reopening the case on new evidence any time he feels like it."

He blanched at that. "And you expect me to supply such evidence? You've got to be real new at this."

She let it go. "As long as Mary's death is listed as an accident, you're vulnerable. If you're satisfied to leave it at that . . . It's up to you."

Langner drained the last of his beer. Then he crushed the can and tossed it into a wastebasket. His hands trembled so that he had trouble lighting a cigarette. Finally, succeeding, he took a deep drag. He held the smoke in his lungs so long that Gwenn thought there wouldn't be any to exhale. There was very little.

"The marriage happened fast. Which one of you was in a hurry?" she asked.

"Neither of us was in a hurry; we were both eager. Look, I made a play for Mary to get Stella off my back. Mary was so pathetically grateful that I was touched. I thought, why not marry the girl? Why not? She was crazy about me and she had money, not a lot but enough. Maybe she was what I'd been looking for all along and didn't know it. Maybe we could have a good life together."

Raising his forefinger, Clark pointed at Gwenn. "All right, the fact is she paid off my gambling debts. I was in real deep; I was desperate. She offered to bail me out. She sold her grandmother's jewelry and gave me the money on our wedding day. That was the deal. She kept her part and I meant to keep mine."

Gambling, Gwenn thought. Clark had so many vices, why not that too?

"After she paid your gambling debts, you had no more use for her."

"I didn't need to kill her to get rid of her. All I had to do was walk out."

"Or make her so unhappy that she'd walk out on you," Gwenn suggested. "Is that what you were trying to do?"

He took a long time answering. "I don't know. I'm not sure. I've known Mary since we were kids. We went to the same school. I felt comfortable with her. Maybe I even loved her. But I felt trapped."

"And how about her? How do you think Mary felt?"

Obviously, he'd never considered that. "Scared," he answered after a while. "That was it, I guess; that's what was wrong. She was shy and I was demanding. I scared her."

"You mean there was no prenuptial sex?"

"That was different. We were both free agents then. Know what I mean?"

Yes, she knew. Gwenn answered silently and intensely.

"After the minister spoke the words over us, everything was changed," Clark went on. "It felt different. I couldn't get used to it. I was rough with her. After the first night on board, she denied me. Night after night, she wouldn't let me near her. As soon as I made a move, she'd run out. So I drank. What else was I going to do? The last night I thought—the hell with it! I took her down to the cabin and left her there and went back up to the bar. I felt damn sorry for myself—it was my honeymoon too, after all. So there was a redhead looking for action. She had a cabin to herself and we went there."

"How long were you with her?"

"I spent the rest of the night. I got back to my cabin around six. Mary was gone. I was too loaded to worry about it."

"When you first told your story you didn't mention this. Why not?"

"I wasn't exactly proud of it."

"Really?"

"Yes, really. Besides, I didn't want to involve the red-head."

"Very considerate."

"Come on, Gwenn, you know what I mean."

"Okay. But once you were arrested, why didn't you speak up then? According to the coast guard record of the tides and the ME's preliminary exam, Mary went overboard around four A.M. This woman could have given you an alibi. She can still. It's not too late."

"Yes, it is. I don't know her name."

Chapter

SEVEN

Angela Fissore wanted to be married in Our Lady Queen of Martyrs Church in Forest Hills where she had attended parochial school. Then she wanted all the guests, mainly her school friends, to be driven by limousine to a big hotel in Manhattan for the reception. She had teased and pleaded, cajoled and sulked, but Emilio Fissore couldn't afford it. It was absolutely beyond his means. He offered to cater the affair himself and hold it in their home in Richmond Hill.

Angela wailed. "Not in the house, Papa. It's too small. Oh, Papa, I won't be able to have half my friends. You and Mama won't be able to invite any of yours."

The argument began in July when she first announced her engagement and continued through the summer.

"We could have it in the yard." Rosa Fissore found herself for the first time in the role of mediator between her husband and her child. "We could rent one of those striped canvas tents . . ."

"There's less room in the yard than in the house," the bride-to-be pouted. "And suppose it rains? Everything would be ruined. Oh, Papa, I want a nice wedding, something I can remember the whole rest of my life. I don't expect to get married but this one time," she said with a twinkle for her father.

Angela Fissore was typically Italian with olive skin, long, straight black hair, smoldering dark eyes. She was small, soft, big breasted, with a narrow waist and wide hips—voluptuous. Later, after the *bambini,* she would be fat. For now, she was tantalizing. She knew it, enjoyed it, used it. Always had. From birth, practicing on her father who had never before resisted her most outrageous whim.

Not so her mother. Physically, Rosa Fissore, thinner, more rigid, her dark hair pulled back and threaded with gray, dark shadows under her dark eyes, was a repressed version of her daughter. When she was young she had been as carefree and as irresponsible. As trusting. She'd learned soon enough there was more to life than satisfying passion. She'd had a good marriage with Fissore. Comfortable. Never lacking for material things. She'd been content. But never happy. No, she'd missed true happiness, she thought in this moment as she watched Angie at Emilio's knee.

Fissore was fifteen years older than Rosa. He was five foot seven. He had fine, bold features but coarse skin. His eyes were soft and brown, but too close together. His shoulders were broad, upper chest well developed, but out of proportion with his short, sturdy legs. Despite being in the food business, Fissore had taken care not to put on weight. Some women still thought him handsome. Subconsciously, Rosa resented her husband's love for the child, feeling he loved Angie more than he did her. How could she blame him? Rosa thought. She'd wanted to give him a son, but it hadn't happened. She couldn't blame him for concentrating his love on Angie. However, Rosa was a volatile woman given to fits of temper and she had on more than one occasion come close to blurting out her own disappointment, her vague sense of resentment. Thank God she'd never done it. She knew that once started she wouldn't be able to stop and the damage would be irreparable for all of them.

Rosa Fissore disliked the man Angie had chosen as much as her husband did. Ed Doran was instantly recognizable as Irish; red hair, freckles, a sparse beard—actually not much more than a golden stubble. He liked to hang out with the guys, watch sports events on TV, and knock off the beers. In high school he had been a linebacker on the team that won the regional championship—his one claim to fame. At twenty-five, he was already getting fat. Emilio had hired him to tend bar in the restaurant. Rosa could hardly look down on him for that; the restaurant was, after all, a family business started right after the marriage. He managed, she was at the cashier's desk, and Angie waited tables. Trouble was, Doran couldn't see beyond the conviviality at the bar. He had neither the interest nor the brains to take on any real responsibility. When the time came for Emilio to retire . . . God willing, that was a long time off.

"The house is small, Emilio." It was not often Rosa took her daughter's side. "A wedding should be an unforgettable occasion."

Their eyes met. Their wedding had been small with family and a few friends. Nevertheless, he couldn't treasure the memories more if it had been held in the ballroom of the Waldorf-Astoria. But times had changed and the young people had no sense of what things cost. Everybody wanted the best of everything—now. He sighed. "If you can keep things going at the restaurant," Emilio told his wife, "and if you're patient," he said to his daughter, "I'll get an outside job and we might be able to afford it."

The girl reached up and threw her arms around her father's waist and hugged him. Then she remembered, got to her feet and went to her mother. She kissed Rosa's brow.

Angela Fissore and Edward Doran were married on Saturday, January sixteenth in Our Lady Queen of Martyrs Church and the reception was held in Manhattan at the

Hilton Hotel. To Angela and those whom she wished to impress it was as elegant as the Plaza or Regency and as glittering as the Helmsley Palace. The affair had been nearly six months in the planning. What had started as a celebration by family and friends had been turned by professional consultants into an extravaganza of useless embellishments.

The wedding gown cost eight hundred and seventy-five dollars. The gowns for the bridesmaids were three hundred and twenty-five each. Hairdressers for the entire wedding party, including the mothers of the bride and of the groom, were provided—by the father of the bride, who else?

Wedding cake: symbol of love and good luck, was decorated to match the bridesmaids' dresses and cost four hundred and twenty-five dollars.

There was music in the church and at the reception. Of course.

There were flowers, not just the bouquets for the bride and her attendants and for the two mothers, but in places neither Rosa nor Emilio in their naivete had ever thought to put flowers—twined around candles, at the ends of each church pew, on the embroidered money satchels provided to accept contributions from their guests.

There was food and liquor. Naturally.

A professional photographer. Expected.

Video record of the entire event—not expected and estimated at anywhere between one hundred and fifty and three thousand dollars.

Then there were the prewedding festivities. Emilio Fissore kept on moonlighting till the night before the big day.

Angie and Ed Doran spent a week's honeymoon, financed by the gifts tucked into the aforementioned embroidered money satchels, in San Juan, Puerto Rico. On their return, Ed went back to work at the restaurant for his usual 3 to 11 P.M. shift. Angie stayed home to fix up the house they had rented. The bride, who had not been able to keep her room in her parents' home neat, was suddenly a compulsive housekeeper. Everything had to be just so. It irritated Doran.

"Hell, honey, a guy's got to have a place to put down his newspaper."

Angie was disappointed that he didn't take the same interest she did in making their nest pretty and snug. Also, she wanted him home at night. "Get a job with daytime hours," she told him.

"I like working for your mom and dad. I got no reason to change."

"The reason is I'm here alone," she pouted.

"I love you, honey, and all that, but I'm not ready to give up my friends and my life-style. If you're lonely here come on back to work with me."

So less than a month after the elaborate wedding celebration, Angela Doran was back waiting tables in her family's restaurant. She watched jealously as Ed served the single women who came in and chose to take stools at the bar rather than a table where she would serve. She took note of every laugh, understanding the women's heightened reaction to Ed's jokes. She recognized the looks they flashed, the hands lingering in his longer than necessary when turning over the money. She knew Ed was more interested in hanging out with his buddies than making it with any babe, at least any that dropped by the Ponte Vecchio. Yet she was suspicious. The acid was eating into her. Then she found she was pregnant. Now her highs and lows were explained. Joy replaced anxiety, but for a while she kept the knowledge to herself, hugged it close. She didn't tell even her father, or her mother, and not Ed. Not yet. She wanted just the right occasion. The first month's anniversary of their marriage would be it.

They both had the day off. Angie prepared dinner at home. She set the table with their wedding china, candles, the best linen, fresh flowers. It occurred to her that she shouldn't have had to buy the flowers herself, that Ed should have remembered. Maybe he still would. Never mind. After tonight, after she told him, everything would be perfect between them again.

He was less than enthusiastic.

"Gee, a kid, so soon?"

"I thought you wanted children. You said so. You said you wanted a family."

"Sure I do. You bet. But I thought we'd wait awhile. Have some fun, just the two of us, enjoy. You know. For Christ's sake, I thought you were on the pill."

"I stopped."

"When?"

"Right after we got engaged."

The whites of his eyes turned red. "You should have told me. You had no right to do that without discussing it with me first."

"I thought you'd be glad."

"Well, I'm not. So get rid of it."

"What?"

"You heard me. Get rid of it."

She started to cry. "I can't do that."

He stared at her, his eyes narrowed to cruel slits. Then without another word, he walked out to the hall and got his coat.

"I won't do it!" she sobbed. "I won't!" she screamed.

His response was to slam the door shut behind him.

A few moments later, Angie heard the motor start and the car pull out of the driveway.

Joseph Lombardi was retired. He lived with his wife, Clara. Because there were no children to come and visit, few friends, and little to talk about, they took an interest in their neighbors. Looking out the kitchen window the next morning as she stacked the breakfast dishes, Clara Lombardi commented that there was no movement around the Doran place. The shades were down. It had an abandoned look.

"They're sleeping late, that's all," Lombardi retorted. "You dramatize everything." He pushed his chair back and got up. It was a sunny day, warm for February, and time to take a walk around the yard and lay out his summer garden.

Joe Lombardi raised tomatoes, cucumbers, and zucchini in a small vegetable patch at the back, but his pride and his neighborhood reputation rested on the colorful display of flowers at the front. He spent a happy morning drawing diagrams of where the marigolds and ageratum should go next summer, the red salvia and white begonias. Maybe he should cut a new bed and put in those new variegated impatiens? While he strolled and considered, he couldn't help but look at the Doran house from time to time. The shades still hadn't been raised.

Clara was annoyed so there was little conversation at lunch. Lombardi was dozing in the den when his wife shook him by the shoulder.

"He's leaving," she said.

He didn't have to ask who. "So?"

"Alone?"

They both knew the Dorans went to work together.

"Maybe she left early," Lombardi suggested.

Clara shook her head. The Dorans went together in the station wagon. She came back alone in the station wagon shortly after ten at night. He either got a lift or came by bus around midnight.

"Maybe she's not going to work today," Lombardi mused.

But his wife was obdurate. "She had yesterday off. They both did. She told me."

Lombardi shrugged.

"She could be sick. I think I'll go over there."

"You'll do nothing of the kind. Mind your own business."

"Where's Angie?" Emilio Fissore asked his son-in-law as soon as he came through the door of the restaurant.

"Home. She's not feeling well."

"Oh? What's the matter with her?"

Ed shrugged. "I don't know. Women's problems."

Emilio and Rosa looked at each other.

"I think I'll call her," Emilio said. He picked up the phone at the cashier's counter and dialed. He let it ring seven times. "She doesn't answer." The comment was addressed to Doran.

"Maybe she went out." Ed went about getting the bar ready for business. "To the drug store. For medicine."

Fissore scowled. "Couldn't you have got it for her?"

"I could if she'd asked."

Nobody said any more. The normal work of setting the tables and the preparations in the kitchen went on as usual. A few minutes before three, Emilio tried the number again.

"No answer." He looked hard at Doran.

The bartender's normally florid complexion grew more so. "All right. Okay. So we had a fight. She's mad at me. Won't talk to me. Probably thinks it's me calling and that's why she's not answering."

"What did you fight about?" Fissore had no reluctance about asking.

"Nothing. She's jealous. God knows she's got nothing to be jealous about. I couldn't cheat on her even if I wanted to; she's got her eyes on me every second." The tight set of his father-in-law's jaw told Ed instantly that had been a mistake. He tried to correct it. "I love Angie. You know that. So maybe some nights I don't rush home right after work. I like to wind down, have a couple of drinks with the guys. That's no crime."

Again Fissore's disapproval was palpable, but he didn't say anything.

Business was brisk, but Emilio found time to call again and again. Without result. Finally, at nine, with both bar and kitchen at peak activity, he turned to Doran. "Go home. Go home and make it up with her."

"You're the boss." Doran threw down his towel and put on his jacket.

"And tell Angie to call me," Fissore yelled after him.

By eleven there was still no word.

"He's had more than enough time to get home," Emilio complained to Rosa as he had over and over for the last hour. "If he went home. He probably stopped somewhere for a drink. He's loaded by now. God knows when he'll turn up—or where. You close up," he told Rosa. "I'm going over."

"Emilio, no! Don't interfere."

"I'm not interfering. I'm just going over there to make sure she's all right. I'm not interfering."

"Maybe the phone's out of order."

"I already checked with the operator, okay? You go ahead and ask again."

"Aren't you going to wait?"

"No." He pulled on a sweater, then put a down coat over that.

He had that stubborn look that came over him only when they argued about Angie, Rosa thought. It meant reasoning was useless. She knew it, but wasn't ready to give up.

"Leave them alone," she said. "They're having a spat. A lover's quarrel. You interfere and you won't get any thanks from either one."

"Thanks isn't what I'm after."

Fissore had to go home to get the car. It was an easy ten-minute walk, but he did it in seven. Heart pounding, he got in and turned on the ignition. His hands were sweating as he gripped the wheel. It was a short run along

Queens Boulevard to the Kew Gardens Interchange and the Whitestone Expressway. He went off at the last exit before the toll booths for the bridge and reached his daughter's house in record time.

It was in the middle of a block of tract houses as alike as paper cutouts. Almost everyone had tried to achieve individuality in some manner; some by the paint job, some by enclosing the front porch, by elaborate landscaping. Angie and Ed's place achieved it by neglect. The rectangle of lawn needed to be raked clear of leaves and rubbish; yesterday's trash cans were still at the foot of the drive. *Slob,* Fissore thought. He noted there was a light burning in the downstairs front room though the rest of the house was dark. It puzzled Fissore and increased his anxiety. He got out and took a quick look into the garage. Doran's beat-up station wagon was inside.

So he'd made it home, Fissore thought. Why hadn't he called? What could have happened for him not to call? he asked himself. Well, suppose Doran got home and he and Angie made up and then went to bed. That was reasonable. They'd gone to bed and made love, and the last thing on Doran's mind would have been to call his father-in-law. He'd plain forgotten just like he'd forgotten to turn out the downstairs light. Who could blame him? In that case, Fissore should turn around and go home himself.

He couldn't. Instead, he parked, switched off the engine, and sat awhile waiting—he didn't know for what. Gradually, the silence his arrival had broken was restored. Slowly, almost cautiously, the small night sounds manifested themselves—vague scamperings of unknown creatures, an eerie sighing of the wind amid the bare branches. Then the fog began to roll in, reminding Fissore that New York was, after all, an island and that one was never far from the sea.

The silence and the mist wrapped around him so that

he felt totally alone, isolated from everyone and everything. He felt empty. He wanted to weep over his loneliness. But Fissore was not one to indulge in self-pity. Sitting there was useless and he couldn't go home without knowing what had happened. Rosa would be furious, but he had to go inside. He couldn't help himself. He got out of the car, made sure not to slam the door, and walked up the path to the porch and the front door and rang the bell.

No answer. He rang again noting the hollow sound it made inside. He tried the door. Locked. What now? He felt his blood tingling. He was burning, but his hands were like ice. If he yelled, he'd wake the whole neighborhood. He went around to the back. The upper half of the kitchen door was composed of four glass squares. One of them had been knocked out, the one nearest the knob.

He entered and turned on the lights. Plates were set out on the serving counter. The good china. Pots and pans were ready on the stove. He flipped on the oven light and through the glass window saw a roast congealed in its juices—it must have been cooked, and the flame automatically turned off. He passed through to the dining room. The table was set with the best silver, flowers, and candles. He continued into the living room.

The light he'd seen from the street came from Angie's favorite lamp with a pagoda-shaped silk shade. Except for the dinner that had been prepared but never served, everything appeared to be in order, normal. Then as he approached the front of the house and the stairs, Emilio Fissore looked over the back of the sofa and saw Ed Doran sprawled out, his muddy shoes dirtying the pale peach upholstery. Asleep. Mouth wide open. Passed out.

"Bum," Fissore muttered. He stood over the man not knowing what to do. He thought about the broken glass in the kitchen door. Could it have been Doran who was responsible? He might have forgotten his keys, Fissore conjectured. He might have rung the bell and Angie, still angry, refused to come down and let him in, so he'd broken the glass. "Lousy bum."

What should he do now? Angie shouldn't be upstairs alone with the kitchen door as good as wide open. He couldn't just go away. He had to go upstairs and look in on her. His hand shook as he grasped the bannister, but he didn't give himself time to hesitate.

He put on the hall light. It lit the way up the stairs and illumined part of the landing. The door of the master bedroom was ajar. At the threshold the light from the street was enough for him to see the bed—rumpled, but empty. He could see that the room was empty, and that the bathroom door was closed.

Later, he couldn't remember opening the bathroom door. He couldn't remember kneeling to reach in across the threshold and raising Angela to cradle her in his arms. He didn't remember how long he cried over her before he called the police. He did hear the doorbell though it sounded far away. When he went down to answer it, his pants were stained where he had knelt in Angie's blackened blood. The front of his coat was smeared with it and it was on his hands.

"There he is!" he told the two Radio Motor Patrol officers, and pointed. "There he is, the murdering son of a bitch! He did it. He killed my daughter."

Doran, still on the couch, barely awake, still clearing his vision, sat up. He took in the presence of his father-in-law and from Fissore's disheveled figure, his contorted face, and wildly staring eyes, he shifted to the cops. "What's going on? What's happened?"

Fissore exploded. He charged at Doran, grabbed him by the lapels of his jacket, and hauled him to his feet. "Murderer!" He cocked his right fist and smashed Doran in the jaw. "Murderer!" Muscles bulging, chest expanded, he hit him again. "Murderer!" The police finally took action.

Ed Doran had both arms up to shield himself, but he didn't try to retaliate. He seemed totally confused.

Restrained by the officers, all that was left for Emilio Fissore were sobs of rage and frustration.

Chapter

EIGHT

Detective Lewis Sackler, Queens Homicide, had just got home from a late date. Carol Lee Landauer was her name. She was attractive, smart, held a good job on the public relations staff of the Metropolitan Opera. They'd been going together for about three months, but the relationship hadn't caught fire. Lew Sackler had the distinct impression, particularly lately, that Carol Lee considered herself superior to him. She was certainly more intellectual, Sackler thought. When they'd said good night, he had routinely added he'd be calling her. She replied she was going to be busy for the next couple of weeks. That was a shock. Sackler was handsome, he had what some considered a glamorous job, and he wasn't used to being given the heave. Okay, it would be easier this way; he could just stop calling without a fuss. Sackler seldom drank before going to bed, but on this occasion he went into the kitchen and got himself a can of beer. It was his farewell to Carol Lee. He had taken only a couple of swallows when the phone rang.

Lew Sackler arrived at the scene shortly before 3 A.M. Nobody from the medical examiner's office had shown up. Probably they'd send a part-timer, someone who had his own private practice and filled in as needed. Those guys

were never in a rush, Lew thought. Never mind, the manner of death was obvious: She had been stabbed repeatedly
and brutally and hemorrhaged profusely. He had to force
himself to look closely. He could see that the wounds were
not fresh, and whoever finally showed up wasn't likely to
estimate the time of death any more precisely than he could
himself. As the murder weapon hadn't been conveniently
left behind, he would need a forensic opinion on the depth
and width of the wounds to determine the size and type
of knife, but he didn't need it to reconstruct what had
happened. The victim was a beautiful young woman about
twenty-two. She was in her nightgown. She had been
stabbed repeatedly on the upper part of her body, front
and back, but her face had been spared. The blood from
the various slashes intermingled, obliterating some; again,
the precise number was not important. The way Detective
Sackler saw it, she had been surprised in bed (it was tumbled), had got up and tried to escape, but was chased into
the bathroom and was cornered there. She had been knifed
in the chest; her bloody arms indicated she had tried to
shield herself. Then she had turned away, cringing between the shower and the basin, and the knife had been
plunged into the back below the left shoulder—reaching
the heart? Was that the fatal wound? She slumped to the
floor and was left there to bleed to death.

The blood was everywhere—on the walls, floor, basin,
tub; yet not a drop outside. There were some smears at
the threshold made by the father as he knelt to reach for
his child, but otherwise the bedroom carpet was clean.
Shouldn't the killer have left tracks? Sackler wondered.

The husband, Edward Doran, swore that when he got
home he had not seen his wife. The house had been dark.
He had assumed she was upstairs asleep and decided not
to disturb her.

"What time was that?" Sackler asked.

Doran lifted his right shoulder in a gesture Sackler would come to recognize as defensive. "I'm not sure. I stopped on the way for a couple of drinks."

"A couple!" His father-in-law snorted. "He was passed out, dead drunk. Ask your officers here. They saw him. They'll tell you."

The RMPs had arrived within minutes of Fissore's call to 911. After pulling him off Doran, they'd sat both men in the kitchen at opposite ends of the table while they used the kitchen wall phone to make the usual notification. Sackler had got there first. By the time the various teams of experts—forensic, photography, fingerprints—arrived, he had ascertained the basic facts and was into the preliminary interrogation.

"We've heard your story, Mr. Fissore. Now I'd like to hear what Mr. Doran has to say."

Fissore clamped his lips together in a straight line of disapproval.

Sackler ignored it. "What time did you get home, Mr. Doran?"

"Ten. Ten-thirty at the outside."

"That's a lie!" Fissore burst out. "I called every fifteen minutes from ten o'clock on and there was no answer. Why didn't you answer the phone if you were here?"

"I'll ask the questions, Mr. Fissore," Sackler said quietly.

Lew Sackler was six foot three, fit and lean, and didn't need to raise his voice to be intimidating. His rugged features were dominated by a high, clear brow from which wavy dark hair swept back. He was twenty-nine and had seven years with the department, three as a detective—first on Burglary, then Neighborhood Relations, and for the last seventeen months, Homicide. Whereas some officers quickly became jaded, hardened to the violence and human degradation to which they were routinely exposed, Lew Sackler had so far remained sensitive and compassionate. He also remained intensely interested and eager to develop his skills. He knew that in a case of this kind, the spouse was always the primary suspect. Here there was the added friction between spouse and father of the victim. It was acting as a stimulus on each so that the last thing Sackler wanted was to separate them.

"Go on," he told Doran.

The freckles stood out on Doran's face like fresh scabs. He looked weak, helpless, scared. "Okay, so maybe it was closer to eleven. To tell you the truth, I wasn't anxious to come home. We'd had a fight, Angie and me."

"What happened when you did get home?" Sackler asked.

"Nothing. The house was dark. I put the car in the garage and came inside. Like I said, the place was dark, so I figured Angie was upstairs asleep. I sure didn't want to wake her, so I figured I'd sleep down here in the spare room. I guess I didn't make it past the couch," he admitted ruefully. "The next thing I knew, Emilio had me on my feet and was shaking the hell out of me and yelling and beating on me. I had no idea what for."

"The hell you didn't!"

It took only one look from Sackler to silence Fissore. He didn't want to be removed any more than the detective wanted to remove him.

"So when was the last time you saw and spoke with your wife?"

"When I left for work this afternoon. I mean, yesterday afternoon."

"Can you be specific?"

"I left a little after one-thirty. Thereabouts."

"You were still arguing?"

Doran had trouble with that. "We weren't talking. At least, she wasn't talking to me."

"But she was all right?"

"Sure."

"You said she wasn't feeling good," Fissore broke in.

"I had to say something to get you off my back," Doran retorted.

The two glared at each other.

"So that was a lie?" Sackler asked.

"No, not exactly. She'd been complaining about not feeling good for the last few days."

"I see. Don't you think it's odd she didn't call her mother or father to inform them she wasn't going to be at work?"

Doran shrugged. "She knew I'd tell them."

Evasive, Sackler thought, going in circles. Lying, he decided, but to what extent?

"How did you know she wouldn't turn up at work? She wasn't speaking to you." He let Doran flounder for an explanation, then raised his hand to stop him before he could give it. "Apparently she was well enough to cook a very elaborate dinner." He indicated the array of pans on the stove and china on the counter. "A very festive dinner." He nodded toward the table in the dining room. "Maybe she had reconciliation in mind? Except that you didn't show up."

"I did show up. The dinner was for the night before last. Tuesday."

"So that was when you had the fight—Tuesday, not last night. What was it about?"

Doran shook his head.

"You're sure Tuesday night wasn't the last time you saw her? You're sure you saw her Wednesday before you went to work?"

"I told you."

"I don't believe you, Mr. Doran. Your wife prepared this festive meal for you Tuesday night, but it wasn't eaten. The dishes weren't used. The meat is still in the oven." To underscore, Sackler pulled down the oven door and then closed it again. "From the looks of the rest of your house your wife was a good housekeeper. Why do you suppose she didn't clear up in here?"

Again, Doran shook his head. Fissore watched him.

"You say you had a fight and walked out. On the Tuesday. When did you get back? What happened when you got back?"

"I got back around four in the morning, yesterday morning. I slept in the spare room."

"That's two nights in a row you didn't sleep in your own bed? The first night in the spare room and tonight on the couch."

"Yes."

"And where was your wife all this time?"

"Upstairs. I suppose."

Sackler fixed him with a hard stare. "Okay, Mr. Doran, one more time. I want a straight story."

Doran swallowed. His face was oily with sweat. "I am telling it to you straight. We had a fight." He took a deep breath. "Okay, she was pregnant. I didn't want the baby. I told her to get rid of it. She refused. I walked out. I had a few drinks with the guys and when I came back the house was dark. I figured she was asleep. I didn't want to wake her and start the argument all over again; I was in no shape for it. So I spent the rest of the night downstairs."

"You left your wife without eating the dinner she'd prepared and went out on a drinking spree. You got home . . . at what time?"

"I don't know. After the bars closed."

"You didn't speak to her then, but you did see her and speak to her later that morning before you went to work? Wednesday morning."

"That's right."

"So what happened? Did you make up?"

"Oh, yeah. Sure."

"You made up and then you went to work. So why didn't she go with you?"

"I told you, she wasn't feeling so good."

"He's lying!" Fissore exclaimed. "He wants us to think

Angie was still alive Wednesday morning so he'll have an alibi. God, it's so obvious."

Sackler glared at him. Things were moving fast. Doran was a strong suspect. Should he now read him his rights? There was some leeway here, at least until Doran was taken into custody. It was a gray area in which the officer could use discretion. Lew Sackler decided to take advantage of it.

"Your wife was dead by the time you left for work on the Wednesday afternoon, Mr. Doran."

Doran gasped. He heaved a couple of times but managed to contain himself. "I didn't do it," he said at last. "I swear to God."

Not once had the man expressed any sorrow or regret for his bride, Sackler thought, only concern for himself. Doran must at that moment have become aware of the same thing because he blurted, "I loved Angie. I loved her."

"Who do you think killed her?"

"I don't know. An intruder. Who else? Everybody loved Angie. It had to be an intruder. Somebody did break in." With rising excitement, the husband pointed to the broken glass of the kitchen door. "Look at that."

"He did that. He did that himself," Fissore said.

"That's ridiculous. I have keys."

"You wanted to make it look like somebody broke in."

"Quiet. Both of you," Sackler stopped them. "Now, Mr. Doran, I want to know the last time you saw or spoke to your wife. You can tell me here and now, or you can come over to the precinct and tell it to my sergeant."

"All right. I walked out before dinner Tuesday and I never saw her again." The full realization that he never would finally hit home. Tears welled up; he blinked them back. "Like I said, I tied one on and got home real late. I didn't go upstairs and I didn't see her the next morning."

"In other words, you slept in this house a part of two

nights without attempting to make contact with your wife? You didn't go upstairs and knock on the door, or call to her? You didn't even go up for a change of clothing? Did you have a change in the spare room?"

"No. I wore what I'd had on the day before."

"In fact, you avoided going upstairs. Why?"

"Because I knew I was wrong. I knew I'd treated Angie bad. Because I wasn't ready to admit it."

"How about tonight when you finally got home? Weren't you ready then either?"

Doran hung his head.

"You didn't call 'Hi, honey, I'm home'? You didn't go up? How did you know she was even there? She could have been out."

"I was drunk," Doran mumbled.

"What? I didn't catch that, Mr. Doran."

"I was drunk!" he shouted.

Sackler nodded. "Well, you'll have to come to the precinct with us and make a formal statement. You too, Mr. Fissore, we'll have to ask you to come along."

"What about my car?"

"One of the officers will drive it home for you."

"Now? You mean you're taking us in now?" Doran asked.

"Right now." Sackler pulled the dog-eared, plastic-covered card from his wallet and began to read the familiar Miranda warning. Doran wasn't listening. He was looking down at the streaks of blood on his white bartender's shirt.

"I can't go like this."

"Change, go ahead. Take a shower," Fissore told him. "Take as many showers as you want, you'll never get Angie's blood off you."

Chapter
NINE

Benjamin Cryder didn't tell his bride of two years the true results of the battery of tests he'd been undergoing during the weeks before they came south. And he'd ordered his physicians to remain silent. He let Tricia think he was cured. He let the outward signs—the return of appetite and resultant weight gain, the surge of energy, his zest—attest to his recovery. But it was only remission. A temporary respite, an illusory and, in a way, cruel period of normality. A false promise. The doctor had told Cryder he had at least six months, probably more, and Ben intended to enjoy every day of it with Tricia at his side blissfully unaware the end was so near. In celebration of what she thought was his full recovery she'd wanted to go around the world. He let her think he turned the trip down because it was physically taxing. She didn't question that. Why should she?

The house in Palm Beach was a favored retreat. It had originally been a small convent. Laid out in the Spanish style around a central patio, it provided a sense of self-containment which Cryder's larger properties lacked and which both Tricia and Ben valued. Though from different backgrounds, they shared many interests; they were compatible. They settled quickly into a routine: a round of golf in the early morning before the day's heat, lunch at the club, back home to glance through the mail sent by his secretary from New York, an afternoon's nap, a planter's punch on the veranda at sunset, dinner with friends followed by bridge to round out the schedule.

During the long lazy afternoons, Ben Cryder took to letting his mind wander back over the years to open doors long shut and peer into dark and forgotten corners. He thought a lot about Anne Soffey. An image of Annie—tall, slender, with long dark hair and luminous eyes—rose before him. She was different now, of course. He'd seen her picture in magazines: She had auburn hair, dressed stylishly, and carried herself with the poise of a self-earned success. Back then in that nearly forgotten past, they had both been nobodies and broke. Well, Annie could always get money from her mother, Grace Soffey, but not in the sums he had lusted for. Now they both had real money and their names were household words. They had both made good, he mused, so his decision had been right. He'd never doubted it. No reason to doubt it now.

It occurred to Cryder that Tricia was very like Annie in many ways and it was one of the reasons he'd married her. He considered confiding in her. Two things put an end to his speculations. The first came in the mail. It was an envelope posted locally. It contained a newspaper clipping.

NEWLYWED'S ANNIVERSARY HORROR
Bride Found Brutally Stabbed

Queens police are investigating the murder of a bride found stabbed and lying in a pool of her own blood in the upstairs bathroom of her house.

The body of Angela Doran—married exactly one month—was found by her father, while her husband, Edward Doran, bartender at the Ponte

Vecchio restaurant on Queens Boulevard, slept
downstairs on the living room couch.

There was nothing else in the envelope, just the clipping.

Shortly after, the pain returned. It was just a stab at first,
quickly gone. Cryder tensed and then relaxed. A leftover,
he assured himself. Two days later it came again; it was
sharper and lasted longer, and the ailing man knew this
was no remnant but a harbinger of what was to come. His
doctors had erred and their prediction had been wildly
optimistic. He tried to hide his suffering from Tricia, but
he was going downhill too fast. She had to notice the
change, to see that he was listless again, tired too easily.
Under the fresh tan, his skin took on a greenish cast. He
couldn't force himself to eat and his weight was going
down. She pretended all was well and for that he was
grateful, but he knew that soon they would both have to
acknowledge the reality and he would have to go back to
New York and the doctors. The time had also come to acknowledge his past and to try to make amends. He was
overwhelmed by a sense of urgency.

He had hired one man, only one, in order to maintain
confidentiality, but that wasn't important any more. He'd
hire more detectives and call his lawyers. Except that he
still didn't want Tricia to know. It had all happened so
long ago that it shouldn't matter to her, but you never
could tell. As neither one of them could ignore the state
of his health any longer, Cryder made that the reason for
going back. He also tried to get Tricia to stay behind.

"It's only some minor thing, I'm sure. Not connected to
the main problem. I'll be back before you know it."

But she wouldn't hear of it. "We'll go up together and
come back down together," she said, firmly maintaining
the fiction. She managed to smile, but her blue eyes be-
trayed her.

* * *

Money couldn't vanquish death, but it might manage to hold it back for a while and to some extent ease the process.

The Westchester mansion was turned into a private hospital. There were nurses around the clock, therapists, a private nutritionist. Two doctors paid house calls on a daily basis to examine Cryder and administer medication. An X-ray machine was installed. A respirator was on standby.

A parade of CEOs from the various Cryder enterprises passed through the sickroom. Sometimes they stayed over for several days. Lawyers and secretaries accompanied them. Papers were drawn up, signed, and witnessed. Benjamin Cryder was putting his affairs in order.

Patricia Garvé Cryder supervised and managed it all—the household staff, the medical team, the comings and goings of her husband's business associates. She took her evening meal at his bedside. It was the only quiet time they had together.

"I wish you'd slow down, Ben," she said one night after two weeks of hectic activity that had become routine. "It's not doing you any good."

"Actually, it is. It's putting my mind at rest. I have obligations. Once they're taken care of, I'll feel better. Then I'll relax."

"Can't I take care of them for you?"

He studied her. She was as beautiful as ever. Her thick, chestnut hair shone in the lamplight. Her eyes were full of compassion. "This is something I have to do myself."

"I only want to help, Ben. To make things easier."

He hesitated. "Everybody makes mistakes. Everybody has regrets, wishes they'd done things differently. Nobody can undo what's done, take back a word or an action. You can't erase the pain you've caused, but sometimes, if you're lucky, you can make a form of restitution. Money can sometimes do that."

Tricia Cryder reached over and put her strong brown hand over her husband's frail liverish one. It was trembling. She squeezed it. "Whatever you want, Ben."

"I want you to know I love you and I won't forget you."

Tears brimmed in her eyes. "We won't talk about it." She leaned over and kissed him. "Go to sleep now. Get some rest."

Obediently, he closed his eyes.

She sat back in the chair and waited till she could tell by the regularity and depth of his breathing that he was asleep. Then, turning out everything but the small nightlight, she went back to the room down the hall which she'd been using since their return from Palm Beach. She went right to bed but sleep wouldn't come to her.

She was awake when the night nurse pressed the alarm button. She ran with the medical team and the rest of the household. The nurse was already applying CPR and the patient was resuscitated within two and a half minutes and placed on the respirator. Both personal physicians arrived within the hour. After consultation, they gave their opinion that Mr. Cryder had not suffered significant brain damage.

Mrs. Cryder wanted her husband to remain at home and the doctors agreed he could do so.

She thanked them and refused the sedatives they offered. After they had gone, she sat in her usual chair beside the bed as she had earlier that night and watched her husband's chest rise and fall, only then he had been breathing on his own; now he was under the control of the machine. She sat there watching and listening to the hoarse rasp of air going in and out of his lungs till first light. Then she went back to her temporary quarters and this time fell asleep as soon as she lay down.

For a period the parade of business associates, lawyers, secretaries continued; in fact the activity intensified as Patricia Cryder gradually took over her husband's affairs. As she became self-reliant, it thinned. Personal visits were discouraged. Problems were handled over the telephone if at all possible. The house emptied and was silent. Only Peter Taplin continued to report on a daily basis and in person.

Peter Taplin looked more like a businessman—could have been any one of those who had been going in and out of the mansion—than a detective. It was his intention to convey expertise without flamboyance, reliability without stodginess. Above all, he guaranteed confidentiality. Cryder had hired him in late August of the preceding year to do an identity check. It was a relatively simple job, and Taplin was able to reassure his client that the young woman in question was indeed who she was represented to be. He was well paid and also received a bonus, generous though not exorbitant. Since in the course of the investigation the detective had learned something of his billionaire client's past, he was not surprised to receive a second call from him shortly after Thanksgiving. He was given Cryder's private telephone number first in Westchester and later in Palm Beach and told to report on a weekly basis. There was no urgency, Cryder said. And Taplin, taking him at his word, was conscientious but didn't drive himself and cashed the paychecks that came in with a regularity to which he quickly became accustomed.

Taplin was forty-two, six foot three, thin as a broomstick. His face was pale and narrow, his brown hair curled at the top of his shirt collar. His mother came from Madrid and his father was of British extraction. So Taplin was possessed of a mix of Latin charm and Anglo-Saxon determination, both good attributes in his line of work.

Like Gwenn Ramadge, Taplin had served his apprenticeship working for a security agency, though one much larger than Hart S and I. He learned fast. One of the things he learned was that his efforts were the basis for the fee charged to the client, but he received a very small percentage of that fee. So he set up his own shop.

The next thing he found out was that clients were not

waiting at his door. What he got were referrals—jobs other agencies didn't want or were too full up to handle. Most were divorce cases. Taplin had no false pride about accepting them, always assuming the money was right. If somebody was determined enough to get rid of a spouse, he was not likely to quibble over the cost. Nor did Taplin consider it a dirty job or think of the hours spent on stakeout as spying. If it were proved the spouse was committing adultery, he/she had brought it all on himself/herself. He merely gathered the evidence. If there was infidelity, Peter Taplin would discover it and document it. If not, he did not manufacture it. He established a reputation.

Cryder looked on him as an honest mercenary. Taplin, in his turn, was prepared to serve Cryder with his usual loyalty. Then he met Mrs. Cryder.

He had never known anyone like her. She was a stunner and at the same time she had class. He was sure she had no idea what her husband was up to. Taplin had never had close contact with the really wealthy. He had no conception of the kind of money they handled, no understanding of the world they lived in, nor the standards they lived by, but he had no trouble figuring why Cryder had hired him, and it was plain that Patricia Cryder would be getting the short end of the stick. On the day Mrs. Cryder took her husband to the Staffordshire for the champagne lunch which celebrated his recovery, Peter Taplin took Cryder's doctor's nurse out and learned his client was a dying man.

Rosy anticipation of a steady income faded.

What should he do? He had turned up a couple of strong leads so he could step up the pace, cut a few corners, find what Cryder wanted him to find, and maybe get a bonus. A dying man's gratitude.

Or he could confide in Patricia Cryder.

He would then get paid by both parties. When Cryder inevitably died, the investigation would end, but Mrs. Cryder would surely continue to be grateful. She wouldn't want anyone to know what Taplin had turned up. His silence would be as valuable to her then as ever.

The interview with Mrs. Cryder took place the day before she and her husband left for Palm Beach. He had no way of telling how much Tricia Cryder knew, but from Cryder's manner, the detective had formed the impression that she was totally ignorant. So he passed on only the basic facts and did so as delicately as he was able.

"Why are you telling me this, Mr. Taplin?" Tricia Cryder asked, her luminous eyes fixed on him. She was calm, but there was a light film of sweat on her upper lip.

He squirmed. "I thought you should know."

"If my husband wanted me to know, he would have told me himself."

The words were cold with disdain; the way she said them, sorrowful. Taplin didn't know what to make of the response. He hadn't been sure about the emotional reaction, but he had taken it for granted she would care about the money. Could he have made a mistake? Maybe, but in doing so he had given her information of great value and he wasn't letting it go for free.

"Mr. Cryder didn't tell me why he was undertaking the search, but it seems obvious . . ."

"I suppose he thought it was none of your business," she stated flatly and with finality.

Taplin marveled. She was either unbelievably selfless or a terrific actress. It was easier for him to deal with duplicity than honesty so he settled for the latter. "Mr. Cryder did indicate the matter was urgent. He offered a bonus of a thousand dollars for each week under six months in which the case was solved." Then to support the lie, he added the truth. "I guess he's in a hurry because he's dying."

Tricia Cryder gasped. A spasm of pain passed over her lovely face.

"Did he tell you he's dying?"

Taplin shook his head.

"Are you a doctor?"

"No, ma'am." He flushed.

"Then I'm not interested in your opinion."

"I'm sorry, ma'am."

He had totally misjudged the woman, Taplin thought, and he was ashamed. He'd assumed because she was so much younger than Cryder that she didn't really care about him. That the money was what counted. He should leave her to her sorrow, Taplin thought, but he couldn't just go. So he stood where he was and waited for her to say something. He waited until he couldn't wait any more.

"Excuse me, Mrs. Cryder, but what do you want me to do?"

"About what?"

"About the investigation. About locating this other woman."

"Do what my husband tells you. He's the one you're working for."

Five weeks later the Cryders returned from Palm Beach and on February nineteenth Benjamin Cryder suffered the stroke that put him into a coma from which it was unlikely he would ever recover. The next day, Patricia Cryder sent for Taplin.

He had expected she would now order him to stop the investigation, but she wanted him to continue.

"To whom should I report?" he asked.

"To me, of course."

Chapter TEN

In the two weeks since Gwenn Ramadge had taken on the Langner case she'd made disappointingly little progress. She excused herself on the grounds that the SS *Serena,* the cruise ship on which Mary and Clark had honeymooned, was at sea. Today, at last, she would be in port, and Gwenn had made arrangements to go aboard after passenger debarkation. Meanwhile, she lingered over coffee and the story on page two of the *Post.*

NEWLYWED'S ANNIVERSARY HORROR
Bride Found Brutally Stabbed

Queens police are investigating the murder of a bride found stabbed and lying in a pool of her own blood . . .

Another bride, Gwenn thought, apparently also killed by her husband. She couldn't help but compare the deaths of Mary and Angela Doran. They had married within weeks of each other and each was killed shortly after the wedding. The circumstances were totally different. Mary went overboard, but even if there had been a struggle it didn't compare to the violence of the other bride's death. The killer had plunged his knife into Angela Doran over and over, eleven times, long after she could be assumed to have stopped resisting and probably after she was dead.

The two victims were of different backgrounds, Gwenn continued the comparison, but the theme of the two murders was the same—the snuffing out of a young life at the time of supreme joy. Marriage, even in the present cynical times, Gwenn reflected, was still considered the high point of a life. The murder of a bride within days or weeks of her wedding was shocking. It was replete with what journalists call "human interest." It could and did knock politics and even sports events off the front pages.

While her coffee grew cold, Gwenn reread the piece. It struck her that in addition to the fact that both victims were brides there was another similarity in the cases: In each instance, at the time the murder was being committed, the husband, after a period of heavy drinking, slept. Or so each man claimed. Clark Langner stated he was in the wedding cabin, alone. The other groom, Edward Doran, lay sprawled in a stupor downstairs on the living room couch. Not every man who tied one on and came home drunk was a killer, but as an alibi it wasn't impressive. She reminded herself that the grand jury, in refusing to return an indictment against Langner, had in essence exonerated him. They had cited lack of evidence. She wondered how Doran would fare. She drank off the cold coffee, made a face, and went into the bedroom to dress.

It was her job to find evidence that might, at the least, cause the district attorney to reopen the case against Langner. She had got as much as she could from Clark himself, and she was still unsure about her own reaction to his story. She had never liked Clark; he was totally self-centered, dishonest, a womanizer, and a liar. What was there to like? And yet, at the end, he had touched Gwenn, enough for her to want to be very sure that his side of the events of that last night at sea were investigated. To do that she had to get aboard the *Serena* and today was the day.

She couldn't make up her mind what to wear and changed twice before settling on forest green wool slacks, a green and blue checked jacket, and a navy crew-necked cashmere sweater. The colors were good for her, she thought, surveying the effect in the mirror, but it would be cold on the water, so she added the short mink stroller with hood that was a leftover from the big-money modelling days. Appearance counts, Gwenn thought. People did react favorably to good looks and Gwenn had no qualms about making the most of what she had.

Lucky she'd dressed warmly and lucky she'd gone to the trouble of requesting permission for boarding, Gwenn concluded, as she waited at the foot of the gangplank in the winds gusting off the Hudson while her credentials were checked. She'd paid a personal visit to the Island Star Lines executive offices, but made little headway till she called on Anne Soffey. This time her client's influence had paid off. It was still paying off as she was not only cleared quickly but with profuse apologies for the formalities due to security. She was handed a VIP badge and assigned a thin, gawky sailor—whose adolescent skin marked his youth—as a guide. Probably he was also acting as a watchdog, she reflected, though she wasn't sure what mischief they thought she might get into. All she wanted was to take a look around, examine the cabin the honeymoon couple had occupied, stroll the deck where Mary had spent the lonely nights. She wanted not only to orient herself, but to get the feel of the ship, particularly to look over the sports deck and the jogging track from which Clark had suggested Mary might have been swept by the winds. Gwenn could see no reason for Mary to have been up there at the hour the autopsy indicated she had gone overboard and drowned. If she had, for some unknown reason, been there, Gwenn agreed with the captain that the wind would have had to be of gale force, which according to the ship's log it had not.

She talked to the cabin steward. Mario.

"Yes, Miss." He beamed at her. "I did know that Mr. and Mrs. Langner were newlyweds. The information is provided to the staff so that the service will be appropriate." He paused. "So that there will be no inadvertent intrusion on their privacy," he confided with a cheerful leer which was in no way offensive.

Mario might be quoting the brochure or service manual in his hesitant, heavily accented English, but there was no doubt he favored the policy. "Very thoughtful," Gwenn commented. "What was your impression of Mr. and Mrs. Langner?"

The light died; the pleasure faded. "I saw them together only the first night and then the next morning. After that, no matter when I came, Mr. Langner was always alone."

He knew, or guessed, Gwenn thought, more than he dared say.

Next she spoke to the steward who had served Mary and Clark breakfast in bed that first morning of their honeymoon cruise. Pablo. He too stated he had seen them together in the cabin only that once. Afterwards, every morning, Mr. Langner rang for coffee and toast for one. He, Pablo, had assumed the Senora was an early riser and took breakfast in the dining room. He was too young to regard this as an indication of the state of the relationship.

Next Gwenn looked up the dining room steward, Jacques. As she'd already learned, honeymoon couples were not unusual aboard the SS *Serena,* but Jacques remembered the Langners very well.

"Because they argued?" Gwenn asked.

"Oh, no, Miss. Honeymooners fight: the bride cries; the groom is nervous and unhappy. These two were so . . . polite. So stiff. Formal."

They were remembered because of what had happened afterwards, Gwenn realized. What had happened afterwards—a bride missing at sea, the police coming on board

to question the passengers and crew, the husband charged
with murder and then released—had fixed in their minds
details they might not even have noticed otherwise, certainly would have soon forgotten. The crew, the cabin crew
particularly, must not only have thought about it, but dis-
cussed it among themselves, thus keeping their memories
fresh.

The bartender in the Mermaid Lounge was no exception. Frank. A veritable United Nations, Gwenn thought.
It was part of a bartender's business to know what was
going on. He was a natural confidant to his customers.
According to Frank, the Langners came in together after
dinner each night. They danced to the music of the small
combo. He drank Dewar's on the rocks; she sipped white
wine. They left early.

"How about the last night?" Gwenn asked.

"The last night they left earlier than usual. Most people
do; they turn in to pack and get ready for debarkation the
next morning. But that night, Mr. Langner came back
alone. He got into conversation with a single lady. They
left together."

"Do you remember the lady's name?"

Frank shrugged elaborately.

"Can you tell me what she looked like?"

"She wasn't young, but not so old either. Red hair, not
natural. Plenty of makeup. Still attractive."

How was she ever going to trace her, Gwenn wondered.
"Is there anything else you can tell me about her?"

Frank shook his head. "I'm sorry."

Gwenn thanked him and reached into her handbag for
one of her business cards. "If you think of anything . . ."

"Wait! There is something. The lady sat at the captain's
table."

"She did?" Gwenn immediately grasped the implication.
A place at the captain's table was an honor accorded only
to the elite among the passengers. The captain and his

officers were very well aware of the identity of those to whom it was accorded. "That's very helpful, Frank. Thank you." She wondered if she should tip him? It would go on Ms. Soffey's bill anyway, she reminded herself, and fished for her wallet. Should it be a ten or a twenty?

Evidently the twenty was the right decision because Frank's eyes brightened and he remembered something else. "The photographer was very busy that last night. Everybody was getting his picture taken, especially the passengers at the captain's table."

Would he have remembered without the tip? Would it have occurred to her to check the photographer? Maybe. On the other hand, maybe not.

Chapter ELEVEN

Gwenn hadn't believed the redhead existed. Clark Langner had made her up, she thought. If the redhead didn't exist his alibi would remain in doubt, but there was also no risk that she would come forward and contradict his story.

But there was a photograph of the redhead, in fact, there were several; she was extremely photogenic. She was shown at the captain's table, sunning beside the pool, winning the limbo contest. The photographer, expecting to get paid, had her name. After that it was simply a matter of checking the passenger list. Before calling on Mrs. Maxine DeLloyd, however, Gwenn needed to know the precise time of Mary Langner's death; what had been in the papers wasn't good enough. She could go to the medical examiner's office and ask to see the autopsy report. There was possibly an easier and more satisfactory way—talk to the detective carrying the case. Anne Soffey had given her his name.

"Detective Daniels?"

Jason Daniels had his feet propped up on the bottom drawer of the desk, his head was tilted back, eyes closed. Was he thinking or sleeping? His mouth fell open and he snored.

Gwenn cleared her throat. "Detective Daniels?" she repeated more loudly. Instantly, he opened his eyes, put his feet on the floor, and pulled himself erect all in one motion. He had brown eyes, brown hair, and looked to be in his late twenties. "Yes?"

Gwenn held back a smile. "My name is Gwenn Ramadge." She handed him one of her cards. "May I speak with you for a moment?"

He glanced at the card, then waved her to a chair. "Shoot."

Maybe because they were close in age, or because she had walked in on him when she did, or both, Gwenn felt easy with him. "I'm investigating the Langner case. I understand you're in charge."

He hesitated. "It was my case."

Gwenn's heart sank at the use of the past tense, but she went on. "The victim's mother, Ms. Anne Soffey, hired me. I don't mean to butt in but . . ."

"Don't worry. I know all about Ms. Soffey. You're not stepping on anybody's toes."

"Oh. Thank you." One of the things Gwenn had learned from her interview with Todd Pennock was not to pretend to be more than she was. "This is my first homicide investigation and I need to establish the time of death. I've got a couple of witnesses who saw the victim wandering the decks alone at about three A.M. I know that's not good enough."

"No, it's not," Daniels agreed. "You need the medical evidence. The autopsy will give you a time within two hours and that's probably as close as you'll ever get. Two hours is close enough to prove or disprove most alibis—which I take it is what you're trying to do."

She nodded. "I was hoping you could save me a trip to the medical examiner's office."

"Ah . . ."

Their eyes met. Daniels broke into a grin.

"Why not? There's a copy in my file." He got up, walked over to a row of cabinets against the wall. He pulled out a drawer, found what he wanted, brought it back with him. Humming softly, he ran a finger down the page. "Here we are. She was spotted by an oil tanker near Ambrose Tower at approximately seven A.M. Sunday. *Condition of the body* . . . uh huh. . . . *adiposity* . . . *adherence of marine life* . . . and so forth and so forth . . . *Analysis of stomach contents* . . . *process of digestion* . . . *last known meal.* Put it all together, factor in the strength of the wind and currents and the place she was sighted, and they figure she went over sometime between three and five A.M. Saturday morning."

Gwenn took it all down. Finished, she stood up and held out her hand. "Thank you. I appreciate this. I really do."

"Not so fast. Don't you think you owe me something?"

She flushed. "What?"

He just looked at her for a while enjoying her embarrassment. "Well . . . like the name of the witness who's going to provide Langner's alibi."

"Oh." She should have realized he'd figure why she needed to know. Could he make her tell? She started to fumble through her handbag. "I don't know if I have it with me . . ."

"You expect me to believe you can't remember the name?" Detective Daniels asked, then he grinned. "Don't worry, Ms. Ramadge, I'm not going to cut you out. As far as my lieut' is concerned, Mary Soffey Langner either jumped or fell overboard. The case is closed. No more man-hours are to be expended on it. It's going to take some real hard evidence for the lieut' to change his mind and reopen the case. If you get that kind of evidence, I expect you to come to me. Otherwise, it's all yours. Deal?"

Before coming over Gwenn had told herself that she was running the risk of having the police take over. She'd told herself it wouldn't matter, that she'd be glad to see the case reactivated. It might even be enough to satisfy Anne

Soffey, and she could then withdraw. But now, at this moment, Gwenn Ramadge discovered that she didn't want out; she didn't want to withdraw gracefully or any other way. It was her case and she wanted to see it through.

"Deal," she said, and took his hand and returned his hard, firm grip with one equally hard and positive.

Gwenn Ramadge emerged from the gloom of the Rockaway station house with a wide grin on her face. She wasn't aware of the squalor of the street, the boarded-up stores, the fire-gutted buildings—only of the flaming sky as the sun set. She wasn't aware that as she stood on the steps of the ancient precinct house she blocked the entrance, nor was she conscious of being jostled as people tried to get by. She went on smiling, and harassed cops, surly suspects, anguished complainants merely shook their heads and stepped around her.

Wrapped in euphoria, Gwenn Ramadge walked the short distance to the subway station, actually an elevated, and waited for the train back to the city.

Maxine DeLloyd was thirty-nine. Her hair was a bit too improbably red, but her skin was without blemish. Her large, dark brown eyes were further emphasized by heavy makeup. She was certainly overblown, but still gorgeous. A divorcée, she lived in a luxury condominium—on what was known as "Condo canyon" on the upper East Side of Manhattan—whose mortgage and maintenance payments took up most of her alimony allotment. She had to scrimp to cover food and clothing and there was little left for dining out or entertainment. The friends of the marriage had split preponderantly to her husband. She wasn't the kind of woman other women sought out as a friend, so she had little social life. The Caribbean cruise had been the door prize at a big charity affair, but with the ticket— paid for by her husband's company and a leftover marital perk—Maxine DeLloyd's luck had run out. She had hoped to meet new people on the trip, but they had all been couples. She hadn't met any men. Except for Langner. And that had been a mistake. A terrible mistake.

When the police came aboard to question the passengers, Maxine had been shaking with nerves, but she had passed through as easily as the rest. Langner wasn't going to mention her, she thought, and their encounter had not been noticed. She promised herself to be more careful, more selective, in the future. So Gwenn Ramadge's call came as a shock, worse because she'd thought the danger was past. Gwenn explained how she'd traced Mrs. DeLloyd, and Mrs. DeLloyd couldn't deny what had happened. It would be better to unburden herself to a private investigator, a woman, than to the police, so she agreed to receive Ms. Ramadge the next day.

"May I offer you something—tea, coffee, a drink?"

"Nothing, thank you," Gwenn replied.

Maxine DeLloyd lit a cigarette and took a deep drag. "Frankly, I expected someone older. More . . . stern. Like a school teacher."

"I hope you're not disappointed."

"Oh, no." She inhaled another lungful. "In fact, I'm relieved. I'll tell you the truth straight out, Ms. Ramadge. I didn't know Clark Langner was married. I certainly had no idea he was on his honeymoon or that he was having problems. Apparently, a lot of the passengers did but I wasn't one. I swear. Otherwise, believe me, I would not have got involved." She puffed some more, but in a more relaxed way. "He was alone. I was alone. He came on to me. I came on to him. We were both drinking heavily. What can I tell you? I'm sorry it happened. I'm as sorry as I can be."

"But you found out the next morning," Gwenn said. "You found out all about Langner, that he was married and that his wife was missing and presumed overboard.

Why didn't you say anything? Why didn't you step forward?"

"Why should I? When I heard he was suspected of having murdered his bride, naturally I was shocked, but I had nothing to do with it. It wasn't my fault. I thought under the circumstances he would bring me into it. I waited for the captain to ask me and I was prepared to tell the truth. But Clark kept quiet, so I kept quiet too. And I've been a nervous wreck ever since, I want you to know. I jump every time the phone rings. When I heard the case was going to the grand jury, I was really scared. But nobody contacted me, and then the grand jury refused to indict. I thought it was all over."

"And then I turn up." Gwenn offered a sympathetic smile.

The redhead nodded.

"I'm just interested in clearing up a couple of points," Gwenn told her. "I'd like to know how long you and Langner were together that night?"

"Why? If he's been cleared, what does it matter?"

Gwenn knew very little about Mrs. DeLloyd beyond what she'd learned from the ship's register, the bartender, and cabin steward. She knew she was divorced and lived alone. Where she lived indicated she was well off. Her reluctance to be involved was understandable. However, given today's moral standards, or lack of them, her nervousness seemed excessive.

"The case was dismissed for lack of evidence," Gwenn explained. "That doesn't mean the district attorney can't try again, any time. With new evidence he could go back to the grand jury and maybe get an indictment. Then the case would go to trial."

"That's not my problem," she shrugged.

"If that happened, Clark Langner might be forced to name you, to bring you into it. You could be called as a witness."

"You mean I'd have to appear in court?"

"Possibly. Probably."

"I couldn't do that."

"You wouldn't have any choice," Gwenn told her.

"No." Maxine DeLloyd shook her head.

"Maybe if you'd answer my questions, it wouldn't come to that."

The woman hesitated. The deep frown cutting in the center of her forehead, the working of her lips back and forth till all the lipstick was gone, these were indications of an inner struggle. "No," she decided. "No, there's nothing to tell. I can't help or hurt Clark. I don't know anything. Nothing happened between us. We had a few drinks at the bar and then we went out on deck for a while. I said good night and went down to my cabin alone."

Gwenn started to protest, but Mrs. DeLloyd did not allow it. "I don't care what he says. You can't prove otherwise."

Gwenn just stared. What had gone wrong? The woman had seemed, if not forthcoming, at least willing to answer direct questions. By implication she'd acknowledged that she and Clark Langner had sex. Now, she was denying it. Gwenn was at a loss. She looked around the large, opulently furnished room searching . . . for what? It was filled with the currently fashionable and expensive clutter—porcelain, silver, crystal, large and small bouquets of dried flowers, a battalion of photographs in silver frames. All of it could be bought by the boxful in any of the good antique shops on Madison or Columbus avenues. Even the photographs, Gwenn thought, though Mrs. DeLloyd herself appeared in several, so obviously not the photographs.

"I'm sorry, Ms. Ramadge, I have another appointment. I'll have to ask you to excuse me."

Gwenn looked more closely at the pictures. "Is your divorce final, Mrs. DeLloyd?" she asked, still not sure where she was heading.

"Yes."

So there could be no anxiety that her behavior might affect the settlement. Nevertheless, instinct drove Gwenn to pursue the subject. "How long since it was finalized?"

"That's none of your business. I'm asking you once again to leave. Otherwise I'll have to call security to escort you."

Gwenn felt a surge of excitement. "Did your husband file or did you?" she asked, but the answer was there in front of her in an eight-by-ten color photograph of a boy in a sailor suit, fair hair slicked down, eyes round, chubby face grave with the importance of sitting for a formal portrait. He looked about five years old.

"Is this your son?"

Maxine DeLloyd's whole body sagged. She nodded. "His father has custody. I get to see Roger one afternoon a week and his father's trying to cut that down. A scandal like this would play right into his hands." She was on the verge of tears as she reached for a cigarette from a Jensen's silver box forgetting there was one already lit and smoldering in the Baccarat crystal ashtray.

So that was it, Gwenn thought. "I'm sorry, Mrs. DeLloyd, honestly. I'd like to tell you that the encounter between you and Clark Langner will never be brought up again, but I can't." She paused. Anything else would be leading, even encouraging her to provide an alibi. "I think the truth will serve you best. I think the truth is your best chance to put it all behind you," she finished lamely.

It was this honesty that decided Maxine DeLloyd. She stubbed out the cigarette she'd just lit.

"Clark came into the bar a little after ten. It was about half full. I was alone as I'd been for the whole cruise and I was disgusted. Anyway, I spotted him looking around. I couldn't believe I'd missed a good-looking guy like that so I waved him over. I'd already had a few—so had he—and we continued drinking together. There was no real attraction. We each needed release. Nothing else was ever implied. Around one A.M. we went down to my cabin. We had sex. It wasn't particularly satisfactory. I don't know when I fell asleep, but it was already light when I woke; according to my clock it was six-thirty. Clark was sitting at the side of the bed, his back to me. I didn't speak. I watched as he got up and quietly started to dress. When he was ready, he turned around, but I closed my eyes and pretended to be still sleeping. I had nothing to say to him. Apparently, he had nothing to say to me."

"You're sure about the time?"

"The time I woke up? Oh, yes."

"Is it possible that while you slept Langner could have left you for a while and then returned?" Gwenn asked. "Without your being aware of it?" she added.

Maxine DeLloyd considered. "You mean he used me for an alibi? He picked me up on purpose so he'd have an alibi?"

"Possibly."

"God!" The redhead groaned. "And I thought I picked him up." She frowned. "But if he did leave me and go up on deck, find his bride and push her overboard and then came back again to me—well, wouldn't he have wakened me and said goodbye, made sure I was aware of the time he was leaving?"

"It would seem so."

"And later when the police questioned all of us, wouldn't he have called on me to verify his story?"

"He says he didn't remember your name."

Maxine DeLloyd flushed; her face was as bright as her hair. After a few moments she was able to set aside her embarrassment. "If he was using me, wouldn't he have made sure to remember my name?"

Ever since her meeting with Detective Daniels in Far Rockaway, Gwenn had been on a high. She thought she'd done well with the interrogation with Maxine DeLloyd too. But by the time she left the twenty-second-floor apartment and reached the lobby, her satisfaction was beginning to dampen. Out on Third Avenue in the bright winter sun and the raw, gusting wind, it turned to dismay. She had been hired to find proof of Clark Langner's guilt and what she'd just done was prove his innocence.

She'd found a witness who could, and she now believed would, support Langner's alibi. The time of Mary Langner's death was officially fixed at between 3 and 5 A.M. Langner and DeLloyd had been together at that time. Doubt could still be cast, but Gwenn believed a jury would decide that Langner had not left DeLloyd's bed in the interval. Furthermore, she thought the assumption that they had been together the entire time was strong enough to preclude the DA's reopening the case.

Gwenn was herself convinced of Clark's innocence. She couldn't go on with the investigation. She was certain Anne Soffey would no longer want her to.

Chapter
TWELVE

Having read him his rights, Detective Lewis Sackler took Ed Doran to the station house for further questioning. In this type of crime the spouse was always the primary suspect, so he was following routine. But Lew was also convinced that Doran was in fact guilty. Sure there were holes, inconsistencies, but he didn't foresee any difficulty in clearing them and making a case. He let Doran stew while he took the father-in-law's statement, and then set about breaking Doran.

But Doran held fast. Inconsistent and illogical as the account was, he didn't change it. In fact, he clung to it. Stubbornly. Desperately. Through what was left of the night and well into the morning.

Till Sackler began to have doubts. The assistant medical examiner, when he finally showed up, had refused even to estimate time of death. Sackler, who had at first thought it might have been around midmorning on Wednesday, was inclined to move it back. Because of the table set for dinner and the food laid out in the kitchen, it seemed to him that Angela Doran must have died some time Tuesday night.

A neighbor, Joseph Lombardi, saw him drive off some time after 8 P.M. on the Tuesday. He observed the station wagon in the driveway the next morning but had no idea when Doran had returned. Neither did Doran. He'd come home after the bars closed; that was as close as he could put it. He had not gone upstairs or tried to communicate with his wife. Not at that hour and not in his condition. His wife would have been madder than ever to see him like he was, Doran kept repeating. He clung to the argument as justification for his having spent the night downstairs.

Actually, Sackler had no problem with that. It was reasonable that after the quarrel Ed Doran would actually be avoiding his wife when he came home that night. And the next morning, too, though not even going upstairs to get a change of clothes seemed stretching it. He'd buy it, Sackler decided. One night, yes. Two nights . . . ? Could Doran really have come home the second night again to a dark and silent house and simply pass out on the living room couch? He had serious doubts. Yet that was the suspect's story. The story was so dumb, Sackler was beginning to believe it. Then he reminded himself that Doran had been doing some extensive, heavy drinking. Under the effects of the booze, he could have done what he said. Sackler scowled and clenched his teeth till his jaws ached. Or under the effects of the prolonged drinking, he could have committed the crime and blacked out. In which case, Doran would believe he was telling the truth and further questioning, for the time being, was useless.

The best thing he could do, Lew Sackler decided, was go home and get some sleep.

Sackler enjoyed Ranger hockey at the Garden, theaters, a good meal in a good restaurant, but he couldn't afford to live in Manhattan, not without a roommate to help pay the rent. He was past the age for the adjustments and accommodations necessary to make such an arrangement work. The solution was a small, but modern, comfortable apartment near the new Van Wyck station of the Independent

subway line. It was a five-story red-brick building overlooking the Expressway. It gave him ready access to the
city by train and his battered, still reliable Volvo got him
to the precinct and anywhere else he needed to go. One
night he came home to find a cat inside the apartment.
She'd climbed up the back fire escape and entered through
the partially open window. He kept putting her out and
she kept coming back, and he didn't have the heart to shut
the window against her. He called her Minerva and after
a while he didn't even go through the motions of trying
to lose her.

Sackler kept the Volvo in a small private garage in the
neighborhood only a scant three blocks from the building
where he lived. As he trudged home that morning of the
Doran murder, it seemed farther. He got there only to
discover the elevator was out—again. That meant five
flights up. On the last flight, Sackler heard the phone ringing in his apartment. He didn't rush. There'd be a message
on his machine. By the time he unlocked his door, the
ringing stopped. He didn't bother to check the recording.
It was much too soon for the autopsy report and at this
moment it was all he was interested in. This case, though
it would surely get a big play from the media, was of little
importance as far as the brass was concerned and therefore
would have little priority with the medical examiner. Angela Doran would have to wait her turn with all the victims
of violence throughout the city that night. As far as Sackler
was concerned whoever was on the phone, whatever it was
about, could wait.

After putting down Minerva's dinner, he shucked off
his clothes and fell into bed. He'd reported for duty yesterday at 4 P.M. It was now sixteen and a half hours later.

Due to political complications involving the police department and the city and various civil rights associations, the
department was dangerously short of officers at the level

of sergeant. The list of patrol officers who had passed the exam and qualified for promotion had been challenged on several points, among them that not enough minority officers qualified to take the exam, and that the exam itself had been biased against minorities. The promotions were held in abeyance while the argument went back and forth. Before it could be resolved, the time limit for appointment from that particular list ran out. Another exam had to be given. Many of the men and women who had taken the first test and passed nevertheless had to take it once again. This time the charge was that the questions had been leaked. It was not possible to know who had bought the questions and answers in advance so everyone was disqualified. Meanwhile, new recruits were admitted to the force as the budget allowed, but the numbers of those to supervise them remained frozen. The strain on these men increased with each day the situation remained unresolved.

Sackler's boss was Sergeant Elijah Powell, a tall, good-looking black man, son of a minister in the Church of the Holy Spirit and the Angels. Elijah was an only son brought up by his father to follow him in the ministry. He had a fine presence, a resonant voice, but he lacked the tact for dealing with the hierarchy. He had the unfortunate habit of telling the truth. Anyway, Elijah Powell was looking for something which would offer more action and more excitement. He joined the police force. It is customary, even standard, to represent police work as tedious, to underscore the plodding, boring routine of hours spent canvassing, dreary days on stakeouts. For Elijah Powell these only intensified the culminating moments of high drama when the net was drawn and the perpetrator apprehended.

It did sometimes occur to Sergeant Powell that perhaps his timing had been bad. If he'd waited awhile longer he might have become a part of a TV ministry. Think what that would have meant, his wife Phyllis would remind him all too often with a lugubrious sigh. When Powell was first appointed sergeant he had eight men under him. Standard. Involving the direct supervision of every detail of each man's duties, it was a manageable number. During the period in which promotions were delayed, his squad grew to twelve—a burden but possible. Now it was up to eighteen, and not only Powell but all the other sergeants complained. Nevertheless, TV ministry or no, if he had it to do over Elijah Powell wouldn't change a thing.

On reading the initial report Sackler had left for him, Powell considered the Doran case open and shut. The husband did it. It should be cleared in a matter of days. He was not pleased when Sackler came in that afternoon with second thoughts.

"As far as I'm concerned, all of what you say points to Doran's guilt, not his innocence," Powell said. "I wouldn't suppose he'd leave the murder weapon and his bloody clothes around the house for us to find. Probably he buried the stuff. If he was real smart he dumped it in a sewer and we'll never find it. But go ahead. Take another look. Go through the house. Check the grounds. Use dogs."

"If he was smart enough to get rid of the incriminating evidence, then why wasn't he smart enough to pretend that he found her dead when he came home and call us right away?"

"If all the perps were smart, we'd never catch a one," Powell snorted. "Let me ask you, if it wasn't the husband, then who?"

"Doran says an intruder."

Powell could see that Sackler was genuinely worried and he wasn't the kind of supervisor to dismiss this kind of concern. "He stabbed her . . ." Powell referred to Sackler's report which was in front of him. "You don't even have a count yet on the number of times. He had to have been a homicidal maniac."

"Yes."

"But a careful maniac. He made sure not to leave any

tracks," Powell pointed out. "Okay, so we'll give Doran the benefit of the doubt for now. Check the victim's background—her family, her friends, her enemies. Maybe there's a jilted lover somewhere. Try to find out where Doran was doing his drinking. But just you, not Finnister." Jim Finnister was Sackler's partner. "I can't afford to waste two men on a hunch."

It was a lot more than a hunch and Powell knew it, but Sackler didn't argue. "Thanks, Sarge," he said and got out fast.

At his desk, he dialed the ME's office. The first thing was to get an official time of death.

"You're telling me that Clark Langner is innocent?"

Anne Soffey sat at the large, elaborate desk in her large, eclectically decorated office. Behind her was the mandatory status-symbol picture window and panoramic view of the Manhattan skyline. Floor and walls were pale beige. The furniture was French provincial, and against the right wall a glass vitrine served to display the products from face creams to perfumes for which Soffey Cosmetics was famous. This was Anne Soffeys' domain. She was surrounded by the aura of her power. She appeared composed, but Gwenn sensed turmoil. She sat a little straighter as she prepared to deal with it.

"He has a very strong alibi."

"It can't be broken?"

"No, I don't say that. I say that I believe the alibi is genuine. Also, there's negative evidence in his favor."

Anne Soffey's face was hard. "Such as?"

Detective Daniels had shared the details of the autopsy with Gwenn so she could answer. "There was alcohol in Mary's blood, low level, but as Mary was not accustomed to drinking, even a small amount might have caused her to lose her balance and fall off the jogging track."

DA Hirsh had already suggested the possibility of suicide, and Gwenn had hoped that she wouldn't have to bring it up again. "Things weren't going well with Mary and Clark," she pointed out. "Several of the cabin crew noticed it and some of the passengers were aware of it. Clark would escort Mary down to their cabin around ten each night. About half an hour or so later Mary was back up on deck alone. She spent the nights on deck. The last night they went down together as usual, but this time it was Clark who came back. He went to the Mermaid Lounge. He picked up a woman and left with her and spent most of the night with her. Mary, if she was on deck as she had been every other night, could have seen them. It would have been the final blow, the rejection she couldn't deal with. The alcohol intensified her despondency. She believed the marriage was doomed . . ." Gwenn left it there.

Anne Soffey, however, had recovered. "I'm not paying you to guess."

"I know that. You hired me to find evidence of Clark Langner's guilt. Instead, I've found strong indication of his innocence. I believe in it. You don't. So it's only right that I withdraw from the case."

"You give up easily," Anne Soffey remarked. "I'm surprised. Considering the confidence Cordelia had in you, I didn't expect a quitter."

Gwenn flushed. "Cordelia taught me to be honest."

"So you've given me your opinion. Fine. Now I'll give you mine. My daughter did not fall overboard and she didn't jump. She was pushed. If Clark didn't do it, then somebody else did."

"Why? What was the motive? What reason would anyone other than Clark have to get rid of her?"

"That's up to you to find out."

"Me?"

"You've come this far; don't you want to see it through?"

* * *

To her own surprise, Gwenn had answered yes. During
the course of her investigation, pity for Mary's tragic death,
for the abrupt ending of what should have been the beginning of a new life, had grown within her. She did not
know why, but she felt personally involved, as though she
had a commitment to the dead girl. That Anne Soffey
thought enough of her to accept her conclusion of Langner's innocence and still be willing to authorize her to go
ahead in this new direction settled the matter.

If Clark had been the one who had gone overboard,
Gwenn would have started by looking up his old girl-
friends. But Mary had no old boyfriends; nobody who
would have killed her out of jealousy. So rule out passion.
That left money. Clark had admitted that Mary had paid
his gambling debts, but her death brought him nothing
more. Was there someone who did stand to gain by the
bride's murder? Young as she was, Mary was an heiress
and as such must have made a will. The executor for Mary's
estate was the same man who handled all of the Soffey
family affairs, Graham Dussart.

Graham Dussart received Gwenn in the study of his Park
Avenue apartment, which also served as his office. He had
bought the place back when $25,000 was considered a lot
of money. He wrote off most of the maintenance costs as
business expense, so he lived almost rent free. He offered
Gwenn a rich Colombian coffee served in a Georgian silver
pot and poured into bone china cups, but he had prepared
it himself.

Dussart was fifty-six, silver-haired, tall, distinguished. He
had a high brow, sharp features, and full, sensuous lips.
Though not rich himself, he moved in the circles of old
money. He lived well but carefully, padding his small income with the stipends earned by serving on the boards
of various large and prestigious corporations. For over

twenty years he had been the friend and constant companion of Anne Soffey. He'd helped her start her company, get financing, and owned a percentage of stock, but he was not involved in the day-to-day operation. He had proposed marriage so many times it had become almost ritual. His suit had been favored by Grace Soffey, Anne's mother; she had wanted him for a son-in-law. Disappointed that Anne stayed single, Grace Soffey had bypassed her daughter and left the entire estate to Mary.

"I know that by the terms of her grandmother's will Mary was to have the use of a part of the income from the estate beginning with her eighteenth birthday," Gwenn began. "The management of the capital remained in the executor's hands. That is, in your hands."

Dussart nodded benignly.

"Upon reaching her twenty-sixth birthday, that is two years from now, everything would have passed to Mary."

"Yes."

"And then she could have done anything she wanted with it."

"Right again, young lady. You've done your homework."

"But as she died before reaching age twenty-six, the money goes to her mother and Clark Langner gets nothing," Gwenn concluded.

"Correct." Dussart picked up the coffee pot, felt the side, pursed his lips together. "I can make some fresh, if you'd care for it, Ms. Ramadge?"

"No, thank you."

"It is hardly likely that Clark was aware of the provisions of the will," Dussart pointed out. "He didn't come to me, and if he had I wouldn't have told him. How else could he have found out?"

"Ms. Soffey might have told him in order to discourage the marriage."

Dussart's lofty brow furrowed. "Aren't you supposed to be working for Ms. Soffey?"

"Ms. Soffey makes no secret of her feelings about Clark. That's why she hired me. It could be that Mary herself told him. Revealing the provisions of her grandmother's will might have been a way of assuring that the marriage would last at least the two years." Could Mary have been so completely in thrall? Gwenn wondered. "As it now stands the only one to benefit financially is Anne Soffey."

"That is so, yes."

"The company's in good shape?"

"Excellent."

"I've noticed the price of Soffey shares dropped dramatically in the stock market crash last October nineteenth. It has not recovered on par with the rest of the market."

Dussart's laughter was both disparaging and indignant. "What are you suggesting?"

"You hold a large block of Soffey shares, don't you, Mr. Dussart?"

He went very still. The patrician aura seemed to solidify into an armor casing. "Perhaps you can save yourself some effort by checking the SS *Serena*'s passenger list. You'll find that no one in any way connected with Soffey Cosmetics nor with Mary and her mother were on that cruise."

"Yes, sir, I know that." Gwenn hesitated then decided to show her hand. "It doesn't preclude the possibility of a hired killer."

"The shares of Soffey Cosmetics which I own have dropped in value, that's true, but unless I sell them it remains a paper loss," he told her. "I've known Mary Soffey since she was two months old. I was her godfather. I gave her away in marriage. I've known and loved her mother since before Mary was born."

Chapter THIRTEEN

As Lew Sackler suspected, the doctor who reported to the scene of Angela Doran's murder was a freelance, one of the city's twenty-nine part-time medical examiners, most of whom were doctors or surgeons in private practice. They were inclined to take their time getting to the body and put the demands of their own live patients over that of the city's corpses. The corpse could wait, Sackler thought, but he couldn't. He telephoned Dr. John Keyser at his office.

The doctor was resistant. "I understand your situation, Detective Sackler, and I would like to help you, but I can't."

"All I want is a ballpark estimate."

"I conduct my private practice from this office, Detective. It is completely separate from . . ."

"Yes, I know that, but . . ."

"Please, let me finish. I don't have my notes here. My notes and everything pertaining to my duties as an assistant medical examiner are in my other office. I couldn't possibly give you any kind of opinion without them."

"You mean you don't remember?"

"Of course, I remember," Keyser retorted. "I remember every single victim I ever examined going back to my first assignment and I expect to remember every one till my last. But you're going to take what I tell you and base an investigation on it, right?"

"I'll use it as a guideline only," Sackler promised.

"I'm scheduled to do the autopsy tonight. Can't you wait?"

"My sergeant's on my back to come up with new evidence or I'm off the case," Sackler pleaded.

Keyser thought about it. "Okay. Unofficially, I'd say the death occurred sometime between eight P.M. and midnight on Tuesday the sixteenth."

"That early?"

"You asked me and I told you. Now you're going to argue with me?"

"No, Doc, no. I appreciate your confidence. Thanks." Sackler hung up.

The next day, Saturday, John Keyser narrowed it down to between ten P.M. and midnight. Apparently, it was good enough for the ADA handling the case because he filed a charge of second-degree murder against Edward Doran— the death penalty being outlawed in New York State, that was as high as he could go. At the preliminary hearing, he argued against allowing bail and the judge ruled for him. Not that it mattered. Bail, if it had been set, would have been too high for Doran to raise. Bewildered and desperate, Ed Doran could only continue to protest his innocence. His memory served him too conveniently—clear on some points and blank on others. His Legal Aid lawyer was not impressed. Sackler, who lost most of the day in court giving evidence, couldn't blame him. Doran didn't look good.

For instance, Doran insisted he left Angie on Tuesday night a little after eight. He made the rounds of the local bars and didn't get home till after closing. He got up around noon on Wednesday, dressed, and without even taking a cup of coffee, without having seen or spoken to his wife, left for work.

He was more exact about the next segment. He reported

for work at the Ponte Vecchio at two and was under the direct gaze of his in-laws until nine-thirty that night. At that time, Emilio Fissore sent him home with instructions to make it up with Angie and to have Angie call. Everybody agreed on that. But instead of going straight home, Doran again hit the bars. It was the kind of alibi nobody took seriously. Anyway, the alibi was for the wrong night.

By the time Ed Doran got home Wednesday, his bride had already been dead close to twenty-four hours.

As for Tuesday night, the night of the actual murder, Doran claimed to have hit a series of bars, but could only remember one. It turned out to be enough. Doran had been loud. He'd attracted attention. On purpose? It wasn't really necessary. The bartender at Paddy's Shamrock on Queens Boulevard, Hank Slattery, was an old buddy of Doran's. He agreed that Doran had come in at around nine, which was early for him because he didn't usually get off work till ten, but, of course, he'd had that day off. Also, he was already high. He continued to knock off the Johnnie Walkers till Slattery refused to serve him. That infuriated Doran. They made a deal—Slattery to put one last drink on the table and Doran to give up his car keys and wait till closing so that his buddy could drive him home. There was no further argument because he passed out in one of the back booths.

"You drove Doran home?" Sackler asked. "He didn't tell us that."

Slattery shrugged. "He's real macho about being able to hold his liquor."

"Under the circumstances that shouldn't be a consideration."

Slattery hesitated. "Could be he doesn't remember."

Sackler looked hard at him. They were alike, he and Doran, the detective thought, grown men with adolescent values. He knew guys like that; some of them were cops. "Did he black out frequently?"

Once more, Slattery hesitated. He had been holding
himself erect, shoulders squared, gut sucked in. Now he
let it all sag. "He drank more than he should have."

"Did you drive him home on other occasions?"

"Not since he got married."

Sackler nodded. "So you closed up and then you drove
him home. In his own car? Then what?"

"I helped him out of the car and walked him to his front
door."

"He wasn't able to navigate?"

Slattery understood the importance of the question.
"Not without help."

"Did you go into the house with him?"

"The house was dark. I didn't want to wake Angie."

"You knew Mrs. Doran?"

"Oh, sure. We went to school together. The three of us.
I used to date Angie, but it was always Ed she liked, really
liked. Anyway, I knew she didn't approve of Ed's drinking
and I didn't want to get caught in the middle, so I unlocked
the door with Ed's keys, put them back in his pocket, and
pushed him inside."

"There was no activity upstairs? No lights came on? Mrs.
Doran didn't call down?"

"No, sir. I turned on the light in the hall, got him as far
as the couch in the living room, and left him there. I was
as quiet as I could be."

"So as not to disturb Mrs. Doran?"

"Right. She would have blamed me for getting him
drunk. She thought I was a bad influence on him. I wanted
to get out while I could."

"So Ed Doran did not call up to his wife? He did not go
up to their bedroom?"

"Not while I was there."

"How long a drive is it from your bar to the Doran
house?" Sackler asked, though he had a pretty good idea
and would check it anyway.

"Late at night like that? Twenty minutes."

"What time did you close?"

"Four A.M."

Sackler wondered just how far Slattery would stick his neck out for a friend. "How did you get home, Mr. Slattery?" he asked. "You said Mr. Doran gave you his keys, so I assume you drove his car and left it in the driveway. How did you get home?"

"One of the waiters followed us in my car."

So now there were two witnesses who would support Doran's alibi.

While the mortal remains of Angela Fissore Doran reposed at the medical examiner's office, the wake was postponed. However, the Fissores closed the restaurant and received the condolences of their friends at home. They were both restless. It would have eased them to be at work, but it would have been unseemly, lacking in reverence and respect. So instead they kept occupied by cooking and serving at home, passing around the food, one dish after another, hour after hour, through the long days.

Fissore was a different man from the one Lew Sackler had encountered at the scene of his daughter's murder. That man had been out of control, shaking with rage, soft eyes pinpointed into lasers of despair. In this man, the fires were spent. There was no fight left. His barrel chest was concave as though the air had been sucked out. He was drawn. His hair had gone white. He greeted the detective like a friend come to mourn. Sackler asked if there was a place they could talk privately, and in that small house filled with neighbors the restaurateur could only take him up to his and Rosa's bedroom. On the way they passed a room with its door slightly ajar. A draft from downstairs blew it open and Lew saw that it was empty, completely empty, devoid not only of furniture, but of carpeting, curtains, pictures—stripped. He looked to Fissore.

"That was Angie's room," Fissore answered the unspoken question.

Sackler merely nodded, but he was shocked. Very often people clung to the material reminders of those they had loved and lost, keeping the room, especially that of a son or daughter, exactly as it had been during life. They turned it into a shrine. Others found the reminders too painful and got rid of everything. But so quickly? Lew thought. Why so quickly? It seemed almost ruthless.

Without another word, Emilio Fissore stepped in front of the detective and pulled the door firmly shut.

Once in the other bedroom, sitting on the end of the king-sized bed, he showed no reluctance about talking about Angie, about reminiscing. Angie was beautiful, full of a joy that somehow transmitted to others, he said. Started, it seemed he couldn't stop. He lost himself in memories and Lew Sackler, sitting on Mrs. Fissore's vanity bench, was content to listen to his anecdotes—about Angie's first communion, her sweet-sixteen party, her high school graduation. How Fissore had taught her to swim and to ride a bike. The bond between father and daughter had been strong, Sackler thought, but that wasn't unusual, particularly in the case of an only child. The mother, by contrast, seemed almost to have been shut out.

"I guess she had a lot of boyfriends," Sackler suggested.

"You bet. From the time she was a little girl with long sausage curls tied in a blue ribbon, from kindergarten to high school, the boys were crazy about her." The eyes flashed and his face lit up with some of the old energy. "The phone never stopped ringing. They lined up to get a date. She could have had anybody, anybody she wanted. She had to go and pick that murdering bastard." Sweat broke out all over his face. "We tried to talk her out of it, but she wouldn't hear a word against him."

"What did you have against him?"

"He's lazy, drinks too much, has no ambition, no sense of responsibility."

"How about a criminal record?" Fissore shook his head. "Had he been married before?"

"He's just no good. But she wouldn't see it. She'd made up her mind. She wouldn't hear a word against him."

"Had she ever been interested in anybody else? Among all those young men she'd dated wasn't there one she took seriously besides Doran?"

Fissore thought about it. "There was Paul. Paul Castell, son of a neighbor. He's an English teacher. Steady. Makes a decent living. He was crazy about Angie. Asked her to marry him—I don't know how many times. She liked him, but I don't think she ever seriously considered him. Maybe we pushed too hard for him. Had the opposite effect."

"Can you give me his address?"

"What for?"

"Routine, Mr. Fissore," Sackler assured him.

"No, not routine. I know you police. You don't waste time. You're not here listening to my stories to pass the time. Something's gone wrong. What? I want to know."

"Tying up loose ends, Mr. Fissore."

"What loose ends? He did it. The drunken lout killed my baby. What's the problem?"

"No problem, sir." Sackler held up both hands, palms out, in a gesture of giving up.

"If Ed didn't do it, then who?" Fissore demanded. "Everybody loved Angie. Everybody."

Chapter _____
_____ FOURTEEN

Public interest in the case of Mary Langner waned. The murder of Angela Doran took its place. The tabloids kept that to the fore. Each day there was another account; another aspect of the violent crime was presented and examined, not to say exploited. They played up the victim's youth and beauty, the brutality with which she'd been killed. And always, Gwenn thought, there was the tragic undercurrent of happiness turned into horror. As she followed the newspaper accounts, Gwenn Ramadge became more and more convinced that somehow the cases were linked. On February twenty-third, she read:

GROOM CHARGED WITH
BRUTAL SLAYING OF BRIDE
Grand Jury Returns Indictment
Doran Held Pending Trial

And decided to do something about it.

She took the F train to Roosevelt Avenue, Jackson Heights, walked upstairs and waited on the wind-swept elevated platform for the Number 7 to Flushing. It was a long walk from Shea Stadium to the precinct and by the time she got there a raw, cold mist had formed. Dressed in a shearling coat and high boots, Gwenn hardly noticed.

"Detective Sackler, please." His name had been in the papers, so she knew whom to ask for.

The desk sergeant, a woman in her mid-thirties with sharp eyes and blonde hair pulled back and held by a black barrette, consulted the duty chart. "Not in."

"When will he be in?"

"Can't say."

"Oh." Gwenn wasn't sure what to do.

"Your name?" the sergeant asked.

"Gwenn Ramadge."

"How do you spell that?"

Gwenn spelled it. "When does Detective Sackler come on duty?"

"He's on duty now. Address and telephone number?"

Gwenn started to reply, then changed her mind. "I'll wait." She headed for one of the benches.

"I wouldn't advise it. It could be all day. Why don't you leave your number and he'll call you."

Sure, when he has nothing better to do, Gwenn thought. "Thank you. I'll try another time."

The sergeant shrugged. Gwenn walked to the door and out.

Standing on the sidewalk in what had become a heavy drizzle, Gwenn debated making the long trip back to Manhattan. As long as she was here she ought to wait a while anyway, she decided. If only she knew what Detective Sackler looked like she might be able to spot and intercept him as he came in. But she didn't, so . . . There was a phone booth across the street. She could call every fifteen minutes or so. Sooner or later she was bound to get him.

An hour and a quarter later, with the rain coming down hard and the wind blowing it into the partial shelter of the booth, her optimism was just about gone. She'd try the number just once more, she thought. She was counting the fourth ring on Sackler's extension when the phone was picked up.

"Homicide. Sackler."

She'd given up and the surprise left her tongue-tied. She'd planned it all in her head, rehearsed it mentally, and now nothing came out.

"Hello? Who's calling?"

"My name is Gwenn Ramadge."

"Yes, ma'am?"

"It has to do with the Doran murder. I understand you're carrying the case."

"I'm working on it, yes, ma'am."

"I'd like to see you and speak with you."

"If you could give me some idea of what it's about?"

"Actually, I'm interested in another bride murder. Mary Soffey Langner? She went overboard on her honeymoon cruise. That was . . . let's see . . ." Suddenly, Gwenn wasn't even sure of her facts. "Just about six weeks ago. Yes, that's right . . ." She was getting flustered.

"I did read about that. But I'm not familiar . . ."

"Detective Sackler, this is very difficult over the telephone. If I could just come over . . ."

"Sure. Yes, Ms. Ramadge. Why don't you give me your number and I'll get back to you and we can set up . . ."

"No." On this Gwenn was firm. "Give me ten minutes of your time now, that's all I ask. Then if you're not interested, well, I won't bother you any more."

"I'm on my way out, Ms. Ramadge. Give me your number and I promise I will get in touch as soon . . ."

"I'm calling from right across the street," she told him. "I can be over there in less than one minute. If you advise the desk sergeant to let me come straight up, I can be at your desk in three. See me now, Detective Sackler, and you can get rid of me once and for all."

"You've made me an offer I can't refuse. Okay, Ms. Ramadge, but I'm going to hold you to the three minutes."

But Gwenn had already hung up and was sprinting across the street, dodging traffic. Inside the station house the blonde sergeant grinned and waved her on to the stairs. By the time she reached the squad room door she was out of breath, but could spare a few moments to regain her composure; she wanted to make an assured entrance. She wasn't aware that her hair was wet and plastered to her head, that the shoulders of her coat were soaked, that her face was flushed and dewy with rain and sweat intermingled, and that her green eyes were sparkling. She looked around. A man at the last desk on the right stood up.

He waved her over.

They stood face to face. Neither said anything. Each took time to examine the other and the long silence was no embarrassment to either. Finally, Gwenn held out her hand. Sackler took it. His grip was strong. Hers matched it. It was not clear which one broke away first.

"You're all wet, Ms. Ramadge," Sackler said, then flushed. He would have liked to sit her before an open fire, pull off her boots and rub her feet. "I mean, your coat's wet. Would you like me to hang up your coat?"

"Oh. Yes, thank you." He was tall, she thought as she struggled to get it off. She had to tilt her head back to look up into his face. But she was not intimidated, not in the least. To the contrary, there was something reassuring about Detective Lewis Sackler and it had little to do with his obvious physical prowess. She took the chair he set out for her and the mug of hot coffee he placed in her hands. Those amenities observed, there was another silence, this one awkward because it concerned not their reaction to each other but the business they had to deal with.

"What can I do for you, Ms. Ramadge?"

This time Gwenn had come prepared. She'd typed a brief outline of the Langner case covering the events and

her investigation. It concluded with the evidence Maxine
DeLloyd had provided. Composure restored, she now set
it before Sackler.

He went over it quickly but thoroughly. "Just how are
you involved?"

"Oh? Didn't I tell you? I've been hired by the victim's
mother. Here." She handed him one of her cards.

"Well." Sackler looked at it then back at her. "Well.
Shouldn't this report go to . . ." He searched through the
account. "Detective Daniels?"

"As far as Detective Daniels is concerned, the case is
closed."

"Why come to me?"

"Because the two cases, yours and mine, are so similar.
You do see that, don't you?"

"There are some points . . ."

"Some!" She leaned forward, green eyes intent as she
ticked them off on her fingers. "They were both brides.
Each was killed shortly after the wedding—Mary Langner
within a week, Angela Doran on the first month's anniversary. In each case the marriage was already in trouble.
And in each case the husband had been drinking heavily
and claimed to have passed out at the time the murder
was committed. In each case, the husband was not just the
obvious suspect but the only one."

Sackler was intrigued but far from convinced. "Let me
point out the differences, Ms. Ramadge," he said. "To start
with, we're dealing with two completely separate and dis-
associated groups. There is no connection between them.
They live in different communities; they are of different
classes. The Soffeys and Langners are society, not high
society, but we can certainly call them upper class. The
Fissores and Ed Doran are lower middle class. One set lives
on Long Island, the other in Flushing. They've never met,
never had any contact."

"Yes, but the psychological undercurrent . . ."

"It's sad for a bride to be killed so soon after her marriage, but not that unusual. And it is usual for the husband to be the one who did it. Unfortunately."

"Clark Langner has an alibi," Gwenn pointed out.

"And you have no other suspect."

"No. And no other motive either," she admitted.

"So you want me to see what I've got and try to make it fit. That's why you're here."

"I thought, if you should have doubts about Ed Doran's guilt, we could help each other."

"I wish I could. Believe me, I do. But it's just not there, Ms. Ramadge. I'm sorry." He looked down at the report. "Your point is well taken. There are psychological similarities, but you don't go to court with that."

"So your man, Doran, your suspect—you've got an airtight case against him?"

"The DA is satisfied."

"I read that in the newspapers."

Sackler considered. He would have liked to be open with her, to share what he knew, but until the DA accepted the testimony of Doran's friends and dismissed the charges, he couldn't speak. "I'm sorry."

"So am I. Thanks for your time, Detective Sackler." Gwenn got up and went for her coat.

"Ms. Ramadge." He ran around the desk and got there first. "Tell you what—let me keep that." He indicated the report she had brought. "I'll go over it once more. Maybe something will occur to me. And if something comes up in my investigation that seems at all pertinent, I'll be in touch."

"You're going on with it?" Gwenn's eyes flashed. She tilted her head back and looked up at him. "That means you do have doubts about Doran. You're not sure he did it, are you?"

It was okay to admit that much, Sackler decided.

"No, I'm not," he said.

* * *

Tricia Cryder sat at her husband's bedside, eyes fixed on the waxen image of his face. The only sound in the big master bedroom which had been transformed into a hospital room was the harsh rasping of the respirator. Tricia had been sitting there, neither reading nor in any way distracting herself, for two days—since that brief incident of false hope. She hadn't been with him when it happened. She hadn't been present when suddenly in the middle of the night and for no fathomable reason, Benjamin Cryder's eyes had twitched; a spasm passed through his heretofore unmoving body, and he had wakened.

She'd been out for a drive at the time. Stressed by trying to deal with intricate business affairs for which she'd had no training, shouldering the unaccustomed responsibility, and at the same time forced to cope with the reports of the doctors, reports which offered no hope and predicted that the end, when it came, would be painful, she had literally fled. The storm had passed so she'd taken the convertible and despite the cold put the top down so that the air washed her heated cheeks and blew away her anxieties. When she got back, the two nurses and the staff were waiting for her; the doctor had been sent for. She rushed up to the sickroom in time for Ben to see her once more. With that ghastly tube down his throat, he couldn't speak; he could only make the horrible strangling sounds. She ran to him, took his hand, held it to her bosom tightly. He looked into her eyes for a long, long moment. He knew her. There was no doubt in her mind nor in the minds of those present that Benjamin Cryder knew his bride. Then he closed his eyes. At first they all thought he'd fallen into a normal slumber. But he had not opened them again.

Nevertheless, Patricia Cryder waited. She spent her waking hours at her husband's bedside spelled by one of the registered nurses only when she needed sleep, and then she was close by in what had been his dressing room. She did not leave the house again. She didn't need the doctors to tell her that he could go at any moment. It had been in his eyes. There had been something else in that last look; she wasn't sure if she had read it right. She got in touch with the detective her husband had hired.

Chapter
FIFTEEN

As the doors opened for the 4:20 departure of the Samuel I. Newhouse ferry to Staten Island, the crowd in the waiting room surged forward, Rebecca Hayman in its midst. It was the start of the rush hour and the start of the weekend, and the terminal at the foot of Whitehall Street was jammed with anywhere from three to four hundred people. She should have known better than to choose that time, Rebecca thought, particularly with a bulky suitcase and an awkward tote slung over her shoulder. She couldn't avoid bumping into someone front or back, nor jabbing someone in the ankles as she rolled the awkward valise along. But the people were tolerant. She got a few dirty looks—being a born-and-bred New Yorker, Rebecca Hayman ignored them.

When Gerald told her he had the use of a friend's house for the weekend, Becky Hayman had been thrilled. The enthusiasm dampened when she found out it wasn't a cabin in the Adirondacks or a villa in the Caribbean. Staten Island wasn't exactly a romantic destination. There were rural sections, Gerald said, woods and lakes and streams. There were beaches where, when the fog rolled in and shrouded Manhattan and Brooklyn and Jersey, you could imagine yourself hundreds of miles away. The best part, and the only part that counted, was that they'd be together for two and a half days with no alarm clock to get them up for work and no roommate to burst in unexpectedly. And with that Rebecca Hayman agreed wholeheartedly.

However, this was not her idea of how to get there. She'd wanted to rent a car and then they could have driven over together. Gerald, ever thrifty, vetoed that. There was a car at the house and his friend had said they could use it. They'd take the ferry. The ride was spectacular. *You'll love it*, he promised. Then at the last minute, he'd called to say he was running late and she should go on ahead; he'd meet her at the house. Gerald Goelet was a resident at New York Hospital and this wasn't the first time this kind of thing had happened. So here she was, alone, struggling with baggage, depressed, sweaty. The cabin was too hot and she was overdressed. Her long brown hair felt matted under the wool cap. Rebecca pulled a small face mirror from her handbag and surveyed the ruin of her makeup. What a way to start a romantic weekend!

Dragging the suitcases, she went out on the open deck and found a place at the rail. A stiff wind quickly cooled her flushed cheeks and as the deck began to throb under her feet and she watched the land fall away, Becky began to feel almost elated. She could imagine she was setting out on a real ocean voyage. The towers of lower Manhattan glistened in the rosy rays of the setting sun. The cranes of the Brooklyn shipyards were outlined like giant birds against the fiery sky. The Samuel I. Newhouse passed Governors Island, then Ellis Island—she could identify the recently restored central reception area through which the immigrants had entered. The biggest thrill was to see the Statue of Liberty from so close up. Gerald was right, she thought; it was a wonderful trip. Free weekends didn't come their way often; they were events. In fact, any time together was to be treasured.

Becky Hayman was twenty-five, outwardly self-assured, fiercely determined to conform with the modern feminine ideal. But in fact, she gave lip service to the relationship between her and Gerald while inwardly she yearned for marriage and a family. She had a good job as a computer programmer and could have afforded to pay for a trip to Bermuda or Puerto Rico for both of them. Gerald wouldn't accept it. He wouldn't even let her pay for a night at a hotel. He was old-fashioned that way and she found it endearing. Since she shared her apartment with another woman and Gerald slept mostly at the hospital, it cut down on their love life. Nevertheless, she wouldn't have wanted Gerald any different.

The twenty-minute crossing was all too short and Becky Hayman was almost sorry when the ferry docked. She let the crowd get off ahead of her. The landing area was well organized with trains and buses waiting for the commuters. She let them load while she stood and looked back toward Manhattan, a gray blur in the distance. When the passengers had dispersed and the buses and trains pulled out, Becky turned her back on the city and walked over to the taxi stand. The whole, wonderful weekend lay ahead.

Gerald had prepared her for the house's being in a built-up area, so it was a pleasant surprise to find it on a quiet, dead-end street and backing on a wooded tract that was probably parkland. The house itself was Tudor style, nestled in the snow which in New York lay in dirty trenches along the streets but here was still pristine. Pretty, she thought, and her spirits lifted even more. She paid the driver and found the key under the potted plant beside the front door and let herself in.

The living room took up most of the first floor. It had a cathedral ceiling, dark oak beams—false, of course—and a fireplace—real. There were also stained-glass windows, of all things. Becky was delighted.

The bedroom was upstairs. It was decorated in plain American maple. She didn't care. She checked the closets. There were two—one full of men's things, the other empty. She unpacked, took half of the empty closet, and left space and hangers for Gerald. It was close to six. She didn't really expect Gerald for another hour so she ran a bath. Just as she was about to get in, the phone rang. She hesitated. It could be someone for the owner, but it was probably Gerald. She felt a sharp pang of anxiety. Oh, God, don't let it be an emergency at the hospital. Don't let it be Gerald saying he couldn't come.

"Hello?"

No one answered. There was certainly somebody there. Becky could sense the line was open, alive, crackling with energy.

"Hello? Who is this? Hello?" Becky Hayman repeated. The caller hung up.

Nothing unusual in that kind of call. It happened often enough to everybody. Usually, it was a wrong number, but it made her nervous. This time, because she was in somebody else's house, it also made her uncomfortable. If it was a friend of the owner's, well, that was his problem, she thought. At least, it hadn't been Gerald. The weekend wasn't canceled. That's all that really mattered. She went back to the bathroom and got into the tub.

He came while she was still soaking. She heard the front door open and close and the footsteps. She called out. He called back. He came running as she rose out of the warm water.

Gerald Goelet was thin, sallow, and wore glasses. His complexion was not helped by the lack of sleep and the haphazard meals that were part of the training regimen of his profession. To Rebecca he was handsome and he represented her future.

Becky was not glamorous either. She was, in fact, over-weight. The shape of her mouth was spoiled by a slight overbite which should have been corrected in her child-hood, but her parents had not been able to afford to have it done. Her skin, a pasty color, was now rosy from the bath. As she emerged naked before him and held out her arms, to Gerald she was Aphrodite.

He stripped off his clothes. They bathed together. They dried each other. They made love.

Dinner was late. Becky was no cook so Gerald had brought a selection from their favorite brand of gourmet frozen foods. They settled on the Boeuf Bourguignonne and from the basket of wines chose a New York State sparkling burgundy. Becky set the table in front of the fire. They ate and drank and made love again. Then fell asleep as the fire smoldered into glowing coals.

Becky hadn't mentioned the phone call. She'd forgotten. But even if she'd remembered, there seemed no reason to say anything.

BRIDE-TO-BE VANISHES
Goes for Walk in Woods
After a Night of Love Making

Another one, Gwenn thought. Oh, my God, another one!

She was sitting up in bed with the Sunday *Times* spread out around her. The story was detailed with unusual thoroughness considering it was a late breaker. What was even more significant was its positioning—on the lower right of the front page of the Sunday edition. After all, the victim wasn't actually a bride yet, she thought, and she was missing, not dead, yet someone on the editorial staff shared Gwenn's instinct that there was more to come and more to reach back to.

According to the fiancé, Dr. Gerald Goelet, a resident at New York Hospital, he and Rebecca Hayman had dined, made love, and fallen asleep in front of the fireplace. He thought that was around midnight. When he woke, the fire was out, and Rebecca was gone. He wasn't alarmed,

not then. He assumed she'd just wakened and gone upstairs. He was supported in this assumption by finding
himself covered with a blanket which hadn't been there
before. He wrapped it around himself and went upstairs
intending to get into bed, too, but Rebecca wasn't there.
The bed was empty though it had been slept in. That was
at 2:45 Saturday morning.

Still half asleep, tired from a long day at the hospital
and from arduous lovemaking, and partly hung over, he
decided Becky must have gone out for a breath of air. It
was a quiet, respectable neighborhood, and he had no fears
for her. He put on his pajamas and robe, went down,
rekindled the fire, and settled to wait.

The next thing he knew it was morning.

Gwenn scowled. The scenario was all too familiar. She
decided that young Dr. Goelet either had a clear conscience
or had been very tired indeed. She read on.

Alarmed (at last, Gwenn thought), he got dressed and
went out to look for Rebecca.

He searched through the woods at the back of the house.
Becky liked to walk in the woods, he said. He thought she
might have fallen and injured herself, twisted an ankle
maybe. He ran into a group of bird-watchers. He gave
them a description of Becky Hayman and asked it they'd
seen her. They hadn't. Emerging from the woods to a
blacktop road, he stopped a police patrol car and went
through the same procedure. Nothing. Distraught, he returned to the house. He fixed himself lunch, but he
couldn't eat. Finally, he stopped trying and did what he'd
known from the beginning he'd have to do and that was
notify the police. It was 2:10 P.M. Saturday.

Gwenn reached for the phone beside the bed and dialed
Lew Sackler's office.

"It's not my case, Ms. Ramadge," he told her. "It's not
even in my jurisdiction."

"I realize that, Detective Sackler, but I figured you must know what's going on."

"There's a search being conducted. Until they find her . . ."

"You think she's alive? You honestly think that?"

There was a pause. Again, Sackler found himself struggling over just how much he could tell her.

"I don't know."

"You think she could have had an accident?" Gwenn persisted.

"It's possible."

"How about the boyfriend? How about Doctor Goelet? Are they holding him still?"

"I wouldn't think so. There's nothing to hold him on."

"The similarities don't strike you?"

"To what?"

"Oh, come on, Lew, you know what I'm talking about."

"That's right, Gwenn, I do. Yes."

From artificial courtesy they had progressed to honest argument, but neither was aware of it.

"That's what worries me about you, Gwenn," Sackler went on. "You're jumping to conclusions. You're twisting the facts to suit your theory. The woman could be alive. Probably is. She could turn up any time—back with her lover, back home, at work, or even reporting to the precinct. If they'd taken Goelet into custody they'd look pretty foolish, wouldn't they? Not to mention he could sue them for wrongful arrest."

Incredible, Gwenn thought. He was like a doctor afraid of malpractice. Defensive law enforcement, is that what they'd come to? "So you're not going to do anything?"

"It's not up to me."

"I know that. What I mean is that you could advise them of the similarities . . ."

"It's not appropriate at this time. An APB, All Points Bulletin, is out on the missing woman. Okay? The woods around the house where she and Goelet were staying are being searched by a team of men with dogs."

Apparently, he knew more and was more interested than he was willing to admit, Gwenn thought. It made her feel better. It eased her disappointment in him. "The search is on now?"

"As we speak," he assured her. He didn't tell her he was on his way to Staten Island to join the search. She might, probably would, ask to go along. It would be hard for him to say no. In fact, Lew Sackler had a suspicion that saying no to Gwenn Ramadge would become increasingly difficult.

When Lew Sackler arrived at Clove Lake Park the search for Rebecca Hayman was in full swing. According to the 911 log, Gerald Goelet had reported his fiancée missing at 2:10 P.M. on Saturday. By the time the detectives arrived, questioned him, and canvassed the neighborhood, it was nearly dark. So an organized search was postponed till the following morning, Sunday, just after dawn. The body was discovered shortly after noon hidden in a ditch approximately three quarters of a mile from the shore of the lake. It was covered by snow and leaves and wrapped in a yellow-flowered shower curtain. The folds were parted so Gerald Goelet could make identification.

He knelt in the snow beside the mound of earth and sodden, rotting vegetation which had been spread over her. She was wearing slacks and a pea coat, a thin T-shirt but no bra, shoes but no socks. Goelet's gaze left her face, then traveled down to the generous hips and thighs he had so recently caressed. Remembering their warmth, he shuddered.

"It's Becky," he said.

He looked once more at her face. As a doctor he had to note the cyanosis, the small circular ecchymoses in the galea of the scalp and the small pinpoint asphyxial hemorrhages in the whites of her wide open, staring eyes. "She's been smothered." He let himself be led away to the backseat of one of the police cars to wait while the usual notifications were made and the machinery of a homicide investigation activated. It took nearly three hours before the medical examiner arrived. While the police stamped their feet and flapped their arms fighting the cold, Gerald Goelet sat in a stoic daze.

Lew Sackler had been present when the clumsily camouflaged grave was discovered and present during the cursory medical examination. The official opinion was the same as the young resident's—Rebecca Hayman had died of asphyxia. As there was no mark of a ligature or clear line of lividity, the ME also concluded the victim had suffocated. Due to the cold weather and the dampness of the snow and leaves in which she'd been lying, he did not offer an estimate of the time of death. The local detectives didn't push for it, and Sackler thought had he been in charge he wouldn't have either. Finally, Rebecca Hayman, still with the plastic curtain around her, was placed in a body bag and hoisted into the morgue van. Gerald Goelet was transported to the station house to make a formal statement. Lew went along continuing in the role of unofficial observer.

He got home at 2 A.M. Much too late to call Gwenn, he thought as he let himself into the apartment. He'd promised to let her know if Hayman was found and she'd said to call any time, but she hadn't meant two in the morning. All the while he rationalized, Sackler knew he wouldn't wait.

The phone rang several times before Gwenn picked it up. "Hello?"

"Gwenn? I woke you, didn't I? I'm sorry."

"Lew?"

"I did wake you."

"No, no, it's all right. I was watching the late movie. I must have dozed off. What's up?"

"Listen, go back to sleep. I'll call you in the morning."

"You might as well tell me now. I'm awake. If you don't tell me, I won't be able to go back to sleep."

"I'm sorry."

"Don't be sorry. Just tell me. You found her, right?"

"Right."

"Alive?"

"No. She was buried in the woods back of the house where she and Goelet were staying. Actually, she wasn't buried; she was lying in a shallow ditch with snow and leaves covering her. I don't know whether that was because the ground was frozen too hard to dig a grave or because the perpetrator didn't have a shovel."

"She was transported to the spot?" Gwenn asked.

"Oh, sure. The tracks were scuffed up but they led from a blacktop and they were single tracks."

"So you think she was transported by car and then . . ."

"Carried to the ditch," Sackler finished for her. "Yes."

"Does the boyfriend have a car?"

"He had access to his friend's car. It will be thoroughly examined, naturally, but as the body was wrapped in a plastic shower curtain . . ."

"Does the shower curtain come from the house?" Gwenn asked.

"The curtain is missing from the downstairs bathroom."

Gwenn was silent for a while. Then she asked, "How was she killed?"

"She was suffocated."

"Not strangled? And you're sure she wasn't killed at the scene?"

"Her shoes were dry. So were her clothes. If there'd been a struggle, if she'd been forced down into the snow, there would have been indications. There were none.

Also," he paused significantly, "she had no underwear on or stockings."

"Ah . . ." Gwenn sighed. "What does the fiancé say?"

"Same as before. Sticks to his story."

"Has he been charged?"

"Not yet."

"Any other suspects?"

"None. I don't think there's any doubt this time about who did it."

"Doesn't seem to be."

"That doesn't mean you're wrong about the other two cases." He tried to ease the disappointment.

"Thanks."

"Listen, if I hear anything, if anything else turns up, I'll let you know."

She didn't answer.

"Okay, Gwenn?"

"Oh, yes, sure. Thanks again, Lew. Good night."

Though she hadn't expected to be able to get back to sleep, Gwenn not only fell asleep quickly but slept well and awoke with renewed optimism. The case against Rebecca Hayman's lover was too pat. As it stood everything pointed to Gerald Goelet. All indications were that Goelet, for some unknown reason, suffocated his lover. Maybe in love play, unintentionally. Anyway, he panicked. He dressed her, forgetting to put on her underwear, and then wrapped her in the shower curtain. Why? To protect his friend's car? Was it necessary? There was no blood. At any rate, that was what he did. He put her in the car and drove around till he found a spot to hide her. There must have been a shovel or some kind of digging tool in the garage; why didn't he take it with him? Possibly he didn't think of it till he was already at the site. So he did the best he could—put her in the ditch and covered her with snow and dirt and leaves and then went back to the house. He waited till an hour passed when he could reasonably make an appearance and start pretending to look for her.

However you reasoned, it came out too much like the other two cases.

Lew had been unexpectedly open about the facts, Gwenn thought. Did that mean he had doubts too? As a professional he couldn't intrude on another cop's case, but she, being a private investigator, was under no such restriction. She could call on Dr. Goelet and ask whatever questions she wanted. She didn't even have to read him his rights.

After spending half an hour shunted from wing to wing, Gwenn finally ran down Dr. Gerald Goelet on the geriatrics floor of New York Hospital. She handed her card to one of the nurses at the nurses' station and was surprised not only that he did come out, but at how promptly.

He looked first at her, then at the card.

He wasn't what she'd expected, she thought ruefully. Under six feet, thin, he had bad skin, stringy and unruly hair which he kept sweeping back from his brow with a nervous gesture as he peered through thick, rimless glasses. He wore a wrinkled, dingy lab coat that flapped over a white shirt and baggy tweed pants. Not the standard image of a man carrying on an illicit affair. Nor of a murderer either, Gwenn thought.

"Thank you for seeing me, Doctor." She held out her hand.

He barely touched it before dropping it. "To tell you the truth, Ms. . . . ." He looked at the card. "Ramadge. I've got very little time to spare. I'm in the midst of writing up my charts. I shouldn't even have come out. All morning I've had a procession of detectives—from Homicide, the DA's office, I don't know what all. I thought I was through with that. You're the first private investigator." He gave her a bleak smile. "I was curious."

The smile did something for him, Gwenn thought. And

for her. It revealed not only a troubled man but a grieving one.

"I'll be as brief as I can, Doctor. I believe I can help you."

"Help me?" he exclaimed. "No one's offered to help me. In what way?"

She looked around the busy corridor and nodded toward the nurses' station to indicate they were being observed. "Is there anywhere we can be private?"

Goelet led her to the end of the wing to a latticed double door that opened on what had once been a terrace but was now enclosed and served as a doctors' lounge. Though there was nobody there, the television was going full blast. Goelet didn't bother to turn it off; he was totally insensitive to it, and Gwenn decided it would serve to cover their conversation should anyone walk in unexpectedly.

Goelet waved her to a sofa at the far end of the lounge and pulled up a chair to face her. He brought out a pack of cigarettes and lit up.

"How can you help me?"

"I don't believe you killed Rebecca Hayman," Gwenn told him straight out.

It overwhelmed him. He blinked behind the thick glasses and the tears that had so far refused to come brimmed over. "Thank you." He removed the glasses, wiped his eyes, and put them on again. "What makes you believe my story?"

"I didn't say I believed your story. I said I didn't think you committed murder."

He stared at her trying to read her. "I have no money," he said at last.

"I don't want money from you, Doctor Goelet, just information. I want to know all about Rebecca. Everything you can tell me. How you met, who her friends were, where she worked. Who she was going with before you. Everything."

"If you're thinking about another relationship, forget it. There wasn't any. No previous lover. Not on her side and not on mine."

"I see."

"I wish I could say otherwise, but I can't. It had to be a chance encounter. She went walking in the woods and someone attacked her."

"And suffocated her? How?"

"With a scarf? I don't know."

"Almost any other method would have been easier, don't you think?"

He didn't reply.

"All right. The two of you made love and fell asleep in front of the fire in the living room, right?" He nodded. "You want us to believe that sometime during the night, Rebecca woke and decided to go out for a walk—alone and in unfamiliar surroundings. She put her clothes back on, but didn't bother with underwear or stockings."

He nodded but he looked very worried.

"It was cold outside, Doctor," Gwenn reminded him. "There was snow on the ground, but her shoes were dry. How do you explain that?"

"I can't. All I know is that I woke up and she was gone."

"All right. Let's start there and take it a step at a time. What happened next?"

"I went upstairs and she wasn't there either."

"But the bed had been slept in?"

He scowled. "Yes. I didn't do it. I swear to God, Ms. Ramadge, I didn't do it."

"All right, Doctor, all right." She tried to calm him. "When you woke on the floor in front of the fireplace, you had a blanket over you, right? Presumably, Rebecca put it on you and then went upstairs to bed. Let's assume somebody broke in. She wakened again. To stop her outcry, the intruder grabbed a pillow and put it over her face and suffocated her."

Goelet nodded.

"Why should he then dress her, smuggle her out of the house, and hide her in the ditch? Why go to that trouble when all he had to do was leave her where she was and let you take the blame?"

The resident groaned and with a shaking hand swept back an unruly lock of hair.

"And the shower curtain? Why would a stranger bother to wrap her in a shower curtain?"

"They're going to get me for this, aren't they? There's no way I can beat it, is there? My God, there's no way!"

"You might try telling the truth, Doctor. You won't be any worse off than you are now."

"I am telling the truth."

Gwenn sighed and tried again. "This stranger you want us to believe is responsible—how did he get in? There was no sign of forcible entry."

"I don't know. There were lots of ways. The back door. Through the garage. A window."

"You didn't check to see everything was secure?"

"No. I had other things on my mind."

"You made it easy for him. On purpose? It almost looks that way. It looks as though you had an accomplice outside."

"No!"

"Maybe all you wanted was to show entry was possible."

"You said you wanted to help, but you're making it worse."

"I need you to name someone who might have had a motive for killing Rebecca. Besides yourself. If you can't . . ." She shrugged and got up.

"I would if I could. I don't know of anybody."

As long as she knew the truth, was getting him to admit it of any value? Gwenn asked herself. It wouldn't help him with the police; they wouldn't believe it. So, she sat down again. "How did Rebecca get along on the job? Was there

any jealousy there? Did anybody resent her? Was she promoted at anybody else's expense?"

"She was a computer programmer—good, but not ex-
ceptional. She wasn't stepping on anybody's toes."

"How about family? Brothers, sisters? Jealousy over an
inheritance?"

"Nothing like that," Goelet answered. "Both parents are
dead. She was an only child. In fact, she was adopted."

"Oh? Did Rebecca know who her real parents were?"

"No, she didn't. I asked her once. I asked her wasn't she
curious? Didn't she want to try to find out? She said she
wasn't interested. She loved her adoptive mother and father. They were the ones who'd wanted her, who'd raised
her and loved her. Her natural parents had rejected her."

"So she made no effort to discover their identities or to
locate them?"

"Definitely not."

But, Gwenn thought, that didn't mean *they* hadn't tried
to find *her.*

Chapter

SIXTEEN

Mary Soffey had been born out of wedlock; everybody knew it and accepted it and by now had forgotten about it. Certainly Anne Soffey had never tried to hide it. She could have, but she didn't. She not only continued to use her own maiden name but hadn't even bothered to put a Mrs. in front of it, though others did automatically. Nowadays her honesty was no big deal, but back in the middle and late sixties, it was an act of courage. Betty Friedan had just published *The Feminine Mystique*. The women's movement was a revolutionary concept. For a single woman to bear a child without even the pretense of a legal mate might not have resulted in complete ostracism by the people of Anne Soffey's class, but it couldn't have been easy for her.

Gwenn's first thought was to rush right out of New York Hospital and call Lew Sackler. He would be skeptical. He would regard the fact that both Mary's and Rebecca's paternity was shrouded as a coincidence. Gwenn couldn't blame him. After all, what she had so far was the merest hunch. Less. Instinct. Though she was firmly convinced she was on the right track, he would want and need more. Best to put off phoning. So instead, Gwenn got on a York Avenue bus that would turn west on Fifty-seventh and take her to Fifth Avenue and the Soffey Cosmetics building.

Anne Soffey kept her waiting less than ten minutes. She

was wearing a severely tailored charcoal gray pants suit with a white silk blouse. She had allowed her auburn hair to grow longer and it softened the gaunt contours of her face. The artful application of her own products covered the new lines grief had etched.

"You have news for me?"

Gwenn had already decided to be direct. If Anne Soffey refused to tell her the truth, there was not much she could do about it—nowhere else to go, no one else to ask. She could try to get hold of Mary's birth certificate, but she had a hunch it wouldn't tell her what she wanted to know.

"I need information about Mary's father."

Anne Soffey gasped. For the first time since Gwenn had known her, the president of Soffey Cosmetics was taken by surprise. "Why?" she asked finally.

"I'm not sure yet. I think I may be able to link Mary's death to that of another bride."

Anne Soffey frowned. "Mary's father is dead. He was in the Navy and he died in a training accident. Before Mary was born. I thought you knew that. I thought everybody knew."

"What's his name?"

Anne Soffey didn't answer. She sat as she was for a long time. Then she got up, walked over to a sideboard on which there was a tray with a Thermos of coffee and cups. She poured for herself, too preoccupied to offer any to Gwenn. She brought the full cup back to her desk, sat, and sipped.

"Did Mary's father know about her before he died?" Gwenn asked.

Every line which art and science had managed to hide now reappeared plus some others. Anne Soffey's stern, determined face sagged. She looked all of her years.

"I didn't think it mattered after all this time. I didn't think I cared. But I do. Yes, Mary's father did know I was pregnant and he chose to walk away from his responsibility."

"Walk away?" Gwenn asked gently.

"That's right. He didn't die while in the Navy or any-where else. He didn't serve in the Navy. He was called up but he was smart enough to duck the draft as he was smart enough to duck his obligation to us."

"Did Mary know her father was alive?"

"Certainly not. What good would it have done her to know he rejected and abandoned us both? No, he wasn't welcome in our lives any more than we were in his," Anne Soffey concluded firmly. She had regained her composure but not her ease. "That part of my life has been closed these twenty-four years. You'll have to give me a very strong reason for reopening it."

"Two other women besides Mary, one a bride and the other a bride-to-be, were murdered recently. There are certain similarities to the way Mary died. I learned just this morning that one of the young women was adopted."

Gwenn had expected her client to dismiss the possibility of a link; instead she smiled bitterly. "I wouldn't put it past Ben to have got more than one woman in trouble. He was not disposed to be faithful."

"Ben?"

"Benjamin Cryder. Yes, *the* Benjamin Cryder," she con-firmed before Gwenn could ask. "Of Cryder Hotels Inter-national. Millionaire. Billionaire, by this time. Back then he didn't have two nickels to rub together. In fact, he tried to borrow from me. He needed a stake for his first hotel and, I think, if I could have provided it, he might have married me." She shrugged. "I didn't have any money, not of my own. Anyway, I wasn't crazy enough about him to buy and pay for him." Both women thought about Mary. "Nor all that heartbroken when he went looking else-where," she added.

"Did your mother know?"

"Oh, yes. Mother saw me through the pregnancy. She was in the delivery room with me. She was wonderful. She

gave me the strength to get through it physically and psy-
chologically—to give birth and to raise Mary and to deal
with the social attitudes. She was the real feminist. At the
same time she wanted to protect Mary from making the
same mistake I'd made."

"That was the reason for the stipulation in the will,"
Gwenn suggested.

"Exactly." Anne Soffey looked off into the past, then
returned. "I don't see Ben involving himself in Mary's
death any more than he had in her life."

"You didn't get in touch with him to notify him that his
daughter was getting married?"

Anne Soffey's temples throbbed as she stared at Gwenn.
"Haven't you been listening?"

Benjamin Cryder was both a rich man and a public man.
Information about him was available through a variety of
channels, and since his marriage to a daughter of one of
the oldest of New York's blue-blooded families, he had
also achieved inclusion in the Social Register. His business
affiliations could be traced through *Fortune 500* and *Standard and Poor's*. From such tomes Gwenn was able to amass
information regarding his various companies, their boards
of directors, assets and holdings. His residences, clubs, philanthropies, awards and honors were part of the entry in
the Social Register. What she found interesting and pertinent was that Benjamin Cryder had remained unmarried
till the age of forty-eight. Single, but certainly not celibate,
she thought, and that was not only according to Anne
Soffey but to the gossip columns. Gwenn was not a follower
of the doings of the socially prominent, but Cryder's name
had been linked with some famous and infamous ladies.
Some relationships had lasted long enough to spur spec-
ulation that they would end in marriage. They had indeed
ended, but not that way. Not till Patricia Garvé.

Using the *Times Index,* Gwenn traced the Cryder story to the announcement of his marriage two years ago.

Once she had the dates, the stories were easy to find. Accounts of the wedding were front-page news. News of his illness, however, was handled more circumspectly. Probably because of the effect it might have on the financial stability of his companies, Gwenn reasoned. She learned that he had been at his home in Palm Beach when he suffered a relapse and was currently resting at his mansion in Harrison, New York.

How could she make contact with such a man? Gwenn wondered. She couldn't simply show up at the front door. If she wrote asking for an appointment she would have to give a very compelling reason for the letter to get past his secretary. What could she say? That Anne Soffey named him as the father of her child, and that child, Mary Soffey Langner, grown up and married, had been murdered on her honeymoon? She couldn't put that in a letter.

It would be a terrible shock for a sick man. The letter might even be withheld from him. And naming Mary would be only the beginning. Before she approached Benjamin Cryder, Gwenn had to establish that he had fathered other children out of wedlock—two, to be precise. Two girls, one a bride and the other a bride-to-be and both cruelly murdered. Learning of Becky Hayman's adoption was the break she'd been searching for, but it was also an obstacle. The adoptive parents were both dead. Adoption records were zealously guarded. The original birth certificate—superceded by a new one issued to the adoptive parents—was set aside as though it had never been. What could she hope to learn from it anyway? The name of the natural mother; the father's name was not likely to be on it. She could try to trace the natural mother—if she was still alive, if she was still using her maiden name. It could take months.

So that left Angela Fissore Doran. There appeared to be no question about her paternity, but unless she too was Benjamin Cryder's child, there was no case.

Birth and Death Records were maintained at the Department of Health at 125 Worth Street, a short walk from Gwenn's office. She merely wanted to verify the parents and the birth date. No big deal. She was handed a yellow application form to fill out. Impatient, Gwenn told the clerk at the information desk, a young fat woman whose police-style uniform was much too tight, that she didn't need a copy of the birth certificate, merely the information.

"I just want to take a look at it."

Her ID as a private investigator meant nothing.

The more she tried to explain, the stiffer the bureaucratic resistance.

"Could you look it up and tell me . . ."

"Are you a relative?"

Gwenn hesitated. There, on the form, in capital letters was the admonition: IF THIS REQUEST IS NOT FOR YOUR OWN BIRTH RECORD OR THAT OF YOUR CHILD, NOTARIZED AUTHORIZATION FROM THE PARENT OF THE PERSON NAMED ON THE CERTIFICATE MUST BE PRESENTED WITH THIS APPLICATION.

"Suppose I were making a genealogical search for my roots?"

"That would be different. You would request a permit and you would be given access to the records."

For a moment it seemed as though the clerk's antagonism had melted. For a moment, Gwenn thought the woman was on the verge of relenting and she smiled. Too soon.

"But you're not making a genealogical search, are you?"

Gwenn sighed. Too late to lie.

She considered coming back tomorrow and trying the

genealogical ploy, but she had made enough ruckus so that she would be remembered. So she could only meekly shake her head.

"Next, please." The fat clerk dismissed her with a triumphant smirk.

Gwenn was frustrated but not finished. She walked out of the building, bought a hot dog from one of the ever-present vendors, and sat down on a bench in Foley Square to eat and to think. She finished the hot dog, disposed of the napkin, and walked over to a section of public phones.

"Lew? It's Gwenn. I need to talk to you. Can I come over?"

He was delighted to see her. He had, in fact, been on the verge of calling her. He greeted her with a big smile and placed a chair for her beside her desk. When he heard what she wanted and why, his pleasure turned to dismay.

"They're not going to let me see that birth certificate, not now. You've put their backs up."

"I botched it. I know."

"Don't feel bad. I wouldn't have got any better results unless I'd shown up with a court order." He stopped her before she could speak. "I doubt I can get one. Frankly, I'm not inclined to try. I don't know what you expect to find out from it."

"For starters, we could compare the date of marriage to the date of birth . . ."

"Which would only tell you if Rosa and Emilio had been fooling around."

"Or if Rosa had been fooling with somebody else."

Sackler groaned. "If you'd ever talked to Emilio Fissore you'd never suggest this. Fissore adored Angela. He lived for her. I can't intrude on his grief and suggest that the daughter he's mourning was somebody else's child."

"He wants her killer found, doesn't he? Especially since

Doran's not a suspect any more." She paused. "I read in the papers he's been released."

Sackler winced. "I'm sorry. I couldn't tell you till the DA made it official. I only found out myself this morning and I was saving it to tell you at dinner tonight."

"Do we have a date?"

"I hope so."

She thought about it. "Make it tomorrow."

"No good for me. How about the day after?"

"Fine."

They grinned at each other.

"Meantime, we could talk to Mrs. Fissore," she suggested.

"We?"

"You want to do it alone?" she challenged.

"I guess not."

"Okay. So if there's nothing in it, Mr. Fissore doesn't even have to know what we had in mind. How about it?"

"Well . . ."

"We can't just ignore the possibility," she insisted.

"Oh, hell! I know that."

The line of cars was gone from the Fissore block. The Fissore house, shades drawn, was silent. The wake must be over, Sackler thought as he and Gwenn walked up the steps to the front door. A week had passed. It seemed both more and less.

Emilio Fissore answered the door. He was in neither better nor worse shape than when Lew had last seen him. Seeing Sackler, he frowned. He barely acknowledged Gwenn's presence till he heard the words "private investigator."

"Ms. Ramadge is working on a case similar to this," Sackler explained. "I hope you don't mind that I brought her along."

At that Fissore gave her a sharp stare. But it was brief.
He shrugged. "When are we going to get Angela back?"
he demanded. "When will they return her to us? How
much longer are we going to have to wait?" He nodded
toward the open arch leading into the empty parlor. "We
want to say goodbye and then bury her. We have to go on
with our lives."

"I'm sure it won't be much longer, Mr. Fissore."

"I've called and all I get is the runaround."

"I'm sorry." It was on the tip of Sackler's tongue to say
how busy they are at the morgue—the homicide rate in
the city had taken another jump—then decided it would
hardly be a consolation.

"Lew, maybe you could call for Mr. Fissore," Gwenn
suggested.

"Sure. I'll do that. I'll get you a definite date, Mr. Fissore,
and let you know." He spoke with more assurance than he
felt.

The commitment earned a look of gratitude from Fissore that included Gwenn. "What can I do for you?"

"Actually, we'd like to talk to Mrs. Fissore," Sackler said.

"She's in the kitchen." He nodded in its direction. He
didn't ask why they wanted to see his wife. He didn't ask
to be present at the interview. He was listless, seemingly
existing through the empty hours till he could get his child
back and have her finally and honorably interred. They
left him, passed through the dining room to the kitchen
door. Sackler tapped lightly, waited a moment, then
pushed it open for Gwenn to enter before him.

Rosa Fissore sat at the big rectangular table, holding a
doll in front of her. At their entrance she quickly lowered
it below table level.

Sackler cleared his throat. "Sorry to disturb you, ma'am.
I'm Detective Sackler. We spoke . . ."

"I remember."

"And this is Ms. Ramadge, a private investigator."

Rosa Fissore nodded without interest.

"That's a beautiful doll," Gwenn remarked. "It's a *Lenci,* isn't it? I had one when I was a little girl. May I see it?"

Rosa brought it out reluctantly at first and then she smiled softly. "It was Angie's."

The doll was exquisite. It had a lovely, natural face, blue eyes and dark, glossy curls. It was an expensive doll, the kind to thrill a little girl but also to disappoint her because it was too delicate for her to be allowed to play with. It was a doll brought out on special occasions and then locked away again. Gwenn had neither seen Angela in life nor in death, but she had studied photographs, and it seemed to her that but for the blue eyes the doll looked a lot like her.

So did the mother, Gwenn thought. Rosa Fissore had the same voluptuous figure, long black hair, and smoldering dark eyes. She must have been, and still was, a remarkably beautiful woman. As a man, her husband couldn't match her. It hardly mattered now, but it must have back when they were courting. Looks were very important to the young. Rosa Di Lucca had surely not lacked for boyfriends—suitors, they were called. And she'd settled on a short, heavyset man fifteen years her senior and went to work beside him running a neighborhood restaurant in Queens.

"Ms. Ramadge is working on a similar case," Sackler explained as usual. "I'd appreciate it if you'd allow her to ask a few questions."

Before replying, Rosa Fissore got up. She went over to a low cabinet, took out a box, and carefully placed the doll inside. Then she put it away, well to the back, and closed the door.

"I thought all the questions had been asked and answered."

Gwenn considered several approaches and opted for the most direct. "I want to talk to you about Benjamin Cryder."

It had all the effect she could have hoped for. Rosa

Fissore's dark eyes flashed and fastened on Gwenn. "He sent you? What does he want?"

"He didn't send me."

"Then why are you here?" Mrs. Fissore frowned. "What do you want?"

"I want to talk to you about Angela's father."

"You tricked me."

"I only mentioned a name."

The woman clamped her full, sensuous lips into a grim line and shook her head obdurately.

"When were you married, Mrs. Fissore?" Gwenn asked.

"June 12, 1966," she answered automatically.

"And how long after was Angela born?"

"That's my business and Emilio's."

"Then why should my mentioning Benjamin Cryder cause you such distress? How did you even come to know him?"

"We're sorry to revive painful memories," Sackler put in, "but your daughter was murdered. It's now clear that Ed Doran didn't do it. Don't you want to find out who did?"

"Ben didn't have anything to do with it," she snapped. "He didn't even know . . . that is . . . Oh, God!" She groaned. "I've been tempted so many times to speak out, to throw it in his face, to make him pay." Her face puckered as she fought tears. "But I didn't want to hurt Emilio. He loved Angie so much. He doted on her. It was Angie this and Angie that; nothing was ever too good for Angie. Whatever she wanted, somehow he managed to get it for her. The big fancy wedding . . . he went back to his old job to pay for it."

Rosa Fissore paused. She was no longer talking to them but rather using them for her own catharsis.

"I resented his love for Angie. I was jealous, jealous of my own child. That's ironic because I always considered Emilio beneath me. I married him because I needed to get married. And he was willing to have me and didn't ask questions. We had a good life, comfortable, never lacked for anything. I was grateful, but not happy. At least, I didn't think I was happy. But suddenly, I didn't want to lose Emilio.

"And I resented Angie's love for him. I felt left out. I wondered what her reaction would be if she ever found out who her real father was. How would she feel about me? When she announced she was going to marry Ed Doran, I was relieved. She was restless, much like me at her age, and I didn't want her to get into the same kind of trouble. I wasn't crazy about Ed, but she wanted him and it would settle her down in a home of her own. Then as Emilio struggled to get the money to pay for the big wedding she'd set her heart on, I saw a way to impress her, to show her I loved her too. She might love me back. At least, she'd be grateful."

"You went to Benjamin Cryder," Gwenn said, and Rosa Fissore nodded. "How did you contact him?"

"I wrote him a letter. I marked it Personal and Private. I said: *Your daughter is getting married. I know you would like her to have a nice wedding.* I rented a post office box and included the number. It took awhile before I got an answer. It was typewritten and unsigned. It asked me to provide certain information and send it to another post office box. About five days after that I got another communication. It told me to be at the public library at Forty-second Street on Tuesday, which was the Tuesday after Labor Day, at noon exactly. I was to wait beside the statue of the lion on the right-hand side and a package would be delivered to me. It would be a wedding gift. There was to be no further contact, no correspondence. I followed instructions and received the package. It was wrapped in brown paper in a shopping bag and contained ten thousand dollars. Naturally, it wasn't easy for me to explain that amount of money to Emilio, but I managed. I told him I'd been

setting aside a little out of my housekeeping money and
that one of our customers at the restaurant had given me
a tip in the stock market."

"Exactly how was the package delivered to you?" Sackler
wanted to know. "Did you have to identify yourself?"

"No. I was waiting as instructed. A man came up to me;
I don't know from what direction. People were coming
and going. It was a hot day. The lunch hour. People were
sitting on the library steps eating, relaxing. I kept looking
around, but I didn't know who I was looking for."

"Naturally."

"He asked me my name and I told him. He handed me
a shopping bag. He said: *Take good care of it,* went back
down the steps and up Fifth Avenue."

"It wasn't Cryder?"

"Oh, no. I was afraid, for a while I was worried, he might
come himself, but I guess he wasn't any more anxious to
see me than I was to see him."

"What did the man who delivered the money look like?"
Sackler asked.

She thought back. "Tall, thin. Real tall and thin, like a
clothespin."

"Would you know him if you saw him again?"

"I'm not sure."

Sackler looked to Gwenn.

"When you wrote to Mr. Cryder, where did you send
the letter?" she asked. "To his home?"

"No. I didn't know the address. I couldn't find it listed,
so I sent it to his office at Cryder Hotels International."

Gwenn nodded.

"I knew it was important that nobody else should see it,
so I marked it Personal and Private, like I told you."

"Yes, of course. Well, thank you for being so forthright,
Mrs. Fissore." Gwenn indicated to Sackler that she was
finished.

"Miss? Detective Sackler?" Rosa Fissore looked from one

to the other. "Does Emilio have to know? He loved Angela so much. He loved her the most, I know that, but he loves me too. If he found out . . . I'm not sure he could go on loving me."

"So what do you think?" Gwenn asked as she settled herself in the front seat of the car. "For all that she marked it Personal and Private, it's possible, even likely, that Rosa Fissore's letter was opened before it got to Cryder. Probably by his personal secretary. On the other hand, this was back in August and chances are the Cryders weren't in the city so the letter would have been sent on. The question is—" Gwenn paused. "Did the letter go to him directly or was it intercepted?"

Chapter
SEVENTEEN

Sackler offered to drive Gwenn home, but she refused to let him go so far out of his way. The nearest subway station would be fine.

"Are you sure you'll be all right?"

"I'm sure."

In fact, it would have been out of his way, Lew acknowledged, and he would have had to work late to catch up.

"You're a nice girl, Gwenn Ramadge, you know that?"

She liked him too, a lot. She felt comfortable with Lew Sackler. She could say what came into her head without having first to weigh all the possible implications. They argued without antagonism. In fact, the arguments seemed to draw them closer. Gwenn found a seat on the E train and fell into that half-dazed state of the habitual subway rider in which one could think one's own thoughts but remain aware of the potentially explosive situation, a situation which changed every time the train stopped at a station, the doors opened, and a new set of riders got on. When the doors closed at Queens Plaza, Gwenn knew there was a long stretch before they would open again in Manhattan and she could relax and think about what Rosa Fissore had told them.

Mrs. Fissore had appealed to the man who had been her

lover for help in financing their daughter's wedding. The letter passed through several hands. The money, ten thousand dollars, which to her was a lot, was delivered through a third party. The third party interested Gwenn because it widened the field of those who knew about Cryder's past. As the train rattled and lurched through the tunnel under the river, it occurred to Gwenn that the money hadn't necessarily come from Cryder. It was possible that Cryder, protected as he was and sick as he was, had never seen Rosa's letter. In that case, who had sent the money? Obviously, someone close enough to the billionaire to have access to his personal mail and someone who didn't want him to renew contact with his past.

As soon as she got home, Gwenn called Avis and reserved a car for the next morning.

It was pretty country, Gwenn thought as she turned off the Hutchinson River Parkway to a two-lane blacktop. Even in the austerity of early March, though the trees were still bare and patches of mud along the shoulder the only traces of the recent snowfall, the air was redolent with the promise of spring. She had set out full of optimism, had marked the route on the map, and so far had made all the right turns. The first obstacle she encountered was the closed gates of the Cryder mansion.

Through the bars she could see a long, winding drive that led up to the house about a quarter of a mile inside. There was an intercom box on the right post. Gwenn got out, walked over to it, and pushed the button.

"Yes?"

"My name is Gwenn Ramadge. I'm here to see Mrs. Cryder." No use asking for Mr. Cryder.

"Mrs. Cryder is not receiving visitors."

"May I ask who you are?"

"I'm Mrs. Alvin, the housekeeper."

"I've come all the way out from New York, Mrs. Alvin."

"You should have called first."

"I realize that now, but since I'm here may I speak to Mrs. Cryder's secretary?" Society women had social secretaries, Gwenn thought.

"Mrs. Cryder's secretary is not here today."

"Oh, dear, now I don't know what to do."

"Call or write."

"But I'm here now, at the gate . . ."

The line went dead.

She had not expected to be turned back at the gate. Was there a back entrance? There had to be a back entrance for tradesmen. Would she have any more luck there than she'd had with Mrs. Alvin at the front? Did the six-foot-high wall enclose the entire property? Maybe there was a break somewhere. Gwenn got back in the car and began a slow tour of the perimeter, examining the wall closely. If she tried to climb it, would she set off an alarm?

The wall was set well back from the paved road, and about an eighth of a mile along Gwenn spotted a tangle of underbrush that should have been cleared but for some reason had not. It would give her a foothold, she thought. There wasn't any cover for her car, but there wasn't much traffic either. In fact, she hadn't encountered a single car since she'd turned off the main road. She could park on the shoulder and anybody who happened along would assume a car had broken down and its owner was trudging to the nearest service station for help. She considered propping up the hood, then decided against it. She might just possibly need to get away fast.

Gwenn stood on a fallen tree trunk and looked closely along both sides of the section of wall she intended to breach. She saw no indication of any kind of electronic device. She had been an energetic athlete in high school. What she'd lacked physically, she'd made up for in dedication and enthusiasm. Short as she was, she'd loved basketball and held the slam-dunk record during her junior

and senior years. In college, basketball went from serious
to grim. They wanted tall girls. Bounce didn't count. At
this moment, stretching, reaching, her muscles felt tight.
She coiled, and jumped and grasped the top of the wall.
For a moment she clung there, then taking a deep breath,
she pulled herself up and straddled the top.

She could see the house. A Gothic structure with wings
and turrets, it was big as a hotel. She was facing the back—
the kitchen and maintenance areas. A small structure in
the same style stood off to one side—a garage converted
from a barn possibly. There was nobody around; still she'd
better climb down before someone just happened to look
out a window and see her. She threw the other leg over,
turned so she faced the inside of the wall. Unfortunately,
the maintenance on the inside was meticulous; there were
no nicks for toeholds to slow the descent. She had to let
go and drop, and in doing so she hit a narrow trench at
the base of the wall and felt her left ankle turn as she rolled
over. Damn. The pain shot through her whole body. Oh,
damn! She bent forward to feel the ankle, to test the movement. It responded. The pain was not unbearable. She
managed to stand up.

Now the house seemed very far away and there was an
open expanse of browned meadow to cross before reaching
it. If she could manage not to hobble too obviously, to walk
neither too fast nor too slow, she might, if she were seen,
pass for someone who belonged. In such a place, Gwenn
thought, there must be a large and anonymous staff.

With each step the pain eased. A sprain, Gwenn thought,
and the best thing for that was to keep active. Nevertheless,
she was relieved when she reached the shadow of the
house. Another few steps and she would be shielded from
the view of those inside. Fine, but she still had to get in
there herself. The wall had turned out to be without any
kind of alarm, but the house must have some kind of security device on the doors and windows. It was not the way

she would have done it if she'd been consulted. For one thing, there must be a constant stream of deliveries, of workers, of maintenance people coming and going. The staff would not want to be bothered with turning the system on and off and on again time after time. It would result in the service section being turned off in the morning and left off till late afternoon.

Gwenn crept up to the nearest window and took a look inside.

Two women sat at a big table in a gleaming, modern pantry having coffee. They were obviously nurses. One was about fifty, buxom, with a mass of dark red curls sprayed to rigidity. The other was anywhere from mid-twenty to mid-thirty, thin and dark. At that moment she looked up in Gwenn's direction. Instinctively, Gwenn dropped down. Then she thought, why hide? She stood up and tapped on the windowpane.

When both women looked at her, Gwenn pointed to the door and limped over.

"Yes?" The elder nurse stood at the threshold.

"I'm sorry to disturb you, but my car broke down," Gwenn explained. "I could see the house, but I couldn't find the gate. I needed to use the telephone, so I climbed the wall and fell." She pulled up her pants leg to show the swollen ankle.

"Oh, my," the redheaded nurse clucked and opened the door wide. "Looks nasty. Come in. Come in and sit down."

"Thank you. I don't think it's anything but a sprain. If you happen to have an Ace bandage . . ."

"I'm sure we do. We've got everything."

"I'd be glad to pay for it."

"Don't worry about that."

"You're very kind. And if I could use your phone . . . ?"

"I'll be glad to call the garage for you," the elder nurse said. "They'll make more of an effort if the call comes from somebody in the house. Meantime, Miss Barnes will get the bandage."

Miss Barnes was up on the instant and heading for the back stairs.

"Thank you," Gwenn said to Miss Barnes. "I'm sorry to put you to all this trouble." This to the senior nurse.

"No trouble. You sit where you are and put your foot up on this." The nurse pulled over a small stool and placed Gwenn's injured leg on it. "You should always keep a sprain high." She smiled encouragingly and bustled off. As there was a wall phone right there, Gwenn presumed it was a house phone and the nurse was going to a phone with an outside line.

She lowered her injured foot, but as soon as she stood on it the pain shot through her. Bad as it was, she had to try to get herself upstairs.

She went the way Miss Barnes had done—up the backstairs. The master bedroom, *suite* in this house, would be on the second floor, she reasoned. So at the landing she opened the door and stepped through from the plain, uncarpeted service stairs to a long, wide passage that was more gallery than corridor. At that moment, one of the doors opened and Nurse Barnes came out carrying a small box. Gwenn ducked behind the draperies of a window enclosure till she was gone. The storage or dispensary closet should be near the sickroom, she reasoned, and the sickroom should be the master bedroom. There was only one set of double doors. She went over and tapped lightly.

No answer.

She tried once more, knocking a little louder but not expecting a response.

The room was large, shadowed from the bright winter sun by venetian blinds. It was hard at first to see, but gradually she made out a large canopied bed at the center of the left wall, fireplace and flanking chairs opposite. The next thing she distinguished was the battery of medical equipment ranged at the head of the bed, an IV stand, and the inevitable bags and tubes. The harsh sound of the respirator was both reassuring and frightening in the silence. Of the man connected to the machines Gwenn could make out no more than a waxen figure propped up on a mound of pillows. She watched in fascination and pity as his chest rose and fell to the dictates of the machine. She noted the screen also at the head of the bed that presented the rhythm and depth of his breathing by means of a luminous green graph. Even from a distance Gwenn knew that the patient was more than just asleep. She was about to step closer when she became aware of another presence, a third person, a woman. She stood at one of the recessed windows, her back to Gwenn, looking out. She too must have sensed Gwenn because she turned.

"Who are you? What are you doing here?"

She stepped to one side so that what light came through the slanted blinds fell full on Gwenn. The woman could see her, but Gwenn could make out only a silhouette—no features, no expression. The tone, however, was commanding.

"Mrs. Cryder?" She waited for a moment, but the woman neither acknowledged nor denied the assumption. "My name is Gwenn Ramadge. I'm very sorry for the intrusion. I had no idea Mr. Cryder was so ill. I apologize."

"You called from the front gate about half an hour ago, didn't you?"

It was surprising that she'd been advised; it was surprising that she remembered Gwenn's name.

"Yes."

"You were told at the time that I wasn't receiving visitors."

"I didn't realize the extent . . ."

"Well, now you do. So please leave."

At the moment Gwenn was inclined to do just that, walk

out, make it back to her car, and go home. Benjamin Cryder was in a coma. His wife was under tremendous emotional strain. To confront her with his past transgressions would be not only inappropriate but cruel. Then she reminded herself of why she'd come. If her suspicion was correct, then Patricia Garvé Cryder did not deserve pity.

"I'm a private investigator, Mrs. Cryder. I'd appreciate a few minutes of your time. I have uncovered certain facts that you should be aware of. You may have found out already, but if you haven't, the sooner you do the better."

Tricia Cryder stepped away from the window and with the light now coming from the side, Gwenn finally got a look at her. They were about the same age, but otherwise had little in common, Gwenn thought. The socialite's beauty was neither classic nor perfect, but it was dramatic. It derived from the contrast of alabaster skin and dark hair and blue eyes. It depended on inner energy. She was tall enough to be a fashion model and she had the figure for it. Above all, she had the inbred assurance of the well born. She was wearing tailored gray wool slacks and a white cashmere turtleneck pullover. Gwenn was also wearing slacks and a sweater. Of course, she'd snagged the pants at one knee and rolled in the dirt, but even in a ballgown she would have felt inadequate beside Mrs. Cryder.

"I don't like vague hints, Ms. Ramadge. Please say what you have to say."

Gwenn looked toward the man in the bed. "Maybe we should go somewhere . . ."

Tricia Cryder shook her head. "He's totally unaware." Then she frowned. "But you're right. It would be unseemly."

There was a light tap at the door. "Mrs. Cryder?"

"Come in."

A man in a light gray uniform opened the door. Security guard, Gwenn thought. Behind him ranged the two nurses.

"That's her. There she is!" The redhead pointed. "She said her car broke down and she sprained her ankle."

"Want me to get the police, Mrs. Cryder?" the guard asked.

"That won't be necessary," she answered. "Ms. Ramadge and I are going to have a talk. I'll call you when she's ready to leave."

That dismissed them. The elder nurse, with a last accusing glance at Gwenn, went in the direction of the service quarters, the guard toward the main staircase, and Nurse Barnes, still holding the bandage as though she didn't know what to do with it, took her place at the bedside.

"This way." Mrs. Cryder led Gwenn down the corridor to a room at the far end.

It was a combination sitting room and lady's writing room with a plump, chintz-covered sofa and matching chairs and a brass-trimmed, Empire-style desk. A bowl of flowers chosen to complement the color scheme, and to judge by their freshness changed daily, graced the desk. Gwenn envied that relatively small luxury more than all the rest. Walking even that short distance had been a strain and she was glad to be able to sit down. Mrs. Cryder hovered for a moment, uncertain whether to take her place at the desk or to sit on the sofa which would certainly be less formal. She chose the sofa.

"Would you care for coffee or tea?"

Noblesse oblige, Gwenn thought; some were still in a position to practice it. "No, thank you."

"Well then, let's get to business, shall we? You want to sell me certain information."

"Sell? I never said anything about selling, Mrs. Cryder."

"I assumed . . ." Patricia Cryder shrugged. "Then what do you want?"

"As I told you, I'm a private investigator and I'm working on a murder case. The victim, a young bride, turns out to have been your husband's illegitimate daughter."

Patricia Cryder's expression remained unchanged. She spoke evenly. "Mary Soffey. Yes. She married Clark Langner and fell or was pushed overboard during her honeymoon cruise."

Totally controlled, Gwenn marveled.

"There was another daughter, Angela Fissore. She married and was killed a month later. Tragic coincidence."

Gwenn was stunned. "How did you find out?"

"Ben told me. We have no secrets from each other, Ms. Ramadge."

"He kept track of the girls over the years?"

"As a matter of fact, no, he didn't. There was no contact with the women or the children. It was all in the past. All over and done with. He assured me of that. He assured me that each was an isolated incident which he regretted and on which he'd closed the door. He told me partly because he thought I was entitled to know and partly in case of future possible blackmail attempts."

Gwenn decided not to take it personally. "Have there been blackmail attempts? Have you or your husband been approached?"

There was the slightest of hesitations but it didn't escape Gwenn. "No."

There had been a request for money from Rosa Fissore. She had written her Private and Personal note to Benjamin Cryder. Certainly, it was logical, in view of his condition, that the letter had been turned over to his wife. Or that she had intercepted it.

Tricia Cryder's blue eyes clouded. She searched and finally fell back on the truth. "Ben hired a detective to find them. He wanted to make amends. He felt he owed them."

"Money?"

"Yes."

What else? Gwenn thought. For people like the Cryders money solved all problems. Money could make amends for any oversight, any injury, any offense, wrong, neglect.

"I know you're thinking there's no price to be put on a childhood without a father, on twenty years of raising a child alone, single-handed, but at this stage what else could he offer? He asked me what I thought and I agreed he should try to find them and do whatever would ease his conscience."

"You agreed?"

"I just told you so. Yes. If it would give him peace, yes." She opened out her arms, palms up. "That's the story, Ms. Ramadge. There's nothing more I can tell you."

"If you could just give me the name of the man your husband hired."

"I don't think that's any of your concern."

"It's very much my concern. I'm investigating the murder of one of those girls, Mary Soffey. At her mother's behest."

"I thought the husband . . ."

"Neither of the husbands is guilty. You might as well tell me who Mr. Cryder hired. I can get the information by other means."

Patricia Cryder frowned, then shrugged and the perfection of her countenance was restored. "Taplin Investigations."

"And the money Mr. Cryder intended to settle on the girls—is it to be an outright gift, or in the form of a trust, or perhaps they're mentioned in the will?"

"We didn't discuss that."

"But it will be a substantial amount?"

"Ben isn't stingy."

"I assume the provisions were made before Mr. Cryder was stricken?"

"Ben isn't one to waste time."

There was a pause. Patricia Cryder had volunteered knowledge of two or her husband's illegitimate offspring, Gwenn thought. She hadn't said anything about the third, about Rebecca Hayman. Was it because she didn't know about Rebecca's existence or because, being adopted, Taplin Investigations hadn't traced her identity? Did that mean Benjamin Cryder hadn't made provision for his third child?

Gwenn pulled herself to her feet and winced. "May I ask a favor?"

"Certainly." Tricia Cryder was relieved that the unwelcome visitor was about to leave.

"Nurse Barnes was getting me an Ace bandage."

Mrs. Cryder picked up the house phone.

"And if I could have a couple of aspirin?"

"Is that all?"

"Maybe somebody could drive me around to where I left my car."

Chapter
EIGHTEEN

If she'd injured the right ankle instead of the left, Gwenn thought, she wouldn't have been able to drive home. As it was, despite the aspirins and the bandage which Nurse Barnes had, at Mrs. Cryder's insistence, put on for Gwenn, the pain was getting worse. Mrs. Cryder had also seen to it that Nurse Barnes supplied Gwenn with a couple of painkillers to take later. She was warned they might make her drowsy while driving, but later they would ease her and help her to sleep.

Gwenn tried to forget the pain by dwelling instead on the case. It was important not to lose sight of the social attitude toward a woman bearing an illegitimate child in the late sixties and now. Now, what with teenage pregnancies, in vitro fertilization, surrogate motherhood, illegitimacy was called single parenting. The woman was no longer ostracized. Back then, when the mothers of Mary Soffey, Angela Fissore, and Rebecca Hayman had their fling and became pregnant, *The Feminine Mystique* was capturing the enthusiasm of the nation. Women's Lib was a call to true emancipation, but few women had the conviction and courage to proclaim pregnancy outside marriage, to reject abortion, and to live the rest of their lives flaunting the scarlet *A*.

Gwenn had come close to it herself and she realized all

at once and for the first time why she felt such empathy for these mothers and their daughters. She understood her commitment to getting at the truth. If she had not lost her baby, if she had carried it to term, what path would she have chosen?

Would she have acted like Anne Soffey?

Anne Soffey had found the inner strength to have her child and raise her alone without a man's help. Yet for all her courage, she had implied that a marriage had been intended but the father killed before it could take place.

Or would she have taken Rosa Fissore's way?

Rosa found herself a man who believed he was the father of the baby in Rosa's womb and who was eager and happy to make her his wife and take responsibility for siring the child.

Or would Gwenn, like Rebecca Hayman's mother, have put her baby up for adoption? Nobody could answer such a question in the abstract, Gwenn decided. It puzzled her that Mrs. Cryder, who had been so forthright in acknowledging her husband's first two children, had not said a word about the third. Was it possible she didn't know about Rebecca?

Gwenn was puzzled by her own motive for not mentioning the third girl. Why had she kept quiet? She couldn't answer her own question. Though she was following the same route back to the city that she had taken out and the traffic was still light, the throbbing of her foot demanded she stop analyzing and concentrate on the driving.

Five hours after she'd started out, Gwenn Ramadge recrossed the Triboro into Manhattan, but she was in no shape to take the car back to the Avis garage. Tomorrow would be time enough. She searched Seventy-second from York to Second avenues till she found a parking place that would be legal till the next morning. She limped back to her building, into the elevator, and finally to her own front door. Inside, she tossed the keys and purse on the sofa, dropping her coat on top of them. She made it to the bedroom and sprawled, exhausted, on the bed. It wasn't just her ankle; every bone in her body ached.

After a few minutes, she reached over and turned on the telephone answering machine. Eyes closed, she leaned back and listened to her messages.

Regal Cleaners, Ms. Ramadge. Your dresses are ready, but we can't get that spot out of your tan slacks.

DuBarry Jewelers. The watch repair comes to twenty-five dollars and will take three weeks. Should we go ahead?

Hi, this is Lew.

Gwenn opened her eyes and paid attention.

I've been trying all day to get you. Where've you been? Anyway, we didn't set a time for tomorrow. Is eight okay? If I don't hear otherwise I'll pick you up at eight.

Should she call and tell him what had happened at the mansion? Actually, nothing had happened. She had fallen and hurt her ankle, that was all. She hadn't turned any new evidence, hadn't even gained any useful insight. If anything she was more perplexed about Patricia Cryder than before. She got up, found an old icebag, and took it to the kitchen to fill. What had she done with those pills? Oh, yes, they were in an envelope in the pocket of her coat. She went out to get them but left the coat and purse where they were. She tore the envelope open. There were two pills, but she decided one would be enough. She took it and went back to bed. She propped up her pillow, adjusted the icebag on her ankle, and using the remote control turned on a small black-and-white television set on the bureau opposite her bed.

When she lay down it was daylight and she couldn't have slept long because it was still light when she was wakened by the ringing of the telephone. She was groggy. Her body felt heavy. The phone was right beside her bed, but by the time she reached for it the answering machine had been activated. She listened to her own voice announce she wasn't home and ask the caller to leave a message. Then she waited.

There was no message. The tape hummed, and then as the caller hung up, clicked off.

Nothing odd about that, Gwenn thought. Plenty of people resisted leaving messages on the machine. Undoubtedly, whoever it was would call another time. Closing her eyes, Gwenn drifted off again.

The next time she woke it was to darkness. The only light was provided by the flickering images on the screen. The volume was normal, neither too loud nor too low, just at the level to cover other sounds. Yet a sound other than the television had wakened Gwenn. As she strained to listen, to discover what had reached to her subconscious, she became aware that her ankle was blissfully numb. Thank God for that, she thought, and continued to lie very still, all senses alert. The bedroom door was ajar and the other room was in darkness, but she knew somebody was there. She was sure of it.

Her next thought was to get her gun. Only it was in her purse and her purse was where she'd tossed it—on the couch in the other room under her coat. No use moaning. She couldn't get to it, so what could she use instead? A knife. Fine. The knives were in the kitchen and to get to the kitchen she had to go through the living room.

Who was out there anyway? A burglar? There was money in the purse. If he found it, he'd find the gun too. Quietly as she could, almost holding her breath, Gwenn swung her legs around and over the side of the bed. As she tried to stand, her left ankle gave way and she nearly toppled to the floor. The gasp sounded thunderous in her own ears, but it must have been louder in her imagination because there was no indication the intruder had heard. Somewhat more confident, she took a few moments to recover and then got herself to the bedroom door and peered around it. She could make out the figure of a man, at least she thought it was a man, though his back was to her and he was hunched over. He was at her desk and with a tiny, pinpoint flashlight he was rummaging through her drawers.

What was he looking for? Whatever it was, if he found it, would he leave her alone? If she stayed very quiet, would he ultimately go away?

It would be sensible not to disturb him. It would be even more sensible if she had a weapon. That was the advice the police gave. If you got mugged, let the thief have your purse; it was better losing your money than your life. If he broke into your home, let him have the jewelry—be quiet, lie low. The police couldn't offer protection and their counsel served notice to the criminals that they could break and enter at will—at the very least. Gwenn's indignation swelled as she thought about it. She refused to go along. No way. Whoever he was, whatever he wanted, he wasn't going to get it, not without a struggle. However, to make the struggle anywhere near even, she had to have her gun. After taking her keys she hadn't bothered to zip the purse up again, so it was just a matter of getting to it.

Keeping watch on the intruder who was on her left, Gwenn cautiously made her way into the living room. She was at the sofa within arm's reach when she tripped, tripped over the damned new magazine rack she'd just bought! Before she could regain her balance, he grabbed her from behind, one hand over her mouth to stifle her screams.

She kicked backwards. She jabbed with her elbows. She squirmed and twisted. She ignored the pain that accompanied every movement. She would have bitten the hand he held over her mouth but he was wearing gloves. She couldn't get free. She was wasting her strength in the attempt and maybe exciting him. God forbid. So, for a moment, Gwenn Ramadge went limp and tried to think.

That was a mistake. A big mistake. He seized the moment. Keeping the one hand still over her mouth, he could now move the other from her waist up to her neck in a hammerlock. She choked. She gasped. She could feel herself losing consciousness, slipping . . . slipping into darkness. Her chest burned. She felt as though her lungs would burst. The darkness was shattered by shards of color, but before it could return and become absolute, Gwenn flung up both arms and reached for his hair. It was thick, good thick hair! She exulted and twined her finger in it and yanked.

He screeched. Like a cat with its tail caught in a trap, he yelled. And let go.

Gwenn dove for the sofa and the purse.

"I've got a gun. Don't move," she warned though she was still fumbling to get the gun out.

He didn't wait. He was past her and flinging the door open, ran into the hall.

She fired into the lighted corridor.

The door slammed shut.

By the time she was able to get to the door and open it, he was gone.

The single bullet she'd fired was embedded in the opposite wall. There was no blood anywhere. She hadn't intended to inflict serious injury, but she hadn't meant to miss him completely either. Damn! Wounding him could have turned out to be a form of identification. She'd goofed. She'd never before had occasion to actually shoot at anyone and she had the uneasy sense that she hadn't really tried to hit him, that subconsciously she'd meant to miss.

Lew came as soon as Gwenn called. He found her charged up, eager to pour out every detail of the encounter. She was drinking coffee, but he took the coffee away from her.

"What happened to your ankle?"

"Nothing. I twisted it."

"How?"

She licked her lips. "I fell."

"Tonight? Just now?"

She shook her head.

"When? Where? How?"

On the phone Gwenn had told him only that someone had broken into her apartment and that she'd shot and missed him. She hadn't mentioned the trip to Westchester and the talk with Patricia Cryder. While waiting for Lew to arrive, she'd had time to think, to try to make sense out of what had happened. It had been no ordinary, chance break-in, she was sure of that. Somehow, it was connected with Mrs. Cryder. Was she behind it? Having appealed to Lew for help, she now had to tell him everything.

"I'm inclined to agree," he said after she was through. "This was no random break-in. I think the intruder wanted to find out just how much you know and what kind of evidence you have to back it up."

"Maybe this Peter Taplin?"

"Could be." Sackler had never heard of Taplin, but there were plenty of private investigators and agencies he didn't know. "It would have made sense to go through your office files first. What could he have found?"

"Not much. Notes, mostly, and copies of the reports I submitted to Mrs. Soffey."

"Hmm. I don't suppose you have much of a lock on your office door either?"

Gwenn sighed ruefully. "I didn't think I needed one."

"You deal in security," he pointed out. "Okay, okay, so he gets in, goes through your files without finding anything significant. So he figures, if you have hard evidence, maybe you're keeping it here. Counting on your having taken the painkiller Mrs. Cryder provided you with . . ."

Gwenn gasped.

". . . he figured it would be safe to come in and take a

look around. I don't suppose you bothered to put the chain on your door."

She was too embarrassed to do more than shake her head.

"Fortunately or unfortunately, I'm not sure which, the pills didn't have the full effect."

"I only took one."

"Ah . . ."

"Only because I don't believe in sedatives and painkillers, not because I suspected anything. I'll know better next time."

Sackler reached for her hand. "It might be very different next time," he warned. "Whoever is behind this now knows that you have no hard evidence involving the Cryders. All you have is what Anne Soffey and Rosa Fissore told you and what Mrs. Cryder admitted. Each woman spoke to you privately. If something should happen to you, they could deny everything, including ever having the conversation. If I tried to go to court, the testimony would be ruled out as hearsay."

"I could give you an official signed statement."

"I don't know how much weight it would carry, or how much protection it would provide for you."

"So?"

"You could drop the case."

She just looked at him, green eyes wide.

He grinned. "It didn't hurt to try. Okay, but we had a deal, remember? We were going to keep each other informed. You should have told me what you were up to."

"I thought you'd try to talk me out of it."

"Would it have done any good?"

"No. But was what I did so wrong? Was it such a bad mistake?"

"Except for putting yourself at risk, no, of course not. Having established the link between two of the victims we would have had to interrogate Mrs. Cryder sooner or later and she would have found out she was a suspect." He shrugged. "Later might have been better."

"It all points to Patricia Cryder, doesn't it?" Gwenn asked. "It makes perfect sense that way, yet I can't see her doing it. Or ordering it done. She's so young. She's still almost a bride herself. And no matter how much money Cryder assigned to his daughters there'll be plenty left over for her. A couple of million more or less shouldn't matter."

"Not to her maybe."

"To whom then?"

"Could be she has a boyfriend."

Chapter NINETEEN

Gwenn needed no more pills to sleep through the rest of the night. She awoke at eight to a miserable day: sleet was mixed with snow and blown by gusty winds. The ankle felt pretty good, but she wasn't sorry she'd promised Lew to stay in. She swung her legs over the side of the bed and got ready to stand. Good. Very good. She moved slowly to the kitchen to make breakfast and found the electric coffee pot filled and ready to be plugged in, the bread already in the toaster. Lew, of course. He'd insisted on making hot tea for her last night before he left and he must have done this at the same time. As she poured the coffee and buttered the toast and put it all on a tray to carry back to bed, Gwenn thought about Lew. She assumed their date for tonight was still on. One of these days, if things progressed between them as she thought and hoped, she'd cook dinner for him. Not tonight. Cooking meant marketing and she wasn't up to that.

Nevertheless, she felt restless. There was plenty to do around the apartment, but Gwenn wasn't much of a housekeeper. She kept things neat as she went along and seldom indulged in any compulsive, down-to-the-bone cleaning. It occurred to her that last night neither she nor Lew had thought of checking her desk to see if anything was missing.

After half an hour, in which time she cleared out bills, receipts, coupons, calendars, stacks of blank checks from closed-out accounts, Gwenn found no indication of a prior search, but she did have a very neat desk. She recalled the intruder had been wearing gloves so there was no use dusting for prints. For lack of anything better, she did it anyway.

No doubt he had been just as careful in her office. Still, she shouldn't take it for granted, she thought as the icy rain beat on the air conditioner. She would check it out, but there was no rush. Sitting at her well-ordered desk, Gwenn placed a yellow pad on the blotter in front of her and wrote:

Benjamin Cryder's paternity.

Cryder was the natural father most certainly of the first two victims and very probably also of the third, Rebecca Hayman. She had no doubt that Cryder had left each young woman a substantial amount in his will. Cryder's young and beautiful wife had indicated it. Would Tricia Cryder have admitted her husband's paternity and his intent to make amends if it weren't true? So that was the link she'd been searching for.

Will.

Checking the will wouldn't be easy. Maybe it might not even be possible, not with Cryder still alive. The only way would be if he gave permission, but he was still in a coma, a coma from which he might never wake. There was no way of knowing what the provisions were in the event of the death of the beneficiaries. Would the money go to their next of kin or revert to Cryder's estate and thus to his widow? An irrelevant question since the girls were dead and Cryder was still alive.

Rosa Fissore stated she had sent the letter asking for money for Angie's wedding almost six months in advance of the wedding date. That letter was the trigger. That appeal wakened Cryder's memories, nostalgia, sense of guilt. But Cryder was a shrewd man; he wouldn't accept Rosa Fissore's word that Angela was his child. Once he paid her money he admitted paternity and opened himself to all kinds of further claims. So before doing anything he had to have her investigated. That's where Peter Taplin came in.

When precisely did Cryder hire the detective?

Obviously it had to be after Rosa sent the letter. Once Rosa Fissore's claim was proved legitimate and he acknowledged Angela was his child, Benjamin Cryder, a dying man, had an attack of conscience. He was driven to make amends not only to Angie but to his other progeny. Having hired Taplin to investigate one of his daughters, he now ordered him to trace the others.

Gwenn reached for the phone and dialed Lew's number. He hadn't said anything about interrogating Taplin, but of course he must be intending to do so. He picked up on the third ring.

"Homicide. Detective Sackler."

"It's me. Gwenn."

"Well, hi." His pleasure was evident in his voice. "How are you feeling?"

"Not bad."

"Are we still on for tonight? If you're not up to it . . ."

"Oh, no, no, I'm fine. Why I called . . . You are planning to see Peter Taplin some time today?"

"Yes," he admitted cautiously.

"I think it would be helpful if I sat in."

"You're supposed to stay home with your foot up."

"I know, but I'm okay. Honestly. If I could get a look at him I'd know whether he's the one who was here last night."

"You said you couldn't give a description because it was too dark. You said he grabbed you from behind."

"Right. But the hallway was lit. When he ran out I got a general impression."

"From the back, before the door slammed shut, right? So, was he tall or short, thin or fat, light or dark?"

"Oh, Lew . . ."

"You said he yelled when you yanked his hair; would you be able to recognize his voice?"

"Give me a break, Lew. I won't say a word. I'll sit in a corner and you won't even know I'm there."

"That'll be the day," Sackler muttered. "You're sure your ankle's okay to get around?"

"No problem."

"All right. I expect to be at Taplin's office at one."

Peter Taplin was located just west of Fifth Avenue on Forty-seventh Street, the heart of the wholesale jewelry district. The merchants were everywhere, occupying cubicles in large street-front stores, or upstairs within the buildings behind steel doors. Along with them were the estate appraisers and the lawyers who served them and who were in turn served by them. But everybody in the trade knew everybody else. Diamond merchants walked the streets with hundreds of thousands of dollars' worth of gems in their pockets and deals were made on the sidewalk or in the lobbies and hallways and sealed with a handshake. Nobody could afford to renege or steal, not if he wanted to stay in business. That was the best security, Gwenn thought. The area impressed with its aura of integrity and the rents were probably low.

The Taplin Agency was on the sixth floor. Gwenn rode the small automatic elevator and walked along a corridor covered with gray asbestos tile. She rang the bell and was buzzed in. One look and she knew instantly this was a one-man operation just like hers. The minuscule reception area had a desk, a typewriter, and a phone. Nobody sat at the desk—ever; it was all for show. But Gwenn was willing to play the game. She took one of the three chairs lined up against the wall and sat. Almost immediately the inner door was opened by Lew Sackler.

"Imagine meeting you here." He grinned and motioned her inside. "Peter Taplin, Gwenn Ramadge."

Taplin rose from behind his desk. He was thin, with a pale narrow face and curly brown hair he wore at medium length. He held out a hand and as she took it, Gwenn was aware that Lew was waiting for an answer to the unspoken question: Was this the man who had attacked her last night? Had she twined her fingers through his wispy hair? She remembered the coarseness of the hair, and answered Lew's look with a slight shake of her head. Also, Taplin was too tall, well over six feet, and she was too short— reaching backwards she couldn't have got a good enough grip. What was someone as distinctive as Peter Taplin doing in the detective business? How could he shadow anybody? How could he melt into a crowd? She might ask the same of herself, she thought. Neither she nor Taplin made much of a first impression on a prospective client. Her office at least was better than his. For one thing it didn't have an ugly fire escape blocking the view.

"How's your ankle?" Taplin asked.

"Good, thank you. Very good."

Having with that one question indicated that he was informed about Gwenn's visit to his client, Taplin sat down. "What can I do for you?" he asked Sackler.

"I have some questions. When did Benjamin Cryder hire you?"

"Mr. Cryder telephoned on August sixteenth."

"Cryder called you himself?"

"That's right. Direct. No secretary. He told me he wanted me to trace the whereabouts of a certain woman. In his youth he'd had an affair and there had been a child. He hadn't been in a position to marry and he'd had no money either. So he walked out.

"Recently, this woman out of his past had contacted him. She'd married another man and passed off the girl she bore as his, or so she was claiming. Her request was modest. The girl was grown up and intending to marry and there wasn't enough money for a really nice wedding. The mother wanted to give her child a day she would remember for the rest of her life. Mr. Cryder was touched. But he was wary. What he wanted was for me to check out the woman's story, make sure she was who she claimed and that the girl was his. The woman signed herself Rosa Di Lucca, her maiden name. She was, in fact, Rosa Fissore, and the girl was Angela Fissore Doran.

"I remember the day I brought him the results of my search. I reported to his office, but I had to wait because he'd been with his doctor. From his manner I assumed it was a routine visit. I found out later it had been anything but. Anyway, I told Mr. Cryder that in my opinion Rosa Fissore was genuine and there was a strong likelihood that Angela Fissore was his daughter."

"Did you arrange for a DNA test to determine positive proof of paternity?" Sackler asked.

"Mr. Cryder didn't want it," Taplin replied. "As long as the blood types were not incompatible, he was satisfied. However, he did request that Mrs. Fissore provide details of their relationship and the dates of the conception and birth. She was able to do that and he was pleased. Very happy in fact, though still leary of revealing himself. He was reluctant to acknowledge paternity and thus make himself vulnerable to further demands. He wanted to avoid contact with Mrs. Fissore or the girl. So I suggested he let me deliver whatever money he'd decided to turn over as a wedding gift. Apparently, Mrs. Fissore wasn't any more anxious than he to have their relationship known, so a meeting between me and her was easy to arrange. She showed up. I handed her the packet. It all went without a hitch."

"This was right after Labor Day?" Sackler asked. "And then?"

"He called me two weeks later. From the hospital. He'd had an operation. Cancer. He wanted to see me. He was pleased with the way I'd handled things and had another job for me. He confided that Angela was not the only child he'd sired. There were two others. He wanted me to find them. His conscience had been roused and he wanted to make restitution. He gave me two names: Anne Soffey and Nadine Janssen and as many dates and facts regarding each as he could remember. Ms. Soffey, of course, is well known. No problem checking out her history. It's no secret she bore a child out of wedlock. I needed only to confirm the relevant dates."

"So Mary Soffey married and then died by drowning approximately three months after Benjamin Cryder put you on the case," Sackler said.

Gwenn remained quiet as she'd said she would.

"Exactly," Taplin agreed quickly. "There was no reason for me to make any connection."

"Angela Fissore married and was murdered little more than a month after that," Sackler pointed out. "Didn't the fact that these two were both brides and half sisters strike you as pertinent?"

"It seemed a tragic coincidence."

Tricia Cryder's words, Gwenn thought, and shuddered.

"It must have struck Mr. Cryder," Sackler insisted. "What did he have to say about it?"

"I don't know. I didn't discuss it with him. He left for Palm Beach right after Mary Soffey was drowned."

"When did he come back?" Gwenn asked; she couldn't keep quiet a second longer. "It was right after Angela's murder, wasn't it?"

"I think . . ."

"Don't think," Sackler told him sharply. "You've got your records right here. Look it up."

Taplin didn't bother to go through the motions. "I saw him on February twenty-second."

"He sent for you, didn't he?" Gwenn said. "Didn't he?"

Taplin, startled by her intensity, nodded.

"What did he want?"

"He wanted to know what progress I was making in tracing the third child."

"Nadine Janssen's child. And what progress had you made?"

"I'd found out Ms. Janssen had given up her baby for adoption. I told Mr. Cryder I was moving to gain access to the sealed adoption record and should have news for him one way or the other soon."

"And? Was he pleased? Was he excited?" She exchanged glances with Sackler. Whereas Taplin had been forthcoming at the start, now every bit of information had to be pried out of him.

"No," Taplin replied. "No. He said he'd changed his mind and was no longer interested. He ordered me to drop the case."

"Did he say why?"

"No. He didn't have to."

"Didn't you wonder why?" Sackler pressed.

"It was none of my business."

"But you must have been disappointed. It was the end of a very lucrative assignment."

"Nothing lasts for ever."

There was silence in the gloomy, overheated room, the only sound the sighing of the wind and the sharp sting of sleet against the window pane.

"Why do you *suppose* Mr. Cryder called off the search?" Gwenn asked in a soft, low voice. "Was it because he suspected that his girls were being murdered for the money he intended to leave them and he wanted to save the life of his third and last child?"

"No." Taplin groaned. "No, I never thought that. I swear to God."

"So you never did learn the identity of the third child?" It was back to Sackler. This was the crux. This was what the interrogation had been leading up to and what Taplin, finally sensing it, had been squirming to avoid. He had already made one mistake by admitting Cryder had called him off the case. He had boxed himself in. Sackler decided to let him know it.

"If the court granted access to the adoption file, there will, of course, be a record."

"All right. I did learn her identity."

"You went ahead after you were specifically ordered not to. Why?"

"Having got so far, it seemed a shame . . ." he shrugged.

"You figured the information might prove useful. Maybe to blackmail Mrs. Cryder."

"No. Never. I never blackmailed Mrs. Cryder."

Gwenn broke in. "She knew about the girls. She admitted to me yesterday that she knew, but she only mentioned two. She said her husband told her, but I think it was you." She waved off the protest. "Doesn't matter. What matters is that she knew about her husband's intent to make a large settlement on each of his daughters and that he hired you to search for them."

"So, I told her. All right. She was entitled to know. She's a fine woman and I respect her."

"And you saw a way to collect from both ends," Sackler charged.

"No."

"You also told her Cryder had called off the search and it was on her order that you continued, wasn't it?"

Taplin hung his head.

"You verified that the third child was Rebecca Hayman and you told Mrs. Cryder. And now she's the sole heir," Sackler concluded. "When Benjamin Cryder dies all the money will be hers—except that part of it that's promised to you."

Chapter
TWENTY

They sat in a booth at the back of a small coffee shop on the same block as Taplin's office. The lunch hour was long since over and the place nearly empty.

"I'm not hungry," Gwenn said.

"What did you have for breakfast?" Sackler asked sternly.

"All right, all right. I'll have a tuna fish on toast and coffee."

"Is that what you really want?"

"I like tuna fish."

"So do I." He grinned. "Make it two," he told the waitress.

After she'd served them, the waitress retired to have a smoke. Nobody seemed in a rush to get them out for the next batch of customers; there wasn't a next batch. They could dawdle.

"What do you think?" Sackler asked. "Are they lovers, or is Taplin blackmailing her? You've met the lady; I haven't."

Gwenn frowned as she tried to analyze her own reactions. "Tricia Cryder is much younger than her husband. She's beautiful and a blue blood. I believe she cares for Cryder, but she's not passionately in love with him. I sense affection, shared interests. I don't think finding out about his past would upset her. After all, it was a long time ago. She was a child when it happened. In fact, she's about the same age as the daughters." Gwenn paused. "Certainly for all the compatibility between her and Cryder, I don't believe she would have married him if he'd been a poor man. But I don't see her getting involved with a man like Taplin."

"Because he's beneath her? That might be the attraction."

"I don't think she's that type."

"So then it's a business proposition. Patricia Cryder married an older man. Of course, she expected in due course to get his money. She put in two years, not much, but for all we know it was a hard time. The last few months were; she devoted herself totally to his care. It wouldn't be surprising if she resented her husband turning over a large part of what she expected would be hers to total strangers who had done nothing to deserve it."

"The next step is to find out exactly what kind of money we're talking about."

"The next step is—I take you home." Sackler signaled for the bill. "Unless you want dessert."

"No, thanks. You're going to Cryder's lawyers, aren't you? Why can't I come with you?"

"Because my sergeant wouldn't like it."

"He won't find out."

"That's right. Because it's not going to happen. Anyway, I don't know who Cryder's lawyers are and when I find out it won't be a matter of just barging in . . ."

"Graymore, Graymore, and Hantze," Gwenn recited. "Mr. Jonathan Graymore, Sr., handles Mr. Cryder's business affairs. Mr. Jonathan, Jr., handles private matters."

Sackler raised his eyebrows.

"Mrs. Cryder told me. I asked her."

"Really? Well, I doubt Mr. Jonathan, Jr., is going to be as forthcoming."

"We could try. He's only a few blocks up in Rockefeller Plaza."

"Suite number?"

"I'm not sure, but he's on the thirtieth floor."

Lew Sackler just shook his head. How could he put her in a taxi and send her home after that?

Jonathan Graymore, Jr., was more in line with Lew Sackler's projection than with Gwenn Ramadge's hope. However, he did receive them in his private office, which Sackler had not expected. In his early sixties, a short, compact man with white hair and a strong jaw, he gave the impression that there was no situation or problem he couldn't handle. He wondered that a police detective would come on official business accompanied by a young woman, a civilian. Nevertheless, he did not ignore the seriousness of their errand.

"Would you care for anything to drink?" Mr. Jonathan, Jr., asked. "Coffee? Tea? I know you don't take anything alcoholic while on duty, Detective, but perhaps Ms. Ramadge would like a glass of sherry?"

At their demurral, he went around and settled himself at a large, tooled leather desk which showed the scratches and goudges of years of use. As did the office which, though expensively furnished, was shabby. A statement was being made, Gwenn thought.

"What can I do for you, Detective Sackler?" the lawyer asked.

"I'm investigating the murder of Angela Fissore Doran, a bride killed in her home just over two weeks ago. Ms. Ramadge is a private investigator hired by Anne Soffey to look into the death of her daughter, Mary, who went overboard on her honeymoon."

Mr. Jonathan, Jr., reassessed Gwenn. "I know who Anne Soffey is, of course, and I've read about both cases. How may I help?"

"We have reason to believe both victims were the illegitimate daughters of Benjamin Cryder."

Not a flicker passed over the lawyer's countenance.

"We need to confirm the provision of Mr. Cryder's will regarding these women."

"No, Detective. You know I can't give you that information; not without Mr. Cryder's permission and he's in a coma. I'm sure you're well aware of his condition."

"Mrs. Cryder . . ."

"Mrs. Cryder can't speak for him." He didn't add—not while her husband is still alive.

"We're trying to establish motive."

Graymore shook his head. "Sorry."

Sackler frowned and got up. Gwenn did not.

"We want to know, Mr. Graymore, not so much what is in the will as what is not."

Thoughtfully the lawyer regarded Gwenn. He tapped the tips of the fingers of both hands together as he thought it over. "Can you be more specific?"

"Certainly. We don't need to know whether Mary Soffey Langner or Angela Fissore Doran are beneficiaries, how large the bequests, nor even what provision was made should they predecease Mr. Cryder, as they have. All we really need to know concerns a third person, Rebecca Hayman. Is she mentioned in the will?"

"That's all?"

Gwenn nodded. Graymore sought Sackler's concurrence and got it.

"She is not," he replied.

Gwenn sighed softly. She was both relieved that her instincts had proved true and excited because the case had taken on a new aspect.

"But you are familiar with the name?"

This time the answer came promptly. "No, I am not." Jonathan Graymore, Jr., rose to indicate the end of the interview.

Neither Lew nor Gwenn made any attempt to continue. As far as Gwenn was concerned, there was no need. She was bursting with excitement. She could hardly contain herself as she and Sackler walked along the heavily carpeted hall and while they waited for the elevator. The presence of other passengers forced her to keep silent on the way down. As soon as they emerged into the main lobby-concourse, Gwenn pulled Sackler over to a side passage where they were alone.

"Why was Rebecca Hayman killed? If she wasn't in the will, why did they need to kill her?" Gwenn kept her voice low but it throbbed with intensity.

"There was always the possibility that he might wake from the coma and decide to put her in it, after all," Sackler suggested.

Gwenn shook her head. "Wouldn't it have been easier to make sure he never does wake up?"

Though Sackler didn't have his car—he never took it into the city—he insisted on seeing Gwenn home. He made her promise to rest till he came by at eight to pick her up for their date. Then he rode the subway out to the precinct.

"Nice of you to drop by," Sergeant Powell said.

"Things have been happening," Sackler said.

"Is that so? Care to tell me what?"

Sackler swallowed. "Looks like the Hayman case is linked to the other two."

"You mean we're dealing with a serial killer? Somebody who's got a pathological objection to brides? And Hayman, I remind you, was not yet a bride."

"No, sir." Sackler started to sweat: The sergeant knew a lot more than he was letting on.

"What then?"

"I'll put it all in my report, why don't I, Sergeant?" He edged to the door.

"Sure, but I want to hear it first. Sit, Sackler. Sit. I want to know what's going on—why you're meddling into other jurisdictions."

Who could have complained? Sackler wondered. He'd been careful not to step on anybody's toes. He'd made sure to keep in the background during the search on Staten Island and the subsequent interrogation of Goelet. "Sarge, Angela Doran was stabbed on February sixteenth, approximately five weeks after another bride . . ."

"I know all about that," Powell interrupted. "According to Detective Daniels, who was carrying," he underscored, "it could have been either an accident or suicide. The case is closed."

"The victim's mother was not satisfied. She hired . . ."

"A private investigator, Gwenn Ramadge."

"Yes, sir. Ms. Ramadge came to me and pointed out similarities between the Langner and Doran cases. In each instance the marriage had got off to a bad start. There was quarreling between the newlyweds. The husband drank too much and passed out and then claimed a stranger killed his bride. In each case the husband was the logical suspect, was arrested, and then exonerated."

"I'm still waiting to hear something I don't know."

Sackler could only plod on. "There weren't any other suspects. Despite the similarities there didn't seem to be a common link, not till Mrs. Fissore and Mrs. Soffey each admitted Benjamin Cryder was the father of her child."

"Are you going to tell me Rebecca Hayman was Cryder's child too?" Powell demanded.

"It looks that way."

"But she was adopted, wasn't she? By the way, how did you find that out?" he asked with disarming curiosity.

Here it comes, Sackler thought. "Doctor Goelet mentioned it to Ms. Ramadge."

"Did he? Who told Ms. Ramadge she could interrogate him?"

"She didn't need anybody's permission," Sackler reminded the sergeant, and seeing the scowl hurried on. "Goelet's remark to her that Hayman was adopted could turn out to be the major break in the case."

"That remains to be seen. Anyway, that's not at issue. I'm not suggesting you're responsible for her actions, but you did take her with you to visit the Fissores and you took her with you and she participated in the meeting with Jonathan Graymore, Jr. You presented her as accredited to the investigation."

So that was where the complaint initiated! Sackler thought. He should have guessed. "No, sir. I did not represent Ms. Ramadge as having any official standing . . ."

"Maybe not in so many words, but it was the impression you created. What has got into you, Sackler? You ought to know better. The woman's a loose canon."

"She's turning up good leads, Sergeant."

"You get leads from snitches, but you don't take them around with you. You don't treat them like equals."

Sackler flushed. It took a couple of moments to get himself in hand. "She's *my* equal, Sergeant. She's the equal of any officer in this precinct. And smarter than a lot of them."

"Hell, Sackler, I don't mean to offend her or you. My point is she's not a member of the force. I don't want you going around with her as though she was your partner. Got it?"

"I know that was wrong."

"Okay." Powell's scowl eased but was not completely gone. "What you do socially, of course, is something else."

Sackler got up.

"I want a complete report before you leave tonight."

Sackler groaned inwardly. It was now three-thirty and his tour ended at four and Powell knew it.

"I'll get right on it."

He glanced toward the window. The rain was coming down in sheets. Maybe by the time he got through it would have stopped.

Sackler had seen her to her door and left her. Gwenn made herself a cup of hot tea and settled in her favorite chair to watch the storm.

The sight and sound of the icy rain hitting the glass should have made her feel delightfully warm and cozy. She'd checked the lock and made sure the chain was in place, yet she was uneasy. Her earlier carelessness had amounted to arrogance. She'd ignored the advice she gave to others as though she were invulnerable. Well, she knew better now. She also knew that it would be a long time before she would feel safe again. The cup in her hand started to rattle on the saucer. Delayed reaction, Gwenn thought.

The memory of the encounter translated into a physical response. She was hot and cold by turns. She could taste the salt of the intruder's sweating hand over her mouth, experience again the nausea as she fought for air, feel the darkness as a palpable force. Her heart pounded as it had when he'd held her. She couldn't identify the assailant, but she believed it was not Peter Taplin. In that brief moment as he fled, when he'd been outlined by the light in the hallway, she'd had the impression of a shorter, stockier man. Also, it didn't make sense for Patricia Cryder to send Taplin to search her files. Mrs. Cryder knew exactly what Gwenn had and where she stood. She would have sent Taplin only if she wanted Gwenn silenced—permanently.

Aside from Taplin, who could have known she was under sedation? Nobody. Then how come the intruder had thought it was safe to enter the apartment?

She brooded over it for a long time, and the answer came to her in its lovely simplicity. He had called up to find out. And her answering machine had told him she

212

wasn't home. She grinned. Solving that small problem was encouraging, an indication things were beginning to break.

Who could the intruder be? Someone besides Patricia Cryder and Peter Taplin who knew of her involvement in the three cases. Who else knew she linked the murders? Who else knew she was convinced someone other than one of the husbands or the fiancé was the perpetrator?

Anne Soffey, of course. Anne Soffey, who had hired Gwenn and for whom she was still working, knew and so must persons connected with Soffey Cosmetics including Graham Dussart.

Rosa and Emilio Fissore. Rosa, who like Anne Soffey, admitted Benjamin Cryder had got her pregnant, Rosa whose appeal to Cryder for money to make a grand wedding for their child had triggered the whole tragic sequence. And Emilio, devastated by mourning, knew. Would he mourn Angie the less when he found out she wasn't his?

Gerald Goelet. The young resident certainly knew of her interest since he was the one who had given her the lead that resulted in the linking of the cases.

Aside from Goelet, there was no one in Rebecca Hayman's life—no family, few friends—yet Gwenn believed that in her death lay the solution to the deaths of the other two.

Before he slipped into a coma, Cryder had called a halt to the search for proof of Rebecca's identity. He had not included her in his will; he had not even mentioned her to his attorney. Therefore, being named in the will was not the murder motive. Money was not the motive.

For a long time Gwenn stared out at the storm as it rose and fell in intensity.

If money was not the motive for the murder of Rebecca Hayman, then logically it was not the motive for killing either Mary or Angela.

There was only one other possibility, Gwenn thought as the room became prematurely dark. There was only one alternative and interpretation of the facts. She reached to the lamp beside her and turned it on. She got up and walked into the bedroom to the telephone, not giving a thought to whether her ankle hurt or not. She dialed Lew's line at the precinct.

He had left for the day, she was told. She looked at her watch: six—already. In two hours he'd be here, but she couldn't wait. She got her handbag from the bureau and rummaged through it for the card he'd given her at what seemed very long ago. It had his home number. She dialed. A woman answered.

Gwenn was taken aback. "Is this Detective Sackler's residence?"

"Yes, it is."

Young, Gwenn thought; she sounded young. "May I speak with Detective Sackler, please?"

"He's not home. Would you like to leave a message?"

"Who is this, please?"

"A friend."

"Oh, I see. Yes. Well, tell him Gwenn Ramadge called and I won't be able to make our date tonight." She hung up. There, she thought, that should take care of that. But she was instantly sorry. She'd behaved instinctively; she should have left word where she was going. Business was business and personal feelings were irrelevant. Should she call back? No, she decided. If the killer hadn't performed the last rite of vengeance by now, Gwenn rationalized, he wasn't likely to do it at all.

Yet the sense of urgency persisted. The subway Gwenn was riding stopped twice in the tunnel under the East River, each time for no more than a couple of minutes, pretty good as subway delays went, but for Gwenn each stop seemed endless. She got out finally at the Union Turnpike and Kew Gardens station and emerged at the corner of Queens Boulevard to look for a taxi. Though officially the rush hour was over, people still thronged the sidewalk, jostling and shoving and fighting for the few available cabs, then in default lining up for the buses. It was all made worse by the weather that hadn't improved and didn't look as though it would for the rest of the night. Gwenn turned east. She opened her umbrella and bent her head into the wind and started walking. She walked as fast as she could and the closer she got to the restaurant, the more anxious she became.

The plate-glass window of the Ponte Vecchio was steamed up so she couldn't see anything but the soft glow of the wall sconces inside. She burst through the door.

A couple of diners looked up; there weren't many. No one was at the bar. The people who usually stopped for a drink had headed straight home tonight, Gwenn thought. She noticed there was a new man in Ed Doran's place. There was no one at the cash register.

"Where's Mrs. Fissore?" she asked the new bartender.

"In the back."

Depositing the soaked umbrella near the coat rack, she started for the kitchen.

"Hey, wait a minute. Miss! You can't go in there."

But Gwenn was already pushing through the swinging doors before he could run out from behind the bar to stop her. Rosa was not in the kitchen.

"Where's Mrs. Fissore?" she demanded of the kitchen staff at large.

They only gawked.

Gwenn spotted a door marked Office. She squeezed by the salad counter, knocked, and without waiting for an answer, entered. Rosa Fissore sat at her husband's desk.

"Where's Mr. Fissore?"

"He went back to work."

Gwenn frowned.

"The work he used to do before we got married and

opened this restaurant," Rosa explained. "I told you he was moonlighting, taking outside work to make money for Angela's wedding."

"Yes, but that's all paid for, isn't it?"

Rosa shrugged. "He says he needs to get away for a while." Her dark eyes were filled with pain.

"I didn't know you opened the restaurant together," Gwenn observed. "Somehow I got the idea he already had it before you married."

"No, we opened it with my dowry. Brides had dowries in those days."

So at last it was clear. Gwenn knew what had happened from the beginning to the terrible end. She felt sorry for this once-beautiful, twice-abandoned woman, but she couldn't spare her. "Where were you the night of February sixteenth?"

"Me?"

"Yes, Mrs. Fissore, you. It was a Tuesday. It was the night Angie was killed."

"I haven't forgotten."

"Where were you?"

"I was visiting my aunt in Jersey. She's an elderly lady; she lives alone and she doesn't get much chance to go out. I take her to dinner and a movie twice a month."

"On a regular basis?"

"Pretty much. The first and third Tuesdays of the month. She looks forward to it. She plans for it. But . . ."

Gwenn got out her notebook. "That would have made your next visit the first of March."

Rosa Fissore leafed back through the calendar on the desk. "No, I went on the twenty-sixth of February. She called and said she wasn't feeling well."

"What time did you usually get home from these visits?"

"Oh, I don't come home till the next morning. It's too far for me to travel alone at night."

"I see. And did you also stay over with your aunt on the sixteenth and the twenty-sixth?"

"Yes."

Gwenn nodded. The knot in her stomach tightened till it hurt. She needed to ask one more question, only one. "What kind of work did Emilio do before you opened the restaurant?"

Gwenn stumbled out of the restaurant and into the pouring rain, not caring that she had left her umbrella behind.

She was appalled. How could so much love have turned to hate? she thought. Contemplating what she now believed had happened, Gwenn began to tremble. All at once she was overcome by shame. She had treated the case like a puzzle, a game of wits. It was neither. It was a series of brutal murders with a motivation as twisted as . . . she groped for a comparison and had to go back to the ancient saga of Medea and the murder of her two sons.

Who would believe it? Gwenn asked herself. Could she even convince Lew? The killer himself would have to admit his guilt, she thought. But why should he?

The rain soaked her hair and trickled into the collar of her coat and down her back, but she was oblivious. There was a way to make the killer confess, she thought. There was bait she could offer. He might take it; he might not. Either way she would be running a terrible risk, but she couldn't let him sail away without at least trying. She owed it to those sad brides.

Spotting a cruising cab, Gwenn raised her arm and shouted "Taxi!" and stepped into the overflowing gutter.

Chapter
───── TWENTY-ONE

Neither the cold nor the continuing driving rain could depress the spirits of the passengers boarding the *Conquistador*. They were setting out on a European cruise that would last eighteen days. The special attraction was making the Atlantic crossing to Southampton by ship rather than by plane. Despite the rough weather at this time of year there were enough travelers who didn't like flying and had chosen the cruise on this particular basis. After Southampton they would follow the coastline to Antwerp, then Brest, Bordeaux, Santander, Oporto, Lisbon, and Tangier. There would be time for shore excursions, then they would head north again touching Barcelona and Nice, curving into the narrow shelter of the Tyrrhenian Sea to Naples before returning to New York.

Their ship was renowned for its luxurious appointments and unparalleled service. She was the flag ship of the Island Star fleet, a city at sea. She had five lounges, three world-class restaurants, and a promenade of luxury boutiques. The ads boasted there was one crew member for every three passengers. As she made her way out on the pier, Gwenn could see only eager anticipation on the faces around her. The ship's officers, uniforms resplendent with gold braid, were everywhere to help and welcome. The No Visitors signs were prominently displayed. Security concerns had caused cancellation by all lines of the traditional going-away parties. But the boarding passengers didn't seem to mind, Gwenn thought. Sailing out of New York on a magnificent, sleek, white ship was still a glamorous experience whether you could show off to your friends or not.

However, Gwenn had forgotten about the restriction. She had counted on the visitors and the parties and confusion they created to get aboard.

The raucous blast of the ship's horn made her jump. "Is she sailing already?" she asked a porter.

"No, ma'am. That's the coast guard testing the gear on the bridge. She's not raising anchor till eight forty-five."

"Thank you."

She looked at her watch. That gave her half an hour. She should have tried Lew once more, regardless of her feelings, but it was too late now. During the taxi ride back to Manhattan and to the Hudson River pier, Gwenn had had plenty of time to plan. She'd decided she had no hope of getting to the captain, not this close to departure. There would be police around the dock, of course, but if she approached one she would only get involved in a tangle of explanations and red tape over jurisdiction. Even if they believed her story, they'd never let her go on board— assuming they listened to her long enough so she could tell it. She was willing to admit she couldn't offer probable cause that would be strong enough for a police officer to take the suspect off the ship, certainly not to delay the ship's departure. At this moment, Gwenn didn't know exactly what she was going to do, but she did know for sure that she was not going to let the killer of three young brides sail away to the other side of the Atlantic, maybe never to return.

Would her PI card get her aboard? It was worth a try, Gwenn thought, then realized she had something better— the ID badge she'd been given when she visited the SS

Serena. It was marked simply ISLAND STAR LINE and had her name. Please God, she still had it.

She did and with it pinned to her coat, she marched boldly through the gate marked Authorized Personnel. She chose the busiest gangplank and was helped over the coaming to the promenade deck by a pair of young sailors who called her ma'am.

People milled everywhere in happy confusion. Some were searching for their cabins, others lined up along the rail to secure a good vantage point for the moment of sailing. Others toured the ship, admiring the public rooms and the decor. Recently, the entire ship had been restored to its original Art Deco style. The vast lounges and long companionways gleamed with lacquer-and-blue mirrors and inlaid paneling. In the main lounge music came over the loudspeakers and soft drinks were being served. There would be nothing alcoholic while in port, a white-coated steward explained to a red-faced passenger who had already had too much. Threading her way through the crowd, Gwenn reached the central lobby and descended below deck by way of a graciously curving staircase. The farther down she went, the less people there were. D-deck was almost deserted. A set of double doors marked Dining Room were closed, but not locked. Gwenn stepped inside.

It was large and elegant, decorated in shades of gray and sparked with red. The tables, already set for the first meal at sea, gleamed with white damask, sparkling crystal, a single yellow rose in each bud vase. It was the only quiet place on the *Conquistador*.

"Hello?" she called out. "Anybody here?"

The maitre d', a good-looking Latin, wearing his tuxedo without jacket, came out from behind a screen that masked the service entry.

"I'm sorry, Miss. We're not open yet. Seating assignments . . ." Then Carlos Estevez spotted Gwenn's badge. "What can I do for you, Ms. Ramadge?"

"I'm looking for one of the stewards. Emilio Fissore. It's very important I see him before the ship sails."

"He's probably in his quarters. I'll call him." It was evident that Estevez was curious, but he was too well trained to ask questions of a VIP from the head office. From a shallow drawer he drew an ordinary cloth-bound ledger and rifled through the pages.

"Has Fissore been sailing with you for a long time?" Gwenn had to be careful not to ask a question to which she'd be expected to know the answer. This was right at the edge of safety.

"Let's see," the maitre d' concentrated. "He came at the end of August and made three or four crossings. On New Year's he transferred to the *Serena* for the New Year's cruise."

"Ah, yes. Then there was his daughter's wedding and . . . the rest of it," Gwenn commented.

Estevez had already dialed. "Fissore? Please come up. You have a visitor."

"Tell him I have an urgent message for him," Gwenn said. Then she had an inspiration. "It's about his daughter's funeral."

The maitre d' repeated the message and then hung up. "You can use my office," he told Gwenn and passed her through the swinging doors to a small room off to the side. "Please remember we sail at eight forty-five," he cautioned and left.

The room had paneled walls and thick carpeting and barely space for a desk, a chair, and a single filing cabinet. There was no porthole and she recalled that there were no portholes in the dining salon either, which indicated they were below water level. Suddenly, Gwenn felt claustrophobic. She'd never had trouble before with enclosed spaces, but now she found herself breathing in short, labored gulps. The door behind her opened.

"Ms. Ramadge?"

She hardly recognized him. The last time she'd seen him, the only time, he'd worn a cheap, rumpled navy suit and a white shirt that was none too fresh. He had been bent under his sorrow. Now he stood erect, almost proud, and though he could not be called handsome, he wore the white mess jacket with gold buttons with flair.

"What are you doing here?" Emilio Fissore asked, almost demanded.

"You wanted to be notified when Angela's body was released for burial," Gwenn reminded him.

"You could have told her mother."

"I did. She thought you'd want to know."

"All right. Thank you. You've found me and you've told me."

"That's not the only reason I'm here. I think you know that."

He stared hard at her. "You came alone?"

She met his look. "Yes."

They measured each other.

"You could have killed me in my apartment the other night, but you didn't."

The PA speaker crackled, a bell clanged, then a voice announced: *Attention all passengers. Lifeboat drill will be conducted immediately after departure. Please be ready to report to your station with your life jacket. This is the first call.*

"That means we'll be lifting anchor soon," Fissore told her. "You should go ashore."

"The only person you wanted to hurt was Benjamin Cryder."

"I don't have to talk to you. You're not a police officer. You're nothing. You're nobody. I have work to do."

"I'm a private investigator hired to find Mary Soffey Langner's killer."

"I don't know anything about any Mary Soffey."

The name came too easily to his lips, Gwenn thought. "Sure you do. You were on board the SS *Serena* when she was lost at sea. You can't deny it. You're listed on the ship's manifest. You switched from the *Conquistador* to the *Serena* just for that one cruise. Why?"

"Because it was a short turn around and there's more money to be made on short trips. Not that I have to explain to you. Just because I happened to be on board when a poor neurotic girl decides to take her own life doesn't mean I had anything to do with it."

"You were at the Soffey house on the day of Mary's wedding."

He glared. "I didn't know her."

"You rigged a bomb in the newlyweds' car. One of the bridesmaids accidentally triggered it and was blown to pieces."

"I don't know what you're talking about." He was riveted in place.

He could have walked out, Gwenn thought, but he stayed. Though he had searched her home and office for evidence against him and found none, he couldn't be sure that she hadn't turned up something new. He had to make sure. But Gwenn couldn't document her accusations. She hoped to break him by the sheer accumulation of circumstantial evidence.

"The bomb was intended to kill Mary, of course," she went on. "When it failed, you were stymied, but not for long. You learned the couple would be honeymooning on the *Serena*. You were scheduled to sail on this ship, but it's the same line and you had no trouble getting a transfer.

"At sea, you were in a familiar environment and you felt confident of success. Poor Mary in her unhappiness seemed to be making it easy for you by spending most of her nights alone on deck. You watched, you waited, but somehow the moment was never right. By the last night, you were desperate, and then again fate seemed to favor you. On that night, not only was Mary alone, but she'd had more to drink than she was accustomed to. She was sick, leaning over the rail. She didn't struggle. She hardly knew what was happening when you lifted her and heaved her over the side."

"I didn't know the woman."

"She was Benjamin Cryder's child. That's all you needed to know. That's why she had to die."

She waited, but Fissore clenched his teeth as though he would prevent a single word from slipping out.

There was one more way to get at him, one way that could shock him into the truth, Gwenn believed. It would inflict a mortal wound. The question was—how would he react? He was a violent, volatile man. Would he turn on her? She had her gun. In that small space there was no way she could miss. The other question was—would she have the nerve to squeeze the trigger?

"That's why Angie had to die," Gwenn went on talking. "That's why you killed your beloved Angie, because you thought that along with Mary and Rebecca she, too, was Benjamin Cryder's child." She paused, then made her decision. "But you made a mistake."

"Mistake?" Emilio Fissore's eyes narrowed and bored into hers.

This was mental sparring—jab and pull back, circle and jab again.

"What mistake?" he demanded. "What mistake?" His gaze never wavered.

Gwenn, transfixed, knew that the balance had shifted to his favor. She had to give him an answer. The clock on the wall indicated there were ten minutes to departure. He didn't deserve the truth, she thought. Not yet.

"What made you think that Angela was not your child?" she asked. "What made you think Rosa had deceived you? Why, after all these years, did you suspect she'd had an affair with another man, married you, and passed off his child as yours?"

Every line and furrow that crosshatched his big, rugged

face deepened; the coarse pores oozed; rivulets coursed down the channels. He shivered as the cold sweat drenched his body.

"It was Angie's wedding that precipitated the whole thing, wasn't it?" Gwenn persisted. "She was crazy to get married. Neither you nor Rosa cared much for Doran, but Angie wanted him. You couldn't say no to her. You never had been able to say no to Angie.

"So the announcement was made and the preparations for the wedding began. It got bigger and bigger and more and more elaborate and expensive. So it was agreed between you and your wife that she should run the restaurant while you went back to your old job to pay for it all. You reactivated your seamen's papers and had no trouble finding a berth."

She paused. Up to this point Gwenn had been fleshing out what Rosa had told her. Now once again she had to rely on instinct—deduce, infer.

"You were on shore leave in early September when you noticed that Rosa was very nervous. She jumped every time the phone rang. She rushed to answer the door. Then one day she announced she was going into Manhattan for shopping. You were suspicious and you followed her."

In the face of his silence, Gwenn returned to what Rosa had admitted and Taplin confirmed.

"She met a man on the steps of the Forty-second Street library. He handed her a shopping bag and they parted. You couldn't imagine what was going on. At first, you'd thought it might be an affair. But they barely exchanged a few words. Rosa accepted the shopping bag and it was over. You were mystified. You could have revealed yourself to Rosa, demanded to know what was going on, see for yourself what was in the bag. Instead, you followed the man. You followed him just a few blocks to his office. He was a private detective.

"You didn't know what to think. Was Rosa hiring him?

Then why had they met in front of the library? What would she hire a detective for anyway? What was in the shopping bag?"

No need for more detail, Gwenn decided; better, in fact, to keep it nonspecific. An image of Peter Taplin's office—dark, gloomy, on the closed court with the fire escape—came to mind.

"You climbed up the fire escape. You waited till the detective left at the end of the afternoon and then you climbed up." As each part of the story found its place, Gwenn's confidence grew. "You went through his files and discovered Rosa's letter to Benjamin Cryder in which she revealed that Angie was his child." Gwenn paused, watching Fissore closely. He didn't speak, but she sensed the inner desperation. She had to push him just a little farther. "Apparently, the detective had checked Rosa's claim and it was true. Rosa had deceived you; she had tricked you into marrying her."

The ship's whistle reached them faintly but unmistakably. The clock stood at eight-forty. Fissore was aware of neither. Both were crucial to Gwenn.

"Going through Taplin's file, you found out that there were two other illegitimate children, both girls, and on Cryder's orders he had traced them. Cryder intended to mention all three in his will. Of course, you knew who Cryder was. Everybody knows Cryder and his story, how he came up from nothing to become a billionaire and marry a society beauty. Everybody also knows that he's dying. Like most rich men, Benjamin Cryder thought money could right every wrong, expiate every sin. Cryder was dying and he was determined to make restitution. You determined to deprive him of that consolation. You murdered three innocent girls."

"The sins of the father shall be visited on the children."

"Except that you made a mistake, Mr. Fissore. Actually,

it was the detective, Peter Taplin, who made the mistake.
One of the girls was not Cryder's."

Emilio Fissore went very still. He turned a sick green.
"You're lying."

"I'm sorry, Mr. Fissore. I'm more sorry than I can say,
but it's the truth." She watched him and measured the
distance to the door.

As though reading her mind, he edged over. "Which
one? Which one wasn't his?"

Gwenn only shook her head.

"Angie? My God, was it Angie?" He began to tremble.
"I don't believe it. It's a trick. It's a trick."

"That should be good news, Mr. Fissore. You should be
glad. You should rejoice that your wife didn't deceive you
after all, that the child you loved and nurtured was your
own."

His eyes flamed. The pulses at his temples throbbed. "I
should have killed him," Fissore said in a cold voice. "It
was my first instinct. But he was dying anyway. Killing him
would actually have spared him suffering. I didn't want
that. I wanted him to feel more than physical pain; I
wanted him to be wracked with the anguish and regret I
felt. My wife was a woman I didn't know, a woman who
had cheated me and let me build my life on a lie. I could
hardly bear to look at Rosa, even to be in the same room
with her. It was torture to share the bed. And every time
I looked at Angie I wanted to cry. It was a relief to go back
to sea."

He paused. Gwenn waited, almost afraid to move.

"The next time I came home the wedding preparations
were in full swing. Rosa told me she'd been putting aside
a little from the housekeeping money and one of the customers at the restaurant gave her a tip on the market. She
was lying again. I knew it. The money had come from
him—Cryder. Hadn't I seen it passed over with my own
eyes?

"But I wasn't ready to admit I knew. I didn't want Angie to find out her real father was a billionaire, a man who could give her everything she'd ever wanted or could want. The years of happiness turned bitter. The memories I had cherished I now wiped from my mind. It wasn't easy to forget Angie, a toddler, shouting *Daddy! Daddy!* and running into my arms when I came home from work. I could still taste her sloppy, wet, wonderful kisses." He allowed himself a moment of joy. "She always came to me first, you know. Secretly, I was flattered. I knew it was because I gave in to her whims. They were innocent whims, I thought, and went on indulging her. I went right on spoiling her because I loved her and because I believed she was mine.

"She grew up to be even more beautiful than her mother. The boys were crazy about her, but she didn't take any of them seriously. She'd come home after her dates and tell me about them. They were either too short, too tall, too smart, too dumb. Some were wimps. The handsome ones were stuck on themselves. She told me everything. We laughed together. I was her father. She'd known Doran all through high school. After graduation, unexpectedly, she started to get serious about him. She couldn't see his flaws. Nothing I said made any difference. He had her hypnotized." He stopped abruptly.

That was when he began to lose his daughter, Gwenn thought. In the sequence of Fissore's emotional destruction, Ed Doran had come before Cryder. That was why the father had been so careful not to leave tracks when he left the bloody scene. He wanted Doran to discover the murder. He wanted the young husband to step into his wife's blood and mark the carpet with his bloody prints. Only it hadn't worked out like that, and Fissore himself had finally put the brand on Doran.

Now Fissore returned to the subject of the real father. "For twenty-two years while Cryder denied her existence,

228

I raised Angie. I shared her laughter and her tears. I was not going to let him buy an easy death.

"Then I read about the other wedding, Mary Soffey's. I knew she was one of his daughters and the answer came to me like a revelation. I would punish Cryder through the girls. I wouldn't allow him to ease his conscience by giving them money. When he died, it would be with his guilt still on him. It was simple. Logical. Right. From then on I never hesitated."

A blast from the ship's whistle sounded the final warning. Up on deck the band played for departure and the music was piped through the loudspeaker and flooded the small space with sound. The hands of the clock stood at eight forty-three. Gwenn's chest burned and she realized it was because she'd been holding her breath, literally. She let it out in a gush that brought Emilio Fissore out of self-justification to the present. He moved to block the door.

"You can't do anything," he told Gwenn. "You have no evidence. There is no evidence. This was just a conversation between us. Unless . . . are you carrying some kind of tape recorder?"

He shrugged. "It doesn't matter. Did you really expect to get off this ship?"

"How can you stop me?" She tried to sound confident, but her voice quivered.

"I didn't come unprepared." Straightening his left arm at his side, he cupped his hand and let the knife slide into it. Then he raised it almost casually so she could see the blade glisten.

Gwenn swallowed. Her heart was pounding. Clutching the purse under her left arm, she could feel the bulk of the .22 inside. With her right hand across her waist, she loosed the clasp of the handbag all the time watching him and talking to distract his attention.

"I won't make it easy for you," she warned. "I'll scream."

"Nobody will hear you."

No, not down here, she thought.

"I'll fight. Like Angie. My blood will be all over everything. How will you explain my blood?"

He tossed the knife aside; it landed with only a soft thud on the thick carpet. "I'll use my hands." He held them out for her to see—short, strong hands with tufts of black hair growing on the backs.

"I'll fight," she repeated. "Like Rebecca." Inside the purse, her right hand closed on the gun.

He took another step.

"Don't!" she warned and brought the gun out. "I won't miss this time," she warned. How could she miss? she thought. At that range even a .22 would be deadly.

"What will you do with my body? Throw it overboard?" The words tumbled out. "The ship is ready to sail. At any moment the maitre d' will be back. The dining salon will open and passengers will be coming down. Where will you hide my body till you're far enough at sea to dump me over the side? Like Mary."

The floor quivered under their feet and both felt the unmistakable throb of the engines.

"Stand aside," Gwenn motioned with the gun. "Stand aside. I really don't want to shoot." She swallowed. It didn't matter any more whether her voice shook or not. It didn't matter whether he knew she was afraid of the gun in her hand. "I really don't want to shoot. But I will if I have to."

He believed her.

Chapter
TWENTY-TWO

"I don't believe you did that," Sackler shook his head. "I don't believe you confronted a man who had committed three murders . . ."

"Four. Counting the car bombing."

"Right. Four. My God, you went aboard that ship without any backup, without even letting anybody know . . ."

"I couldn't reach you."

"How hard did you try?"

She hesitated. "Not very."

"You went aboard, revealed everything you had on him to the suspect, thus giving him a chance to concoct a defense, and then walked off the ship while he sailed away." Sackler raised both hands high and then dropped them to underscore his dismay.

As it was, she'd barely made it, Gwenn thought. They were actually starting to raise the gangplank when she got up to the deck. Two sailors escorted her ashore. She'd stood on the pier and watched the *Conquistador* in all its majestic awkwardness back out to the open harbor, then under the guidance of the attending tugs turn around and head for the sea. She took the pier elevator down to the street, found a taxi—it was getting to be an expensive habit—and headed for home.

She'd been cold and tired, and her ankle was aching

again. She changed from damp clothes into a comfortable robe and poured herself a glass of sherry, very dry. Sherry, she'd learned from Cordelia, delivered more clout than most people realized. It wasn't the drink favored by little old ladies for nothing. She took her time sipping, savoring, feeling the warmth spread through her body, the kinks loosening. There was no rush, Gwenn thought. Though the tension eased, she was still not at peace with herself. So she'd waited to pour out a second glass before dialing Lew's number.

This time he answered himself. On the first ring.

"I got your message. What's up? Are you all right?"

Not in the least embarrassed or apologetic, Gwenn marveled. "Are you free to come over?"

"Free?" The irony was lost on him. "Sure I'm free. I've been free all evening. What are you talking about?"

She gave it up—for the moment. "Then come over."

But when he arrived, in the shortest possible time, Gwenn made no mention of the woman who had answered his telephone earlier. Instead, she plunged into an account of her visit to Rosa Fissore and how that led her to board the *Conquistador* and how she had maneuvered Fissore into an admission of guilt. She had expected praise. Instead . . .

Sackler groaned. "I thought you had more sense."

"Really? What should I have done? Made a citizen's arrest and tried to take him off the ship? Marched him three levels up to the Promenade deck and through all those people at gunpoint? Given him a chance to grab a hostage? What?"

"Turned him over to the captain."

"Same problem."

"I suppose."

She glared at him.

"You shouldn't have left the ship."

"I didn't feel like sailing to England."

"They would have put you to shore with the pilot."

"I didn't know that. The point is I didn't have enough evidence to go to the captain."

"You've got that right."

They both sulked.

Both got over it and started to speak at the same time. Sackler gave way.

"Look," Gwenn said, "I was the last person off that ship. I stood there on the pier and watched till it was in the middle of the harbor. He did not get off. So where's he going?" She answered herself. "To Southampton."

"True."

"How long does the crossing take? Four days? Plenty of time to make the case. Now that we know where to look."

"I never checked Fissore's alibi. There seemed no reason." Sackler was thinking aloud.

"Rosa Fissore was with her aunt on the night Angie was killed," Gwenn told him. "And also on the night of Rebecca Hayman's death. It was her habit to stay over till the next morning. Fissore would have been counting on that."

"Okay. I can go with his pushing Mary Soffey overboard, and strangling, or suffocating, Rebecca Hayman and then burying her in the woods . . ."

Gwenn started to speak, then decided not to interrupt.

". . . but I have a problem with what he did to Angela. I have a problem with the violence. I can't buy the blood and gore. And his anguish afterwards. I was there. I saw him. The man was emotionally destroyed. He had the victim's blood on him. He attacked Doran. It's hard to believe that was an act."

"Maybe it wasn't," Gwenn replied. "Maybe the emotion was genuine. When Fissore found out the child he doted on was not his, the shock must have been devastating. He managed somehow to hide his pain, but that only intensified it. Even as he planned his revenge, the pain grew. He was forced to wait to carry out his plans and the waiting nearly consumed him. He managed to kill the other two brides without excessive violence. It only needed a push to topple Mary over the railing into the sea. Rebecca Hayman was asleep when he entered the bedroom and held the pillow over her face. Even if she'd wakened, she could have put up little resistance. Neither one meant anything to him except as instruments of his revenge. He didn't care whether Mary's body was ever found. He left Rebecca in the bed."

"What?"

"Why should he move her? Why should he take the risk of moving her? No, it was Gerald Goelet who carried her out and buried her."

"How do you know?" Sackler demanded.

"Because of the shower curtain."

"Oh, come on."

"Just think about it. The two of them, Becky and Gerald, make love and fall asleep downstairs in front of the fireplace. The fire dies; the room cools off. Becky wakes up cold and tries to rouse Gerald. She can't, so she gets a blanket and covers him, then goes upstairs alone to bed. Fissore's been watching from outside and . . ."

"Hold it. How did Fissore know who the third girl was and where to find her?"

"The same way he knew all the rest, by having gone through Peter Taplin's files."

"The weekend hideaway wasn't in the files."

"No, but it wasn't a secret either. All Fissore had to do was call Rebecca, and her roommate would have told him where to reach her." Gwenn waited, but as there was no further challenge she went on. "So he went out to the hideaway and found the victim in a familiar situation. All he had to do was wait for the right moment. When Becky went upstairs to bed, he entered, probably through the garage, did what he had to do, and left.

"After a while, Gerald Goelet wakened. He went upstairs and found Rebecca. He's a doctor. He knew right away

that there was nothing he could do for her. He also knew
he was going to be the primary suspect. So he decides to
protect himself by making it look like she was killed somewhere else. He was the one who moved her, but he didn't
kill her."

"All right, but where does the shower curtain come in?"

"He loved her," Gwenn replied. "He was not going to
put her into the ground and shovel dirt on her face. He
had to provide some kind of shroud, didn't he?"

Sackler's eyes were bright with new respect. "How about
Angela?"

"Ah, well," Gwenn sighed. "On her, Fissore vented all
his rage and despair. Can you imagine her reaction? She
was in her own bed, half asleep, when suddenly there's her
father standing in front of her and he's got a knife. Can
you imagine what she felt when she saw the father she
loved raise the knife against her? She must have thought
she'd gone crazy. She tried to get away. But he cornered
her in the bathroom. There were knife cuts all over her
arms indicating she'd tried to shield herself. He stabbed
her eleven times. He had to before she succumbed. He
had to before she sank at his feet in a pool of her own
blood. And after all that, he was cool enough to walk out
and leave her for Doran to find. He was cool enough to
remember to take off his shoes so that he wouldn't leave
a bloody track."

Sackler nodded.

"He went home to wait for the news that Ed Doran had
discovered the body, but nothing happened. There was no
announcement that night nor the next morning, not over
the radio nor in the newspapers. Nothing. Doran turned
up for work at the restaurant as usual, but without Angie.
He said he'd had a fight with Angie but indicated he was
confident they'd make up as usual. Fissore began to doubt
his own senses. He looked back on the mortal struggle in
the bathroom—had it happened or was it a nightmare of

his imagination and need for revenge? He couldn't bear not knowing so he sent Doran home early Wednesday night expecting a call from him. Again, nothing. So almost twenty-four hours later he was forced to return to the scene, confront the carnage, and report the crime himself. He was a man torn between grief, anger, fear of being caught, and the despair at what his own hands had wrought."

"I'll buy it," Sackler said. "But we need evidence for the DA."

"How about the shoes?" Gwenn suggested. "He stood in her blood. If we could find the shoes . . ."

"It's not likely he'd keep that kind of evidence around." What Sergeant Powell had suggested Doran might have done was equally applicable whoever might be the perp. "He either burned everything he wore that night or stuffed his clothes and shoes down a sewer. Either way he got rid of them."

"But he had to get home first," Gwenn pointed out.

"Sure."

"He drove home, didn't he? It's not likely he drove in his stocking feet."

Their eyes met.

Gwenn re-created the scene for both of them. "There he stood in the bathroom, blood everywhere and a clean expanse of carpet between him and the bedroom door. It was like being painted into a corner. How was he going to get out without leaving tracks? He was trapped—till he thought of taking his shoes off. Once he got out of the house and made it to his car, with the danger behind him, he just automatically put them back on."

"So there'll be blood on the accelerator pedal, the brake, the mat!" Sackler grinned. "Smart, very smart." But his elation didn't last. "He cleaned himself up when he got home; wouldn't he have cleaned the car?"

Gwenn bit her lips. "He never thought he'd be a suspect,"

she argued. "But yes, of course, he would have checked the car." She thought some more. "Would he do such a thorough job that the lab, with all the scientific tests now available, won't be able to find even a trace? I don't think so. Unless . . . suppose he says he got the blood in his car on the second night, the night he ostensibly discovered the body?"

"He couldn't have. No way," Sackler answered promptly. "We took him to the precinct directly from the scene. He rode with me, and one of the patrol cops drove his car back home for him. We've got him!" Lew exulted. "In four days when the *Conquistador* puts in at Southampton we can be standing on the dock along with Scotland Yard waiting."

Gwenn was silent for several moments. "Not me," she said at last. "I'm out of it. From here on it's strictly police business."

Lew had been upset at Gwenn's acting on her own. She was, after all, an amateur and had not only risked letting the killer get away, but had put herself in grave peril. He'd reacted with anger, but he saw now that she was deeply shaken and he should have offered comfort.

He tried. "You've been through a terrible experience. I've dealt with all kinds of killers, but I have to tell you nobody as heartless as Fissore." Looking back, Lew realized that there had been indications of the man's ambivalence. He remembered Angie Fissore's bare room. He recalled Rosa Fissore sitting alone in the kitchen holding the doll in front of her, the only memento of her child that was left, and how she'd instinctively tried to hide it when they came in. He hadn't put the two together. He should have.

"You followed your instincts," he acknowledged to Gwenn. "And you were right. Only next time, get some backup. Okay?" He smiled.

But she didn't respond. "There's not going to be a next time. I'm not cut out for this kind of thing. This is my first and my last homicide."

"You don't mean that."

"I do. I was hired to find Mary Soffey's killer. I have, but I can't offer proof, so what good is it? Even if I had a big staff, I'd still say it's a matter for the police."

Totally out of character, Lew thought. What in the world was bugging her? And how in hell could he help if she wouldn't say what was wrong?

"Tell you what, I'll see to it that you have complete access to any evidence we turn. How's that?"

He could have protested a little more, Gwenn thought. He could have made a little more show of wanting her input. Disappointed, she blurted out, "Who was the woman who answered your phone?"

"What woman?"

"The woman who answered your phone when I called earlier. And please don't tell me it was the cleaning lady. Not that it's any of my business, of course."

"You must mean Christie. My neighbor. Gorgeous brunette. Okay, okay. She's married with two kids. She comes in to feed Minerva, my cat, when I'm working late."

Gwenn blushed and knew it and blushed some more.

"What else? Come on, I know that's not all that's on your mind."

"It was a standoff between Fissore and me. Maybe he thought if I let him go and the ship sailed off he'd be in the clear. But after he's had time to think, he'll realize the authorities will be waiting for him and that he has nowhere to run. Then what will he do?"

"Nothing. He'll probably still think he can beat the rap. Killers tend to be conceited."

"No." Gwenn was very pale. "I don't believe he's thinking about getting away with it. You see, I told him one of the girls he killed was not Cryder's. I let him think that girl was Angie. I as good as told him he'd killed his own child."

Sackler formed a silent whistle.

"Misleading him so that he'd confess was one thing, but

if he takes his own life? I don't know how I could deal with that."

He sat down beside her and took both her hands in his. "I'll radio the *Conquistador* and request that the captain put Fissore in the brig and keep an eye on him till they make port. Okay?"

Gwenn nodded. "Thanks." Surprising them both, she began to cry. "I feel so much better," she said. "Honestly, you have no idea how much better I feel." The tears coursed down her cheeks.

He put his arms around her and held her. After a while she stopped crying.